RISK

SKYE JORDAN

1

Everything she'd ever heard about California was true.

Caitlyn Winters was experiencing it for herself for the first time: long stretches of gorgeous Southern California beach, the sun setting in pink and coral hues over the deep blue Pacific Ocean, multimillion-dollar homes lining the sand, the August day warmed to a perfect seventy-six degrees, complete with a gentle breeze.

Then there was the company—the beautiful people. As in truly, unbelievably gorgeous people, men and women of every age, awaiting the bride.

Caitlyn hoped the flowers she'd secured in Lexi's braid lasted, at least through the ceremony. It had been a long time since she'd braided Lexi's hair.

The harpist played something romantic, and guests chatted in their seats, which were neatly arranged in rows facing the ocean. The wedding planner had extended Jax and Lexi's beachside Malibu home with a temporary wood floor over the sand and hung strings of lights over the large round tables waiting quietly for the reception.

As Jax was a former blockbuster movie star turned

stuntman and Renegades owner, his wedding would draw the kind of attention that could ruin this special day.

The guest list grew from fifty to seventy-five to one hundred, where Lexi drew the line. If it were up to Jax, he would have filled SoFi Stadium, covered it in flowers, and televised the ceremony. But because Lexi wanted quiet, Jax had given her quiet by pulling in a handful of favors to close the airspace surrounding the house.

There was no missing the Renegades team several rows up. Even if Caitlyn hadn't met most of them when she'd arrived, the way they poked fun at each other gave them away. And if the way their suits hung on their big frames was any indication, their bodies were as amazing as their smiles.

They were rowdy even at their most subdued, laughing, joking, talking, issuing challenges. Their significant others sat between each Renegade, probably to help hold them at a simmer. Caitlyn knew how boys worked. She had three little brothers at home. Men, on the other hand, were still a mystery to her and, based on her last relationship, not something she was all that interested in deciphering.

Lexi and Jax wanted quick and informal, and Caitlyn couldn't help but wonder if that was because they knew their chosen family's behavior would skid off the rails if they'd pushed the ceremony over twenty minutes.

The thought made her smile.

She watched the ocean in the distance, the waves rolling onto the sand, then sliding back. Her blood pressure dropped every time she focused on the dark blue water. Pictures didn't do it justice. Video either. The magic of California beaches couldn't be bottled. It had to be experienced.

She hadn't been down to the waterline yet. Honestly, the ocean scared her a little. She would have asked Lexi to go with her, but she didn't want to take Lexi's mind off the wedding, and

Caitlyn didn't know anyone else well enough to expose such a silly fear.

There was still one aisle seat open beside the Renegades team. Evidently, they were missing someone.

Wes, Jax's best friend, already stood at the front, alongside an arch covered in flowers. A sandy blond with an electric smile, Wes was attractive and fit, like the other Renegades.

The minister made his way toward the arch, his back toward the ocean. Everyone's attention refocused as Jax walked down the aisle, swift and determined, taking his place beside Wes.

The Renegades cheered as if he'd done something exceptional and peppered him with "it's about damn time" and "never thought I'd see the day" and "what took you so long?" as well as a couple of "told you he'd make it without fainting, you owe me a hundred bucks," all the jokes in reference to the slow road Jax had traveled to get Lexi to the altar.

Others gave him catcalls for his *GQ* style: simple black slacks, white shirt, white tie, silver vest. He looked handsome AF. Wes said something and elbowed Jax in the ribs. This man, one who would be her cousin-in-law within minutes, beamed with joy.

Tears sprang to Caitlyn's eyes. Lexi had been through a hellish childhood and worked her way into the fashion world with literally nothing. Now, women all over the world sought out a couture LaCroix gown for their own weddings. She deserved a happily ever after with—by all accounts—an amazing man.

The music changed, and everyone turned in their seats, anticipating the sight of Lexi. Instead, they were treated to the sight of a man who could only be another Renegade. Six-two, dark hair, olive skin, handsome, built—and, it appeared, the only Renegade who'd come solo.

He lifted his hands with a grin and said, "Sorry to disappoint," making everyone laugh. His entrance lit sparks in her belly. She could feel his charisma from where she was sitting.

He took the open seat and muttered something to the effect of "wardrobe malfunction" to the questions from his teammates, but he looked damned good to Caitlyn in dark slacks, white shirt, and a gray blazer.

When Solo Renegade turned to look down the aisle, waiting for Lexi like everyone else, his gaze caught on Caitlyn, and she felt the grip of it instantly. She had to fight herself not to look away. She was bold now. She did bold things, like hold a handsome man's gaze.

Then he smiled. Good God, he smiled. A beautiful, bright smile that made Caitlyn's chest tight.

Lexi appeared at the end of the aisle, arm in arm with her best friend, Rubi, Wes's girl. Lexi's gown couldn't have been any simpler or more stunning. Really little more than what Lexi called a shift. Thin straps and white satin, the dress was fitted to her gorgeous body while also tastefully concealing the details.

When she could have had any dress she wanted, Lexi purchased the dress from a local designer who needed a win in her column. Lexi was good like that, always had been.

Her skin was tan, her makeup minimal, her hair up in that simple asymmetrical braid that signified the awful past Lexi had survived.

Today, her smile was as radiant as Jax's. As if he couldn't keep his joy inside, Jax laughed, which made Lexi laugh, which rippled laughter through the guests. Caitlyn's joy for Lexi tightened her throat and stung her eyes.

Her gaze followed Lexi's path up the aisle and paused on Solo Renegade, who was smiling at Lexi. A warm smile. One that reached his dark eyes. Dark eyes that strayed to Caitlyn after Lexi passed.

She took a slow breath to quell the nerves. This was exactly what she'd hoped for—new friends, new experiences, a bold change.

Bold had sounded perfect when she was trapped in Kentucky. Bold now scared the heck out of her.

When Lexi stood before Jax, he took her hand and turned toward the guests. "Miracles do happen."

The audience laughed and cheered.

Then Jax and Lexi faced each other, and the minister greeted them.

The ceremony was short, but beautiful. Lexi and Jax went with vows as simple as the wedding. It was perfect. And when Jax kissed his bride, the guests—read: Renegades—cheered and whistled so loud, it made Caitlyn's ears ring.

2

Duke needed to get over there and talk to her.

They were an hour into the reception, and he hadn't built up the nerve to interrupt one of her conversations to introduce himself. Nor had he found the time with everyone welcoming him back.

Now, Josh, a former Navy SEAL and the director of risk management for Renegades, was telling Duke about the new certification requirement for stunt coordinators and performers while Duke watched Caitlyn over Josh's shoulder.

Duke had learned her name from others at the reception, as well as the fact that she was Lexi's cousin. Which explained a lot about her looks.

"The bottom line," Josh was saying, "is that everyone has to get certified within two years because they recently added a new rule that only certified stunt companies and stunt coordinators can work for SAG."

SAG was short for SAG-AFTRA, the Screen Actors Guild labor union for performers. Behind Josh, Caitlyn was laughing with Wes, Rubi, an A-list actor, and a B-list friend.

There were a lot of stars here—actors, directors, producers

—but she didn't seem any more enamored with them than she was with the bartender, whom she'd chatted with for a few minutes. Duke really liked that.

He also liked the way she filled out that dress. It was a deep pink with beads sparkling everywhere. Thin straps, low V in the front exposing cleavage he wanted to get up close and personal with, and a plunging back that showed her entire spine.

He could already see himself kissing every vertebra on his way toward even more interesting territory. She would taste sweet. So fucking sweet.

God, he hoped she didn't have a guy back where she'd come from—the South somewhere.

"It's good for us," Josh said, drawing him back to the certification thing, which felt as dry as cardboard when Duke had Caitlyn in sight. "They're not grandfathering anyone in, so everyone is starting from scratch."

He still had no idea how to approach her other than offering the same old boring introduction everyone else had used on her tonight. Yeah, he'd noticed. He'd noticed other men notice her. Even men with women on their arm. Fucking Hollywood.

"As much as we work," Josh said, "we'll all be certified before we know it. The requirement also thins the pool, getting rid of the fly-by-nighters, the wannabes, and the purely stupid. And the more of us who are certified, the lower our insurance costs, the more demand and higher profit, which all translates into higher pay."

Duke laughed. "*I'd* pay *Jax* to do this job."

He used to be good at picking up women. Used to have the nerve to saunter up, toss out some ridiculous line that somehow caught a woman's interest, and before he knew it, they were in bed together. Or up against an alley wall. Or in a bathroom stall.

Ah, the good old days. Days that were way too far in the past.

"I've heard rumors they're going to make the certification mandatory," Josh said, "so we really need to jump on it. Two thousand hours is two hundred ten-hour days."

Duke exhaled and refocused on Josh. "That feels daunting. Especially just coming back."

"I know. But a few of the guys are already certified, so we can lean on their creds until everyone is done. We're going to have to expand soon too. We need an explosives expert—"

"Bring Ryker back. He's been in Virginia too long. Did you hear his accent? On Rachel, it's adorable. On him..." Duke made a face.

Josh laughed. "We're talking about it, but we still need people. Especially women. With the trend toward stronger heroines, there's a huge demand for female stuntpeople, and Zahara is working her ass off already. She doesn't get enough time with her baby. But we could also use someone for fire, another fighter, another rigger, another driver. We need to clone everyone to meet the demand. And we've been talking about growing our support staff. The new guys probably won't have as many hours toward certification."

"I'll finish the mandatory safety training on the plane tonight, then start on the written requirements for the stunt coordinator certification." He shook his head. "So much fucking red tape now."

"Remember," Josh said, "if injuries occur on your watch, you could be stripped of whatever hours you've attained and be put on hold for six months. If you're found negligent, you could be banned from certification altogether."

Which would put Duke's job—the only real job he'd ever had and the only one he wanted—in jeopardy.

"Jesus, no pressure."

"You'll start earning hours with this film. You have to keep track and get your hours signed off. Currently, within the guidelines, the producer will be the person to validate hours."

"That seems like a menial job for a producer."

"Not when the producer is ultimately responsible for all safety on the set. The buck stops with him."

"Who's the producer on *American Valor*?"

"Kingsley."

Duke tilted his head side to side. "It should be fine. He's intense, but fair."

Grace, Josh's wife, came up and hugged Duke. "Missed you."

"You too."

They chatted about Kristy and the girls for a couple of minutes, then Josh and Grace greeted more friends and Duke refocused on Caitlyn.

She had Lexi's blonde hair, but wavy and cut shorter, reaching her shoulders. The kind of hair he could really sink his hands into. Her face was a heart shape, and he'd bet money she had blue eyes. Her body left him speechless. And hot. If a man could get wet, Duke would be drenched.

Lexi's beauty leaned toward sophisticated and exotic. Caitlyn's leaned toward spicy girl next door. It really worked for Duke.

He waited until Brad Withermore, an A-list producer, gave Lexi room to breathe and slid in behind him.

"Hey, gorgeous," he greeted with a smile that truly matched the joy of being there.

She threw her arms around him and hugged him hard. "God, it's good to have you back. We missed you so much."

"Baby, you're choking him." Jax came up to Lexi's side. "He's turning red. Looks like he might pop."

Lexi and Duke laughed, and she finally pulled away.

Duke took Jax's hand for a shake and gave him a hug.

"About time, you two. You've restored a chunk of my faith in humanity."

"Welcome back," Jax said. "Really good to have you onboard again."

"Really good to be onboard."

"Did Josh get with you about stunt coordinator certification?" Jax asked.

"We were just talking about it."

"Charlie's hailing you," Lexi told Jax, who looked around and found an older man waving in their direction.

"Heading into battle again." He kissed her temple like he wasn't going to get another chance in two minutes. "Can we leave soon?"

"Duke and I need to catch up," she said, grinning at her husband until he headed toward Charlie. Lexi turned back to Duke, her blue eyes bright and warm. "So? How's Kristy? How are the girls? God, I bet they're so big now."

"They really are. Especially Willow. I swear she was just born. Now she walks around the house telling me 'no' in very clear adult English to everything I say—and I mean everything. Her diaper leaked all over me right before I was getting ready to leave, which is why I ran late."

Lexi laughed. "Pics?"

"Thought you'd never ask." Duke took out his phone, and he and Lexi lost long minutes looking at pictures and talking about the three little gremlins that changed his life.

"How is Kristy holding up?" Lexi asked. "It's got to be hell for her. And it's been going on for so long. I'm sorry she and the girls couldn't make it tonight, but I totally understand why."

"Yeah, the stress of bringing all three girls here was just too much, and she didn't want anything to ruin your special day. We can barely manage them at home. It's wearing on both of us, but this move will be good. She's been taking a few classes at USC remotely to finish her degree. She was able to get a scholarship through some organizations that support battered women. We hope to get her back to campus in the fall, but that kind of depends on the divorce and my work. It's a very precarious balance with the possibility of a fault shift at any second. It all hinges on how much of a bastard Peter decides to be. The final custody hearing is coming up soon. Has us on edge."

"We're here for you. You know that. All of us. If we need to do a round-robin to take the girls off your hands to keep you guys rolling, we're in. And if you need money, please, please, *please* let us know. You know we have more than we can use. It's stupid to have it sitting around in a bank account. We'd never expect it back, so you wouldn't have to feel like you owe anything."

"Thanks. But that's a little easier said than done."

"I know, but it's here if things get tight."

"Thank you." Duke glanced toward Lexi's cousin and cleared his throat. "So, Caitlyn."

Lexi's face lit up. She made a high-pitched *squee* and clapped her hands, but it was all subdued, so she didn't draw attention. "Gorgeous, right?"

"Your family genes definitely run hot."

"Oh, and she's Georgia-peach sweet."

He'd overheard enough of Caitlyn's conversations to catch the Southern accent. "She sounds like a Georgia peach."

"I was hoping you two would notice each other. I didn't see you talking to her."

"I haven't yet."

"Duke," she said with a tilt of her head and a heavy why-not in her tone.

"I'm a little low on confidence at the moment. I can change a diaper, feed a baby, and occupy a toddler all at the same time, but finding my game... I don't even know what field I'm playing on. Tell me about her."

"Not if you're going to use what I say as an excuse not to get that information directly from her."

"I'll get there."

"You might want to move a little faster. You leave Monday."

"Tomorrow night, actually, so I can get in a warm-up climb before the chaos starts. I can't say I've ever had the best timing. Hit me with a few highlights. Is she visiting or staying? Is she with someone or is she available? What does she do? What is she like?"

Lexi's gaze moved around the crowd and paused on Caitlyn, where she was sitting with a group of mutual friends, laughing. Duke liked how easily she seemed to laugh.

"She's here for the foreseeable future," Lexi said. "She got a job at a PR firm. I asked her to stay here at the house, but she wants to do it on her own. Sound familiar?"

He nodded.

"She broke up with a long-term boyfriend before she moved."

Duke groaned.

"It was over a long time before she left the relationship," Lexi said. "It was just comfortable, and she had a lot of family pressure to stay with him. A lot of family pressure to stay home too. Believe me, she's glad it's over, and she's happy to be out of Kentucky. That small town was chipping away at her soul. She just lights up here."

Duke glanced toward her again, and this time, her gaze waited for his. She smiled, a little shy, a little mischievous, then looked away again, and excitement burned through his chest. "She's fucking radiant. Like she's lit up from the inside."

"Oh, she is." Lexi's voice softened with affection. "She's the real thing. Good through and through. When we were kids, she defied her parents to take care of me. Our moms were sisters, and while Caitlyn's parents tried to help us, the money they gave my mom always went right up her nose, so they stopped trying."

Duke had heard the CliffsNotes of Lexi's young life, but he'd never heard it straight from her, so he tuned in.

"My brother and I often went without food and utilities so Mom could get a fix. When the water would get shut off, sometimes I couldn't shower for days. Sometimes weeks. I was getting bullied at school because I was dirty."

"God, Lex. That's awful."

She nodded. "Caitlyn would bring a supply bag to school with her everyday filled with wet wipes, a hairbrush, hair ties, food, a change of clothes. I would clean up while she braided my hair when it was too dirty to wear down." She touched her braid. "Like this. I asked her to do it today for my 'something old.'"

She took a breath and blew it out with a wobbly smile. "I swear I wake up every day sure this life isn't real."

Duke wrapped his arms around her again. "It's real, Lex. And you earned it."

Jax came to claim his bride, and Duke was left to figure out how to approach Caitlyn. Or even if he should. He wasn't sure why this felt so hard, but he felt awkward and clumsy. Over the last two years, Duke had hooked up with only two women. But he'd met each in a bar, and they'd come on to him, making it easier.

She turned away from the table of guests and leaned up against the railing separating the wood floor and the sand, looking out at the ocean. He followed the length of her arm to an empty lowball glass hanging from her fingertips.

An empty glass. That was an idea Duke could get behind. He just needed to do it before someone else struck up another conversation with her.

He strode to the bar. "What's she drinking? The woman in pink?"

"Whiskey, straight up."

"What?" Duke focused on the bartender. "You're shittin' me."

"Nope. Tennessee is known for their whiskey."

He thought she was from Kentucky. He needed a drink to get his head around this woman. "Can I get two whiskeys and a kamikaze shot, please?"

As the bartender poured the drinks, Duke glanced at Caitlyn again, scanning the deep plunge of the dress, the silky skirt that flowed over her curvy backside, the four-inch heels.

But he'd bet the rest of his savings—which would cover only two more months of rent in this jungle—that Caitlyn was more of a Converse girl. He'd bet she liked to wear her hair in a puffy ponytail and only used makeup when she dressed up.

The bartender slid the drinks across the temporary bar, and Duke pulled out his wallet, trading them for a healthy tip.

"Good luck, dude." The bartender quirked a grin. "You don't meet girls like that around here very often. As in.:.ever."

The bartender moved on to other customers, and Duke downed the kamikaze, letting the vodka burn down his throat.

Just do it.

He turned toward the railing and almost walked into someone. "Oh, shit, I'm—"

Caitlyn looked up at him. Surprise rocked his heart. Her eyes were blue. A smoky blue. And she was even more beautiful close up: long eyelashes, smooth skin, full lips. Duke's breath caught for an agonizingly extended moment.

"Sorry. I shouldn't have snuck up on you like that." God, that Southern drawl was intoxicating. "But I knew if I didn't make myself come over, I wouldn't do it."

She leaned into a vertical four-by-four holding up the pergola and gave him a smile that reminded him of everything he'd been missing over the last couple of years. "Hi, I'm Caitlyn, and I'd love a long walk on the beach."

It was so unexpected, it was funny. "I'm Duke." He offered her one of the whiskeys. "I was just bringing this to you. And I think you mean 'Hi, I'm Caitlyn, and I like long walks on the beach.'"

"No, actually, I really would love a walk on the beach, but I don't want to go alone." Her gaze slid to the dark expanse of water. "This is the first time I've seen the ocean, and it's a little intimidating. Even more so at night."

Duke was stunned. "Are you serious?"

"Mmm-hmm." Her gaze returned to his, and her smile deepened again. "Will you take me?"

"Hell, yes." Duke answered before the full question was out of Caitlyn's mouth, making her laugh so hard, she doubled over.

Duke laughed too. "Is someone tipsy?"

She stopped laughing and met his gaze again. Those blue eyes were brighter now. "More punchy than tipsy. It's been one heck of a week."

Duke offered his free hand, and she curled her fingers around his. "Tell me about it."

3

Taking Duke's hand made Caitlyn's stomach float. It was big and warm and peppered with callouses from fingertip to palm, and it seemed to swallow hers.

This felt like a really bold move. Other women might do it every day, but Caitlyn didn't. And this guy was so sexy, she couldn't quite think straight. Thankfully, the whiskey had helped her come up with the guts to approach him.

He'd taken off his jacket at some point since the ceremony ended and rolled up his shirt sleeves, exposing tanned muscled forearms. And the way the fabric of his shirt pulled across the muscle underneath was really something.

He smelled like sandalwood, leather, and tobacco—the leaf, not the smoke. And it wasn't one of those bodywashes that floated around a man, head to toe, like an overwhelming cloud.

No, he was wearing cologne.

Caitlyn ticked another box in the sexy column. He was racking up points at lightning speed.

He led her to the edge of the wood floor, set his drink on a table, and released her hand to lean down and take off his shoes.

"Right, shoes." She followed his lead, balancing with one hand on the railing. "That's how often I walk on sand."

"I can't believe you've never seen the ocean."

God, that voice. It was deep and smooth and did strange things inside her. She'd never noticed a man's voice before, but maybe that was because she'd never heard one like Duke's.

He straightened just as Caitlyn stepped onto the floor without shoes. The relief flooding her feet felt so good, she groaned.

Duke laughed and offered his hand again. "I pegged you as more Converse, less heel."

"You'd be right." She took his hand, and when she stepped onto the sand, she was glad she had. She sank a lot lower than she'd expected, and she was instantly off-balance until they finally hit wet sand, where she stopped to catch her breath. She released his hand, putting both of hers at her hips. "I feel like I just ran a sprint. That's crazy."

"Beach workouts are killers."

"God, could this night be any more perfect?"

He grinned.

"What?"

He shook his head. "I was going to say something inappropriate. Sorry. Outside my family, I haven't had much in the way of female company in a while."

"That's impossible to believe."

He laughed. The sound was deep and rough and so sexy, her knees tried to buckle.

They started toward the waterline at a stroll, hand in hand, the wet sand chillier than she'd expected. Without the lights of the homes that sat back from the water a hundred yards or more, the darkness encompassed her and Duke. The partial moon cast a strip of white on the ocean and gave the setting a beautiful blue-white glow.

She was overwhelmed by the romance of it all. Naive, she

knew. But in her defense, this was only the second man she'd ever held hands with in her life, and not only was he completely and utterly out of her league, but she didn't even know him. So, yeah, it made her a little giddy.

"I haven't been able to stop looking at you," Duke told her. "You're gorgeous."

The compliment felt strange. "I don't think I've ever had a man say that to me."

"Did you grow up in a convent?"

She laughed again. "No."

"Then you're definitely hanging around the wrong men. It's not something anyone could miss."

She gave his hand a squeeze and looked out at the dark water, stretching forever. The waves added a smooth, quiet rhythm to the night. She breathed deep, and for the first time since she was in college, she felt free. Free of all the judgment, obligations, and expectations back in Kentucky.

Here she was, having blown up her life in the South—she'd broken up with Brett, quit the job her dad got for her, hurt her mom, shocked her brothers, and ignored all the advice of her friends. Friends who turned out to be more Brett's friends than hers. They'd all sided with Brett in the breakup.

"I never understood why so many people dreamed of living near the water," she said. "Now I do."

"I don't know how I'd feel if I were seeing the ocean for the first time."

"It's one of those things you can't describe or just see to understand. It's something you have to experience to know."

They strolled in silence for a few steps. She enjoyed the unexpected comfort, but still felt like she was in an alternate universe.

"So, your hands," she said. "Where did the callouses come from?"

He looked at the palm of his free hand. "Climbing."

"Climbing?"

"Rock climbing. You know, where you use ropes and harnesses to scale the side of a mountain?"

"You guys do crazy stuff," she said, shaking her head, her attention split between Duke and the waves, both equally mesmerizing. "Crazy, crazy stuff. Is that what you do in the movies? Rock climb?"

"And a bunch of other things. You have to be flexible if you want to keep work in your corner around here. I can do a little of everything—driving, falling, fighting. But my specialty is climbing—mountains, rocks, buildings, whatever."

"You must love it to do these scary things."

"I do. I can't imagine doing anything else. Tell me about you."

"What would you like to know?"

"Everything."

His gaze was soft, his smile warm. She couldn't remember the last time anyone had paid such close attention to her—including when she'd announced she was leaving Kentucky.

"Can you narrow it down for me?" she asked.

"Lexi told me you're in PR?"

Caitlyn nodded.

"Why PR?"

"Oh, well... That's a bit convoluted. I love art, but my parents said I'd never make any money as an artist, so I veered toward graphic design, which led me to marketing, which led me to public relations. And by that time, I had to decide on something to graduate, so I finished with a PR degree. I kind of like the idea of helping people, you know? People who are working hard to get ahead, but need some help being seen."

"That's an interesting way to look at it, and I guess on the most fundamental level, that's what PR is."

"Why do you say that?"

"I guess because the PR tactics I've seen have been more

about covering up bad behavior than exposing the good. But that's celebrity bullshit."

"I doubt I'll have any exposure to celebrities. I'm sure I'll be stuck in a tiny office with no windows, creating marketing materials, assisting other people with their clients."

"First job out of college?" he asked.

"Oh no. I've been out of college awhile, but where I lived, the closest I got to public relations was designing the city's summer activities pamphlet."

"Small, huh?"

She nodded. "Beautiful, though. Mountains and lakes, historical homes, quiet streets."

"Miss it?"

"Not really. Not yet. I'm sure I will at some point, but right now, I feel like I can breathe for the first time since I went to college."

"What firm are you working for?"

"Excel PR?" She lifted her voice, leaving the statement as more of a question. "Do you know them?"

He shook his head. "We cross paths with quite a few, but never that one. What are you doing for them?"

"I have no idea." She laughed, exposing the nerves she'd developed over that very issue. "They left the job description wide open. I was so excited to get the job, I didn't ask. Amateur move. I'm a little nervous about it, but I figure as long as I can pay rent and eat…" She shrugged. "I'll make it work. I have to. I can't go back."

"Can't go back?"

She looked at him, considering whether or not she wanted to get into this. "Can we sit?"

"Yeah, sure."

They found dry sand and sat. She hiked up her skirt to clear her knees and wrapped her arms around her legs.

"Everyone from my parents to the grocery clerk at the

Piggly Wiggly thought this move was a mistake. They have all kinds of preconceived ideas of what LA is like—whether they've been here or not—convinced I'll fall into evil hands and end up on the streets or something equally horrifying."

"That has been known to happen."

She shook her head. "They were talking out of their asses. Small-town thinking at its finest. If I failed and had to go home... Talk about humiliation. I'd be known as the girl who couldn't hack LA for the rest of my life. No, I'm not going back." She gestured toward him. "It's your turn."

He grinned. "Okay, okay, bring it on."

There was something about the way he said *bring it on* that made everything inside her sizzle, which distracted her from all those questions she'd had collecting in her head just minutes ago.

So she started with the most basic question she wanted an answer to. "No girlfriend? That's crazy."

"But true. You're not the only person with a convoluted story."

"Ooo, now I *really* want to hear this." She slid her arm through his, momentarily stunned at the rock-hard biceps beneath his shirtsleeve. She leaned into him, and he offered counterpressure.

"Just remember," he said, smiling. He had an incredible smile. "You asked for it."

She rested her chin on his arm, and while he looked out at the ocean, Caitlyn looked at him. The slight stubble on his jaw framing full lips. The scar bisecting one eyebrow, another on his chin. The square jaw and a nose that, despite being straight, still looked like he'd broken it at some point.

"No time or space for a girlfriend right now."

"What do you mean?"

"I'm living with my sister and three nieces. We're like little sardines packed into a can."

She hummed in understanding. "I looked for months for something I could afford. I'm sharing with a roommate."

"Money is part of it, but that's because she's going through a really bitter divorce and her ex is a movie producer, so he's got money and power. He's making her life hell. Early on, he moved all their money into accounts she can't touch, and Kristy dropped out of college when she got pregnant so she could raise the girls, so it wasn't like she could get a job that paid enough to justify leaving them at daycare.

"When he hired PIs to get dirt on her in an attempt to get custody of the girls, I stepped in, created a wall, blocked them from most of the press. But the more we hid, the harder he tried to get to us, so I moved her and the kids to our parents' house in Northern California to get some space from the publicity. Which worked, until I'd burned through my savings."

Caitlyn winced. "I know that feeling."

"We moved back so I could work and because our parents aren't in great health and couldn't give Kristy the help she needs with the girls. Especially not when her husband sends people to watch and harass her. But all we can afford right now is a tiny two-bedroom apartment. Kristy has a room, the girls have a room, and I have a couch. But by the time we all wake up, Kristy's got one or two of the girls in her bed, and I've got at least one sleeping on my chest."

"I can't lie, that is one heart-melting scenario." She squeezed his arm. "Sounds like they're lucky to have you."

He smiled, and the expression was so soft, it tugged on every last heartstring. "I'm just as lucky. Those girls, they make every ounce of trouble worth it. They're what keep Kristy and me going."

"Things will get better after the divorce?"

"Hopefully. But it won't be long before he finds out we moved back. She has a restraining order against him and temporary full custody of the girls—the reason he's so bitter—

but the people he hired to follow her can do anything they want."

"Wait, he *hired* people to *follow* her?"

He chuckled. "Welcome to Hollywood. Looney fucking Tunes, I swear. As long as they don't come onto private property, the law can't touch them. And in order to work, I have to be on the set, leaving Kristy with the girls and the problems. We're just taking it day by day right now, grateful the girls are resilient."

"When will it end?"

"When the divorce is final. Hopefully next month. He'll be forced to give Kristy half of their assets. But they have kids together, so there will always be a connection no matter how much she wants to break it. She's going back to college to finish up so she can be stable on her own."

"What major?"

"Business."

"That will be good in the end, but middles are always messy."

"Very. As far as work, I can't wait to go back. But there are new changes there too. A certification that everyone has to attain by a certain date to work on SAG films."

"SAG?"

"A union for performers. Every movie I've ever worked on has been under a SAG contract. It's all about accruing hours and keeping the set safe. Just heard that if there are accidents on your set, you not only lose all the time you've accrued, you're put on a six-month waiting period before you can start accruing time again. And eventually, we won't be able to work unless we're certified. That would be a real problem for me. And for Kristy and the girls."

"Jeez, no pressure."

He laughed. "That's exactly what I thought. I don't mean to dump on you. It's just a stressful time, but we'll work it all out."

"You know, I'm going to be here, so if Kristy needs help while you're gone, I'd be happy to pitch in. I could stay with them if they needed a third party in the house, or I could take the kids off her hands for a while to give her a break. She's going to need time to study. Heck, I could just help her do the laundry. Three little kids make a lot of laundry."

He turned his head and looked at her. Seemed to search her eyes. And she wanted him to kiss her in the worst way. It had been a long time since she was kissed with any passion. And she really wanted to kiss another man. Really wanted to know what that was like.

"That's a really sweet offer." He covered her hand on his biceps with his own and threaded their fingers together. "Thank you. The bartender was so right about you."

"The bartender?" She smiled. "I got one drink and we talked maybe three minutes."

"He said you don't find girls like you around here. And he's right, you really don't."

"Like me?"

"Sweet, authentic, beautiful."

"The hell you don't. You've got"—she ticked off her fingers—"Lexi, Rubi, Rachel, Grace, Ellie, Brook Tessa, and Zahara to prove you wrong."

"The guys have cornered the market on amazing women. None left in all of LA. Until now."

She smiled. "You're a smooth talker."

He laughed.

"Do you have pictures? Of the girls?"

"You really want to see pictures of my nieces? Now?"

Caitlyn rested her chin on his arm, gaze lingering on his. "I have a few alternate activities we could entertain, but yeah, I'd love to see them."

He unlocked his phone and scrolled to his photos, stopping on one with all three girls. He pointed to each. "Scarlett, Paisley, and Willow. Five, three and a very terrible two. And that's Kristy."

"Oh, wow. They're beautiful. Paisley really looks like you, the same eyes. And Willow, she's got your mouth."

Her gaze lowered to his mouth and held. The hand on the inside of his biceps was so close, all she had to do to touch him was lift a finger, and she skimmed it across his lower lip.

Duke's lashes fluttered closed, and he sighed a sound of longing. Without warning, he took the tip of her index finger between his lips.

She pulled in a sharp breath. Her stomach rose until it closed off her airway. Heat melted into her pelvis, increasing pressure between her legs. Heavens, she'd never felt anything so sensual.

Then he pulled his head back to release her fingertip, only to move right back in, taking her whole finger this time. A sound of surprise ebbed from her throat. Her breathing hitched, her mind went blank, and she couldn't pry her gaze from the sight, sure if she looked away, she'd discover it was just a dream.

He stroked the length of her finger with his tongue and sucked as he pulled back again. It made her restless. She wanted to say something. Break the tension. A sexual pull so powerful, she didn't know what to do with it. But how could she? She'd never felt it before.

And therein lay the problem.

"Duke—"

He reached across his body, slid two fingers beneath Caitlyn's chin, and lifted it enough for her mouth to clear his arm, then pressed his lips to hers.

Time slowed. Sound faded. He kissed her the way he'd explored her finger, gentle sucks and slow licks, until her brain was complete mush, and she was leaning in for more.

She now knew what it felt like to kiss someone other than

Brett. She now knew it was a whole different world. A world she'd been looking for while being told it didn't exist.

Duke's mouth was warm and soft. He tasted of heat edged in whiskey. But it was the way he moved his mouth that instantly set Caitlyn on fire. Loose, exploratory, sensual. Hungry.

He gently broke the kiss and stroked her cheek with his thumb. "I'm really interested in those alternate activities you mentioned."

Her brain slugged to life. This was the only alternate activity she'd imagined. It was as far as her mind would let her go. A safety mechanism, it seemed, because she didn't know where to go from here.

Damn, here two days and she'd already jumped into quicksand.

"Yeah," she said, her voice soft. "About those..." She forced herself out of the haze. "Um, I um..."

He was still looking at her as if his mind was already in the bedroom. "Mmm-hmm."

There was no easy way to say this, so she just said it. "I... wouldn't know what to do with a man like you. I knew that from the beginning. I just didn't think we'd ever get, well, here, so I didn't say anything—"

"What do you mean, a man like me?"

"You know." She gestured to him. "This. All this."

He laughed and kissed her again. She instantly melted, opening to him, tasting him. God, it was glorious. Thrilling. Electrifying. The kiss went on forever, yet not long enough. She swore she could feel the desire he seemed to be holding back, and even though it made her nervous, she still wanted it. All of it.

When he finally pulled away, he said, "Feels like you know exactly what to do with me."

Oh, that voice.

She smiled and shrugged. "Well, kissing."

"If that's all we do, I'll still go home happy." He brushed his thumb across her wet lower lip. "I love your mouth."

He dropped into another soul-searing kiss. His moves were varied and slow, his lips demanding but gentle, his tongue searching but satisfied. Like he really could be happy just kissing. Like he really could kiss her all night.

Only, she was wet. Dripping wet from nothing but a kiss. Or maybe it was the promise of that kiss. She didn't know. She didn't know anything right now.

She pulled away, breathless. "You might go home happy, but I'm going to die."

He laughed. Then he laughed harder and pressed his forehead to her shoulder. It felt intimate, like they knew each other better than they did. Like they wanted the same thing, they were just trying to navigate their way there.

He turned his head and kissed her jaw. "What would send you home happy?"

Gooseflesh rose on her neck. Heat slid between her legs. "Things I don't even know exist yet."

She couldn't bluff her way through this. She had to be honest. She pulled away to put space between them and braced for...she wasn't sure what. Disappointment? Frustration? Judgment?

"The truth is, I've only been with one guy, and it wasn't bad, but it wasn't great. So, I can't imagine knowing how to..." She couldn't find words that didn't sound stupid. "Let's just say... I don't think it would be what you're used to. And I think you're pretty great, so I'd rather we didn't get into uncomfortable territory."

For the first time since they met, his smile fell. Mortification crept into her gut. She'd gone and ruined the good moments they'd shared. She felt heat rising in her neck.

"I'm really sorry—"

He put his finger against her lips. "Whoever made you feel like a disappointment," he said, slow and deliberate, "better look in his own toolbox for the fix, because you're not the problem."

She was stunned he'd translated her words that way. Maybe she gave away more of her insecurities than she realized.

He took her face between both hands. "Don't ever think that. And don't let it keep you from searching for more, because you'll eventually find exactly what you want and need, but you've got to look."

Her breath slid from her lungs. Emotions swelled in her chest.

He pressed another kiss to her mouth, then shifted on the sand. "Let's head back—"

She grabbed his arm before he pushed to his feet. "Wait." He stopped and met her gaze, then waited patiently until she found the strength to say, "I want more."

He brushed the hair off her shoulder and cupped her jaw. "You sure?"

"Dead sure."

That got a smile. A smile that left her breathless. "Then come here, beautiful."

He wrapped one arm around her waist and pulled her toward him. She slid one leg across his lap.

"There you go." He coaxed her close. "Now sink in."

She exhaled and let her body relax. Her legs slid wider until the neediest part of her was pressed against the very apparent erection beneath his slacks. He groaned at the pressure, and Caitlyn joined in.

Duke ran his hands up her back, pressed his lips to her neck, and murmured, "I want to eat you."

Good Lord, no one had ever said anything remotely that sexy to her. Ever. And she was so ready for this kind of passion in her life.

She took his face in both hands and kissed him in a way she hadn't kissed anyone in a long damn time. Blatantly hungry and filled with promises she wasn't sure she could keep. But she was going to give it her best damn try.

He took everything she gave, matched her desire, but didn't demand more. She felt the power he was holding back, and she wanted it. All of it.

She rocked her hips and moaned deep in her throat.

Duke broke the kiss and pushed his hands into her hair. The move was powerful, startling, thrilling. The look on his handsome face was hungry and serious.

"I want skin." His voice was low and rough and created tingles all over her body. He kissed her jaw, her neck, her throat. "I want every inch of me inside you."

Jesus. He was *so* out of her league. Still, she heard "Yes" come out of her mouth. "Yes, yes, yes. Where? Here?"

He pulled back and smiled. "Look at you, ready to get naked on a public beach."

She laughed, embarrassed, so completely beyond her scope of experience. "See what you do to me?"

He stroked her neck, let the backs of his fingers slide down her chest and across one breast. Her nipple tightened and her chest ached. "I'm game."

Her entire body fizzed like soda. "You would be."

"Are you calling me slutty?"

"Oh my God, I didn't mean it like—"

"Hey." He dipped his head to meet her eyes. "I'm kidding."

"Sorry." She laughed and rested her cheek against his shoulder, catching her breath. "My room? At the house?"

"Perfect." He tipped his head back and smiled up at her. "Want a little something to tide you over?"

"What?"

He slid the strap of her dress off her shoulder, and the fabric fell away from her breast. Nerves vibrated in her belly.

Then he dipped his head and took her into his mouth, stroking her nipple with his tongue. Pleasure streaked through her chest and slid low between her legs.

"Holy hell," she murmured, eyes closed, soaking in the feeling of this strong, sexy man wanting her. Suddenly, nothing existed but the two of them.

While she was still processing all these new sensations, he slipped his hand under her dress, up her thigh, between her legs.

She sucked a breath. This was crazily intimate. And wildfire fast. She might have had sex before, but she was a total virgin when it came to this kind of passion, this kind of intimacy. She felt vulnerable, both physically and emotionally. She hadn't been prepared for equal attraction on his part. She'd been prepping for rejection or just friendship.

He stroked her, just a light brush of his thumb, and pleasure jolted through her, sinking deep. Her eyes closed, and her head dropped forward. "Jesus Christ."

She couldn't think. Couldn't anticipate what came next. Everything felt so good.

He slipped his fingers under the edge of her panties and stroked her. "Oh-ho, fuck," he half laughed, half groaned against her neck. "You're so wet."

She slid her hands into his hair, breathing hard and fast, her forehead pressed to his.

He touched her like he was exploring, not looking for the end game. Like he was focused on her pleasure, not trying to turn her on so they could get on with sex.

His fingers pushed between her legs and through all that wetness he'd created. Then slid right inside her. Caitlyn gasped, and all her muscles coiled tight.

"Like that?" he murmured.

"Yes."

He pulled out of her, and she felt suddenly hollow. "Don't stop."

"I'm not going anywhere, sugar. I promise I will not leave you wanting for one goddamned thing tonight."

Then his fingers were back, doing things that made her jaw drop and sounds roll out. She fisted his crisp shirt at the shoulders, and rocked her hips toward his touch.

"More?"

"More."

He sure as hell knew all the right buttons to push. His touch was light, his mouth was strong. He pushed deep, but moved slowly. She dropped her head back, eyes closed, body floating somewhere on clouds. "More, more, more."

"I love a woman who knows what she wants." He stroked her, teased her, sank deep again.

"Duke..." She was on the verge of orgasm. How had this happened? She hadn't climaxed with Brett in more than a year. She'd begun to believe she was broken. And she was learning —very quickly—Duke was right. She wasn't the problem.

"Come get it, sugar. I'm right here." Caitlyn coiled tighter and tighter until she had to rock her hips into his touch. "There you go."

She was effectively fucking herself on his fingers—and loving it. Duke seemed to love it too, adding a little more punch than she could create on her own and making her want to crawl out of her skin—in a good way.

"I love the way you move," he said against her skin, biting her throat. "Let go. I've got you."

Her body leapt at the suggestion. She moved one hand to the back of his neck and rocked herself into an orgasm that overwhelmed her, bent her backward and made her moan and shiver. And it lasted for what felt like forever, coming in little bursts of aftershocks.

When she started drifting down, mind blank, she buried her face against his neck.

He lifted his head and licked his fingers, humming with pleasure. "Sweet. I knew you'd be sweet."

Jesus Christ. When she wasn't in the throes of building toward orgasm, she was shocked and embarrassed, but when she was, she wanted it all.

He let her come back to the present in her own time, getting to know her body by touching her everywhere. Cupping her breasts, stroking her legs, letting his fingers follow her spine.

"Can I," she said between breaths, "I don't know. Do something for you?"

He leaned away, cupped her face, and lifted her head to look into her eyes. "Oh, sugar, you already have." He kissed her. "Let me know when you're ready to go. We'll head back to your room and continue this—if that's what you want. If not, it's okay."

She smiled and nodded. "Oh yes, I want."

4

This hadn't been what Duke had expected. The way she handled herself with the guests made her seem confident and savvy.

Turns out, as far as sex was concerned, she was more of a diamond in the rough. And Duke wanted to be the one to polish her to a brilliant shine.

He steadied her as she tackled the deep sand near the house, and when they finally stood at the edge of the temporary patio, there were only about fifty guests left.

"Lexi and Jax must have gone to the hotel," he said.

"Were we gone that long?" she asked.

He looked at his watch and smiled. "Yep. Why don't you head to the room? I'll grab our drinks and shoes and meet you there."

She seemed relieved she didn't have to return to the very public setting. "I like that idea. Thank you."

When she slipped into the shadows, skirting the edge of the property to reach the room, which had a separate entry, he picked up their shoes in one hand, their drinks in the other, and crossed the patio, headed toward the other Renegades chilling by the firepit, now just Wes, Rubi, Troy, Ellie, Zahara, and Chase.

"There he is," Ellie said. "Wondered where you'd disappeared to."

"That was one long walk on the beach," Troy added with a smirk.

"Leave him alone," Rubi said. "He deserves some Duke time."

"More like Caitlyn time," Zahara said. She raised her fist to Duke, and he used the hand holding the shoes to bump her. "Nice choice. We like her."

"Glad you approve. See you tomorrow at brunch?"

They collectively agreed, and Duke continued to the room —really more of a suite—every Renegade had lived in for some length of time at some point over the years.

The lighting was dim, a soft glow coming from a lamp in the corner. Moonlight drifted through the windows, and Caitlyn stood in the middle of the room, worrying her fingers. She was stunning. Simply, stunningly gorgeous, and she had no idea.

Duke set the shoes on the floor and the whiskey on a side table. "Second thoughts?"

"No, just nerves."

Damn, that was adorable. "Sometimes the only way to get through the nerves is to just keep moving. Don't stop to look around, just put your head down and trust yourself to do what you need to do. At least that's how I handle nerves in stunts."

In the dim light, he could see the rosy flush to her skin, the slight swelling of her lips, and maybe a few red marks on her neck. He liked seeing the effect of his body on hers.

"Yeah, I think you're right." She reached up, slid the straps of her dress off her shoulders, and let it drop to the floor.

Duke's jaw dropped right along with it. He was speechless. He'd never seen anyone or anything so beautiful. From the top of her head to the polish on her toenails, she wore nothing but a very tiny pair of lace panties.

Duke slapped a hand to his thudding heart and drank her in. Every naked inch of her. "Sweet baby Jesus."

She laughed softly. "That's something we'd say in the South."

He stepped in, took her hands in his, and held them up and out. "How did God fit all those delicious curves into such a little package?"

She closed the distance and tilted her head back to look into his eyes while she unbuttoned his shirt. "I want you."

"That's the best thing I've heard in a long time." Duke let himself enjoy the moment. The thrill of a beautiful woman wanting him. He slid his hands down her smooth arms and up her back, traced the sweet features of her face. "There is no rush here. We can move as slow as you want."

She pulled the shirttails from his pants and pushed it off his shoulders, took one look at his chest, and froze. "Wow."

While he let the shirt drop from his arms, her hands drifted over his abs, up, and across his chest. Her fingers traced the hills and valleys, creating an electrical current everywhere she touched.

He wanted to lay her down and get dirty. Fuck her until they were both sweaty and exhausted. He could almost feel the rhythm. Only, she wasn't the kind of woman who got dirty. She wasn't someone who fucked for the sake of fucking. And he realized he was glad about that.

When they fucked, it wouldn't be mindless.

"I didn't think this was real," she said. "I mean, like, doable. I thought it was... I don't know what I thought. Maybe something you saw in movies or modeling. I can't even imagine the dedication you must have to achieve this. You're...just...wow. You don't have an ounce of body fat. How is that possible?"

It really had been too long since a woman had appreciated

his body. "Fast metabolism, constant workouts, working the farm."

Her gaze jumped to his. "Farm?"

"My parents live on a farm. My dad supplies hay to the area, and my mom sells at farmers markets and makes jams for local stores."

"That's so cool. But I've seen men who work on farms, and they don't have all this."

"Low body fat is good for climbing. Less effort to get up those mountains."

He lowered his head and kissed her. Tasted her until she groaned. Until she lifted to her toes, pushed her fingers into his hair, and pulled his head down to go deeper.

She had so much to give. How in holy hell had her ex missed all this?

She broke the kiss to work on his belt, but Duke tipped her head back and dove back in for another tongue-tangling kiss.

She laughed and pulled back. "I can't undress you while I'm kissing you. It's like being ambidextrous or something. One amazing thing at a time."

Breathing fast and shallow, she worked on his belt. And he let her. Soaked in the way her pupils dilated, the way she licked her lips, leaving a shine. She wanted this. Wanted him. She'd been dying to step out of her comfort zone. Duke just gave her the means, and he felt like one lucky bastard.

Once his pants were loose, her hand moved in, and her fingers closed around him, forcing "Holy fuck" from his lips.

"I was about to say the same thing."

He saw stars. Felt a wave of lust wash in. He wrapped her in his arms and walked her back to the bed, then laid her down.

"I'm not finished," she complained.

"You are for now." He let his body sink onto hers and groaned at all her soft, warm skin. Loved the press of her breasts against his chest, the curve of her waist beneath his hand. "God, you feel good."

"I'd feel better if you'd let me finish undressing you."

He smiled, caressed her face, then kissed her. Kissed her the way he wanted to fuck her, slow and deep, until she begged for the peak.

She hummed into his mouth, relenting to anything Duke wanted. It was easy to forget some of this would be new territory for her. She was naturally sensual, and she didn't even realize it.

When he pulled out of the kiss to breathe, she pressed her hand against his chest. "Roll over."

"I like the orders." He obeyed, taking her with him. She planted her hands on the mattress and pushed herself up just enough to kiss her way south.

When she hit his waist without any signs of stopping, he grabbed her arms with a playful "Where do you think you're going?"

She lifted her head and rested her chin on his belly. "I want to taste you."

Good God, he wanted her to taste him too.

"Uh-uh. Another time. I'd never last. It's been too long." He pulled her back to him and rolled again so she was underneath him. "You on the other hand, don't have to last."

He kissed her neck, her chest, her breasts, her belly. She grabbed his arms and said, "Where do you think you're going?" with a smile in her voice.

He looked up at her, chin on her belly, imitating her. "I want to taste you."

Nerves jumped in her eyes. "Um... I um..."

He hooked his fingers in her panties and dragged them down her legs and off, then kissed his way up her thigh. The small patch of sandy curls between her legs confirmed what

Duke had already believed—she was a natural blonde. "You, um what?"

"I'm not... I haven't..."

Normally, he preferred a confident woman in bed. At least he thought that was what he liked. But Caitlyn and her mild insecurities were a ridiculous thrill.

"How 'bout we give it a try, and if you don't like it, I'll stop?" Once he got his mouth on her, she'd forget her own name. Stopping wouldn't even enter her mind.

"I guess that's—"

He slid his hands under her thighs, dragged her toward him until she was on the edge of the bed, then made space for himself between her legs. And slowed way down.

He watched his fingers slide through her wet folds, and her scent filled his head, expanded his chest, and added pressure between his legs.

She covered his hand on her thigh. "Oh my God."

"Save that, sugar. You're going to need it."

He began slowly, lightly, teasing her into relaxation. His first lick made her gasp. His first suck made her moan.

Oh, yeah, this was going to be epic.

He opened wide and covered as much of her as he could. She whimpered, tilted her head, and watched him. And he watched her watch him. Her eyes were sultry and heavy lidded, her lips parted, tongue sliding along her full lower lip.

He eased his fingers through her heat again, this time exposing that tight little bud that needed his attention. A sound ebbed from her throat, something between a moan and a whimper. Duke found that pleasure point and flicked his tongue against it over and over, until she made more sexy sounds, until she curled into a partial sit-up, until she closed her fingers in his hair, until she held his head and her legs closed around him as she climbed toward the peak.

He gently pressed her thighs open again and closed his mouth over her, then sucked.

"God." She arched, eyes closed, hand fisted in the pillow above her head. "Oh my God."

He coaxed her and inched her and enticed her until she was on the very edge of orgasm, her body wire tight. Then he eased up.

Her eyes glazed over with need. "Don't...don't stop."

"Like it?"

"Yes." Her answer came quick and decisive. "God, yes."

A giddy bubble rose inside him. He pushed two fingers inside her and covered her with his mouth again, repeating all those moves that made her squirm and pant and arch.

One more round of flicking and sucking, and an intense orgasm ripped through her. And, oh, the sounds she made. Even as her hips bucked, even as she shivered and writhed, Duke kept sucking, kept licking, and kept drawing orgasm after orgasm out of her.

When her eyes started to clear, Duke stood and dropped his pants and boxers. Caitlyn lay limp on the bed, a beautiful display, her gaze following his movements and scanning his body, her eyes popping at his erection.

She moaned, rolled to her stomach, and spun to put her head at the foot of the bed, reaching for him. "Let me. Just a taste."

He released a slow breath. He wanted to let her, so badly. He hadn't had a woman's mouth on him for over two years.

"You don't like it?" Her question pulled some gray matter together, but he still couldn't think.

"What?"

"You don't like blow jobs?"

He huffed a laugh and ran one hand over her hair. "I'm a man. Loving them is required."

"Actually, it's not. But I'm really glad you love them." She looked up at him. "Let me. It's okay if you come."

Duke gave his head a shake. Maybe he'd been wrong about her getting dirty. "I can't think."

"I'll think for you. Come here. Just a taste."

In one step, he was in her hands and his mind was dust.

With her knees bent, legs in the air, her feet crossed at the ankles, she looked young and sweet. Then she licked his tip, and loose sparks floated through his body.

"Closer," she murmured.

He took another step, and he was in her mouth. Duke combed his hands through her hair, let them slide down her back and over her ass. Until she took him into her throat.

He gripped the comforter at her sides. "Fuck."

This was clearly something Caitlyn was good at. She knew exactly how to suck and stroke, and the way she looked at him while she did it made this more of an X-rated show than a simple act meant to please.

He watched her take him deep into that sweet Southern mouth of hers. Watched her tease him with her tongue and trace her lips with the tip of his cock. She created suction that made his eyes roll back in his head, and her tongue was on the verge of making him beg.

"That's...more than a taste." His words came out rough and low and lust filled. She just smiled and sucked until he shuddered.

"I think you catfished me on your experience." When she didn't offer up an explanation he asked, "How the fuck did you get so good at this?"

She pulled him from her mouth to say "porn" before she licked his length and took him deep again.

The answer jolted him enough to pull away. And while she whined in complaint, he lowered to his knees to get on the same level. "Did you just say *porn*?"

She stroked his jaw. “Yeah.”

“Aren’t you just a bundle of surprises?” he said before he kissed her, long, slow and deep. He was damned sure he’d never get tired of kissing this luscious mouth.

She pulled away and stroked the length of his nose with her own, a sweet gesture that tugged at his heart. “I am?”

“You’re Georgia-peach sweet, but you drink whiskey straight up. You’ve only been with one man, but you’re willing to go all in with someone new. You look as innocent as a baby deer, but you watch porn.”

“I don’t watch porn, per se,” she said. “I just wanted to get good at something that pleased a man, and it’s not exactly something you can just ask your friends about over lunch. It’s also something that really turns me on. Seemed like a win-win.” She sat up and offered her hand. “Come here. I remember you saying something about every inch of you inside me.”

5

Caitlyn had never experienced this kind of desire. The kind that reached deep inside her and had the power to make her want things she knew little to nothing about.

Instead of taking her hand to join her on the bed, Duke gripped her waist and lifted her—completely lifted her—off the bed, making her squeak in surprise. He pulled her close, pressed one knee to the mattress, and laid her down again. And when he eased back, he just looked and looked and looked. She'd never felt more beautiful.

"God damn," he muttered.

While he drank in the sight of her body, she reveled in his. She'd seen pictures of buff guys, met a few at college, but Duke was different. His muscle wasn't restricted to just his chest and arms. He didn't just have a nice ass. Every single muscle in his body was strong and sleek, not just the big muscles, but all the smaller ones too. She could see how they connected and created his body. It was really something. Fascinating.

She'd built so many firsts with him already. First time she'd met and had sex with a man in the same day. First time she'd climaxed with nothing but a man touching her. First time she'd overtly told a man she wanted him. First time she'd ever had a man's mouth on her. And she was pretty dang sure she was about to experience the best sex of her life.

She slid her hands up his arms, over his shoulders, through his hair. All while he kissed her.

This was one amazing fantasy she'd never even imagined, let alone expected to come true. She still wasn't sure how this dream had materialized. She kept second-guessing herself. Was this just a typical "California" hookup, or were they flash fire together? Was everything in California just better, the way everything in Texas was just bigger, or was this as exceptional as it felt? Was this all just the thrill of the moment? Maybe the whiskey?

"No, no, no," he said, his voice soft and low. "No thinking allowed."

He sank onto her, and all ability to think vanished. The feel of his skin on hers shut her mind down and heightened all her senses. His erection was hot and pressing against her in a way that made her moan and lift into him, but he just propped himself up on his forearms and did more staring.

No man had ever made her feel more beautiful. More accepted. More valued.

Just a hookup, she reminded herself. *Just a hookup.*

"Okay, talk," he said, patient and open. "What's going through your head? You've got to get it out, or you won't be able to enjoy this. And there's nothing I want more than for you to enjoy this."

"I've already enjoyed the heck out of this." She skimmed her fingers over all the skin she could reach. "It just all feels new again. And so much better. It's been a long time."

"Sounds like we're in the same place."

She laughed softly. "I don't think so. I can already classify this as the best sex of my life, and I haven't even had you inside me yet."

His smile came slow and burned hot. He brushed the hair off her forehead. "And we've still got an entire night ahead of us."

She slid her hand over his shoulder and pulled him close. "Then let's get on with the best sex of our lives."

He laughed, pushed up, and reached for his phone. From the bill holder on the back, he pulled a foil square. Caitlyn bit the inside of her lip as she took it from him, surprising him again. She enjoyed watching his reaction every time she challenged one of her limits, which, let's be real, was about everything they'd done—or would do—tonight.

It had been a long time since she'd used a condom. Years, in fact. Many years.

"Roll for me," she said, voice thick.

When he was on his back, Caitlyn sat up, opened the packet, pulled the condom out, and made a curious face. "I never could figure out which way it's supposed to go on."

Smiling, he reached up and flipped the condom. "That way."

"Got it."

Duke gripped her thighs as she rolled the condom down his length. A very long length. She knew guys varied in size, not firsthand, but she'd seen it in the porn, heard about it from her friends. Duke was quite a departure from Brett. A welcome departure. And, okay, maybe also a nerve-racking departure.

When she hit the base of his cock, Duke pulled himself into a sitting position, wrapped his arms around her, and started to roll.

She pressed her hand to the mattress. "Hold on. I think I'll stay here awhile."

His slow smile burned her up. "By all means, let's stay here awhile."

She rose on her knees and slid his cock against her heat before easing him inside.

The glory of it took her breath. She had to take him slowly, and every inch drove her closer to delirium.

The way he filled her was like the ocean, overwhelming and something that had to be experienced to understand. With her hands on his chest, his cock stretching her, she paused, soaking in the ecstasy, adjusting to his size.

Looking down into his handsome face, she saw a whole new world of sex opening up right in front of her. She was looking at the personification of that nagging inkling that had plagued her for years—*there has to be more.* She'd been right. Duke was that more.

He reached up, slid his hand through her hair, and pulled her down for one of his epic kisses. Damn, the way this man could use his mouth... His passion was white-hot, and his fingers dug into her hips. He pulled her in, then pushed her back.

She broke the kiss on a sharp "Oh God."

She was in so far over her head. Didn't know how to process all this pleasure, but evidently, her body did, because she picked up the rhythm, wringing a deep curse from Duke's lips.

Pleasing him thrilled her. Every word of praise or show of excitement lured her into stepping further and further out of her comfort zone. The pleasure was so intense, she lost track of the rhythm.

Duke took over for her, pulling her in, then rocking her away. She fisted the comforter at his shoulders and just tried to hold on as a monster orgasm took over like a tsunami. And when the wave broke, Caitlyn was flooded with an ecstasy she didn't know was even possible.

She might have screamed, she wasn't sure. All she could focus on was the cycle of need and release, need and release, release, release.

Multiple orgasms were not fictional. Another myth busted.

This time when Duke rolled her, she let him, then lifted her hips to meet his thrusts. Sweat dripped from his temple, hit her chest, and slid between her breasts.

He paused, and Caitlyn focused on his face. His eyes were closed, a mixed look of pleasure and pain in his expression.

"What?" she said, breathless. "What's wrong?"

"Everything's perfect." Sweat slid into his eye, and she wiped it away from his temple. "Too perfect. Trying to pull myself back. It's just...so fucking good. I don't want it to be over."

His pleasure made Caitlyn feel like she could fly.

She sat up, and Duke followed until she straddled his lap. She slid her arms around his shoulders and pressed her lips to his neck.

"Didn't I just hear a reference to having an entire night left?" she murmured against his skin.

He laughed, a breathless huff of air. "You sure did."

She pulled back and smiled at him. "Then we've got lots of time left for it to be so fucking good."

6

The heat woke Caitlyn. A deep heat that made her want to peel off layers. But as soon as she tried to reach for the covers to throw them off, she found her hand wrapped in someone else's.

Duke.

Caitlyn smiled. She smiled and smiled and smiled some more. She smiled until her face hurt, and laughter slipped out.

He was lying on his side, one arm under her, the other one over, the fingers of one hand threaded with hers. His strong body connected with hers from shoulders to toes. No wonder she was hot.

She stared at their hands, fingers interlocked. His so big and rough, hers so small and soft. The sight filled an empty place inside her. One she hadn't known was empty until Duke filled it. Caitlyn rolled to her back and turned her head to look at the man who had single-handedly changed her life. And that wasn't hyperbole. He'd altered her perception of so much—her beauty, her limits, her desirability, her personal power. And laughter. So much laughter. Over family stories, work, friends, sex.

She listened to the soft rhythm of the ocean in the distance for a few long moments, the thick, warm silence in the room. She couldn't remember ever feeling this good. Good from the inside out.

Caitlyn rolled to her back, but Duke didn't move. She sighed and studied him with that gooey warm spot in her chest growing. She couldn't get enough of that face. Long dark eyelashes, stubble highlighting his square jaw and framing his full lips, his dark hair mussed by Caitlyn's hands. The bedsheets were in a tangle, barely covering even one of his perfect ass cheeks. The contrast between the white sheet and his luscious olive skin made her want to touch him.

Heck, everything made her want to touch him.

She cut a look at the clock behind him on the other nightstand, surprised to find it coming up on 7:00 a.m.

Her stomach dropped a little. She now faced a decision she'd been pushing off since she and Duke had stepped into this room—do the morning-after thing or leave?

Hookups weren't supposed to do the morning-after, right?

She turned his hand over and traced the callouses. There was still so much she wanted to know about him.

Her mind drifted through the roughly twelve hours they'd spent together, and the most intense moments stood out. Having to face all the things she'd said and done in the heat of passion created a bubble of anxiety in her stomach.

The night had been so magical. The dark, the beach, the wedding, her new, sexy friend—it had been the perfect storm, and Caitlyn had let the rain pummel her, let the wind take her, let the lightning electrify her. She could honestly say she'd made a bold presence in her new life.

She closed her eyes. Amazing didn't have enough oomph to accurately describe the intensity between them. How would that look in the morning light? Would he be sweet and one hundred percent into her the way he was last night? Or would he be cool and dismissive, with an it-was-great-but-it's-over attitude.

A nagging insecurity told her she didn't want to face the possibility of indifference. It had been, hands down, the best night of her life, and she didn't want a morning encounter to tarnish it.

She slowly moved his arm off her, and when he didn't wake, she eased from the bed. She grimaced, hoping he stayed asleep. The bed coverings were on the floor, pillows all over the room. Duke had complained that they kept him from getting as close as he wanted and tossed them until there was nothing on the bed but the two of them. She pulled her lips between her teeth to keep from laughing.

God, it was hard to let go. But she wanted to keep as much of their time together intact in her memory as possible, and she didn't want those memories to include him walking out that door with a cool, great-fuck attitude. Because it had been so much more than a great fuck to Caitlyn.

She opened the top of her already-unzipped suitcase and pulled on jeans and a T-shirt, moving excruciatingly slow.

When she was dressed, she moved toward the door and smiled at Duke. Last night was forever etched in her memory. In her heart.

She slowly pressed her thumb against the door handle and drew it open just a foot, just enough for her to slip through. She hoped the cold morning air didn't wake him, prayed the hinges didn't squeak.

Her hopes and prayers were realized, but the relief was a mix of pleasure and loss.

Her drive to the new apartment was steeped in sizzling memories, making her so hot, she had to fan her face. But her attention veered to the present when she turned into a very sketchy neighborhood. Like don't-get-out-of-the-car sketchy. A few more turns, and she rolled up to the address.

The building looked like it was from the forties and hadn't been updated since. Peeling paint, patched roof, a board over a broken window.

Her stomach twisted and dropped. So much for the ability of Google's street view to give an accurate rendering of the neighborhood.

She parked at the curb, and tears stung her eyes. Just emotion overload. So much had happened over the last week. She'd be okay in a few minutes.

On a deep breath, she closed her eyes and imagined going into work at city hall, where her father had gotten her a job. Imagined being bored stupid for eight hours only to return home and stream mind-numbing Netflix. Or worse, had dinner with Brett, where she would have to listen to his day as an IT guy, which was, quite possibly, more boring than hers.

Determination renewed, she stood from her ancient Honda Civic. She still couldn't believe it had gotten her here without the engine dropping out or something equally devastating to her bank account. Caitlyn pulled out two big suitcases from the trunk and started up the stairs to apartment 2B. She'd have to get her other things from Lexi's later today.

She used the key the roommate had sent her to enter the apartment and was dragging in her suitcases just as a completely naked man passed through the hall of the apartment. At the sight of her, he stopped, giving her a full frontal view she tried to ignore. He was tall, thin, pale, and scruffy.

While she tried to get some words together, he disappeared into another room—probably a bathroom—and Caitlyn stood there shell-shocked for a long moment.

She took in the low-pile orange-brown carpet, holding stains Caitlyn didn't want to think about. The interior walls were dirty, with handprints on doorjambs and scuffs at every level. And the smell, the musty scent of dirt and life, made her a little sick.

She stared at the ceiling and the dark marks that could only be dried soda. There had been a short span of time when her brothers thought the funniest thing on earth was to shake soda cans and open them in the house. It was short-lived because the fun factor dropped into the negative range when Caitlyn stood there and watched as they cleaned the ceiling, wiped the walls, and steam cleaned the carpets.

"Um, hello?" she called. "I'm Caitlyn. I'm supposed to live here."

A woman stepped out of the room the man had just come from. Her expression wasn't exactly unenthusiastic, it was more deadpan. She wore cut-offs and a sports bra. Her hair was a short brown-blonde blend, and spiked. Somehow, it worked for her. She had more piercings and tattoos than Caitlyn had ever seen, even in Atlanta.

"I'm Andi." Both her tone and her gaze were flat. "Where the fuck did you get that accent?"

Not a great start. "I grew up in Kentucky, but we were on the border of Tennessee, and I was in Georgia for a couple of years, so—"

"That was a rhetorical question, and it's going to bug the fuck out of me."

Last night, everyone had been delighted with her accent. This first meeting certainly wouldn't go down as the best in Caitlyn's history.

"That's your room." Andi pointed toward a door at the end of the hall. "You take your showers at night, because the bathroom is mine in the morning."

"But I—"

"Stay out of my room, and don't touch my stuff, especially not my food. It's all labeled. If you want to keep your stuff, label all of it. I've got a shitty schedule, so when you get home, check to see if I'm asleep before you start making any noise."

"Okay, I—"

"Half the rent, half the utility, half the cable, like we agreed."

"Right."

Before Caitlyn could say any more, the man exited the bathroom and once again stood there and stared. Caitlyn couldn't help but compare his thin, pale body to Duke's, which really wasn't fair. No one compared to Duke. Maybe other Renegades, but honestly, no one else.

"Who's this?" he finally asked.

"Roommate," Andi told him with as little warmth as she'd shown Caitlyn. She wasn't sure why, but it gave Caitlyn hope. "You're going to have to start wearing clothes when you come around here."

"Fucking roommates," he muttered and disappeared into the bedroom that was obviously Andi's.

"So," Caitlyn said, working up a smile for Andi. "It's good to meet you face-to-face."

Before she could say more, her cell pinged, and she looked at the message.

It was from Lexi. *Will you be at brunch?*

"Oh no." She'd forgotten about brunch. A brunch for their closest friends before Jax and Lexi boarded a plane for Fiji—for a month. Duke would be attending said brunch, no doubt. All that effort to sneak out, and she was going to walk right back to him. It was both annoying and exciting.

She texted back. *Can't wait. What time and where?*

Lexi's answers sent a panic through Caitlyn.

I'll be there. May be a little late. Start without me, I'll catch up.

She returned her gaze to Andi, who was waiting with surprising patience. "Sorry. My cousin got married last night, and we're going to brunch before they leave on their honeymoon. Would it be okay if I take a shower this morning? After today, I don't mind showering at night."

She shrugged. "Yeah, that's fine."

The easy answer confused Caitlyn. After the roommate's intro with a bunch of rules, Caitlyn thought she'd have to fight for it. She was absolutely not going to the brunch smelling like sex with Duke, as delicious as it was.

The guy came out and paused in front of Andi. "Text me."

"Dreamer," Andi quipped, poker faced.

Then the guy was gone, Andi retreated into her room, and Caitlyn was left to haul in luggage, find something to wear, shower, and try really hard not to get nervous about seeing Duke this morning.

7

Duke couldn't remember the last time he'd felt this good. Physically and mentally, he was still on cloud nine where Caitlyn had left him. Though he'd slipped a few notches when he woke to find her gone.

He was almost the last to arrive at the restaurant. The huge table was surrounded by the most important people in his life—all the Renegades, their significant others, and a few of the kids they'd had over the last couple of years, including Zach and Tessa, who'd come from Hawaii, and Ryker and Rachel, who'd come from Virginia. Tessa's daughter, Sophia, was the oldest of the kids and acted like a miniature babysitter for the others. Kristy had elected not to come. He understood. Handling three girls under five could really take the joy out of even the most casual outing.

The only other person missing: Caitlyn.

He wondered if she was going to show. There was a seat open for her with far too many people between them for his taste.

"Look, Uncle Duke is here." Keaton passed his boy down

the line of people until the kid reached Duke. Keaton clapped his hands. "Let's eat."

Everyone laughed.

The kid was beautiful, with Keaton's dark hair and big dark brown eyes. Still, Duke grimaced at little Connor. "You look like your dad, buddy. Bad break. It's okay, women are really only interested in your mind."

While the others laughed, Duke stood the kid on the table and started moving the kid's arms and legs like a dancing puppet. Connor was a good sport about it, and Duke got some deep belly laughs before it was his turn to order.

He settled Connor into the crook of his elbow and glanced at the empty chair again, then to Lexi. "Is Caitlyn coming? Should we wait?"

"Since when do we wait for anyone?" Troy asked.

"Caitlyn said she would be running late," Lexi told him, "and to start without her."

At least he'd get to see her again today. Duke ordered and played with the baby awhile before he started fussing and was sent back to his parents.

"Man, that's nice." Duke crossed his arms on the table. "Having someone to hand them off to. I gotta get me one of those."

"They're called a wife," Keaton said, earning an elbow from Brook even as she took the baby from Keaton and offered a bottle. "You should try it."

They talked about the wedding, who was there, what was new. There was a lot of nitpicking, chiding, and laughter. And while Duke often laughed at his nieces and Kristy, this was different. And it felt really good.

When Caitlyn whisked in, she was all apologies and hey y'alls. She wore jeans, white Keds, and one of those off-the-shoulder blouses. She was fresh-faced, her hair flowy, wearing hoop earrings and a necklace that drew his gaze to her cleavage. And, yeah, she was just as beautiful as she'd been last night. It wasn't a figment of his imagination. The woman was simply gorgeous.

Just the sight of her got his engine revving. His body sprang to life in areas that had been neglected until Caitlyn. He sure as hell hoped last night wasn't their only night.

The waitress came over, got her drink order, and offered a menu, but Caitlyn didn't need it. She ordered the largest breakfast they had: eggs, bacon, sausage, country potatoes, pancakes, toast...

"Where in the hell are you going to put all that food?" Wes wanted to know.

"Bless your heart for caring," she quipped, something everyone knew translated into various meanings depending on the setting and the tone. In this case it was a sweet "mind your own business," making the others laugh. "I'm *starving*."

The instant Duke linked her current starved state to the activity the night before, her gaze met his. And she gave him a smile like the one she'd given him before they'd ever met yesterday, a little shy, a little mischievous. But she didn't let it linger nearly long enough.

The table was as rowdy as it always was when they all got together, and their teasing and laughter filled the restaurant.

Caitlyn fit in as if she'd always been part of them. Before the food came, Keaton passed off his boy again, this time to Caitlyn, who got him laughing as deeply and happily as Duke had. He thought of her offer to help with his nieces, and that soft spot inside him grew.

The food came, and Caitlyn handed Connor back to his parents. While everyone was distracted by their plates, Caitlyn gave Duke a sweet smile and a conspiratorial wave.

He couldn't do this. Couldn't just sit here for the entire meal, wondering what last night meant. Was it the beginning of her sowing oats? Or was it something she wanted to continue with him?

Duke excused himself and moved by her on the way toward the bathroom, laying a hand on her shoulder only for as long as it took him to pass. In the hallway, he leaned against the wall and waited. He hoped he knew her as well as he thought he did and was rewarded when she turned the corner into the hallway and stopped short at the sight of him.

"What are you doing?"

"Waiting for you."

She relaxed and moved closer. "Who says I'm here for you? Maybe I just came to use the facilities."

They stood across the hall from each other, both leaning against the wall, in this crowded restaurant with all their friends just a table away. But Duke had never felt closer to her.

"Why'd you sneak out?" he asked.

"I didn't sneak, exactly."

"Then what would you call it?"

She gave a one-shouldered shrug. "Maybe an insurance policy?"

Duke lifted a brow.

"You know, against the ill effects of—for lack of a better choice of words at the moment—buyer's remorse."

He reached out and ran a few fingers along her jaw and down her neck, but steeled himself for the answer to his next question. "Do you have regrets?"

She puffed a laugh. "I meant for you. There wasn't a goddamned thing for me to regret."

Weight lifted off his chest, allowing him to breathe better. He slipped two fingers into the waistband of her jeans and tugged her forward until her body rested against his. Not only didn't she fight it, she swayed into him, and she felt as amazing as she had last night.

"Not one regret here," he told her.

She made a melodramatic show of wiping her brow. "Phew. Disaster averted."

"I know this is bad timing," he said, "but I'm leaving town for a job. I'll be gone four or five weeks."

"Why is it bad timing?"

They either were on different pages or weren't communicating well. "Because we just met. Just started something."

"Oh. Right. Um..."

"Did we? Start something?" he asked. "Or was this morning the end of whatever happened last night?"

"I, um..." She stroked her hands up his arms and over his shoulders. Her belly pressed against his, her breasts pillowed against his chest, and she smelled like a field of flowers. "I was, sort of, thinking about that." She shifted on her feet and bit the inside of her lip. "I just got here, and I still have a lot of knots to untangle, you know? I don't think this would be a good time for me to jump into anything, and I know your life is just as messy at the moment."

"Yeah." His heart dropped. "Life's pretty crazy right now." He stroked her cheek with his thumb. "Bad timing."

"Bad timing," she agreed.

Duke didn't like the thought of letting her go with no guarantee she'd be available or interested when he returned. In fact, he was pretty sure once she'd seen the depth of chaos that was his life, she would be the opposite of interested. Not to mention all the men who would be hitting on her around here. And he really didn't like the hole he was already feeling inside.

"Last night was..." She started, looking wistful and laughing softly, "Amazing wouldn't begin to describe it." She met his gaze. "It was honestly the very best night of my life. You're an incredible guy, in so many ways."

His heart rebounded. "It was. Amazing, I mean. I was disappointed to find you gone when I woke up."

She winced. "I wasn't sure what to do. I've heard some ugly

stories about the morning-after thing, and the night was so incredible, I didn't want to ruin it."

Fuck him to hell and back, he wanted to keep her.

"Where's your job?" she asked.

"Canada. A lot of studios film in Canada now because it's cheaper than the US."

"That sounds fun. I've never been out of the country. Bet you're excited to get back to your friends. Hey, do you want to give me Kristy's phone number? I'll give her a holler next week, once I've got my life in some sort of order."

She offered her phone, and he traded with her. They smiled at each other before adding their numbers into the phones.

He brushed a strand of her hair over her shoulder, cupped her jaw, and lowered his head to kiss her. Her lips felt familiar, in the best possible way. She made a sound of pleasure and relief and took the kiss deeper, tongue to tongue. The embers still burning inside him caught fire again.

She locked her arms behind his neck, stretching her body against his, and opened to him, dragging him right back to the most intense moments of their night, when he was embedded deep inside her, delivering as much pleasure as humanly possible.

The passion in her kiss made him moan, and he slid one hand over her ass cheek and pulled her against him.

"Excuse me."

The annoyed male voice broke them apart like ice water.

"Pardon us," Caitlyn said, squeezing even closer to Duke as the man passed. When he disappeared into the bathroom, Caitlyn pressed her face to Duke's chest and laughed. Then looked up at him. "We should probably get back to the table before those boys eat your breakfast."

"What about your breakfast?"

"Oh, honey, no one would touch my breakfast. They're smarter than that."

He chuckled, then grew serious. “I won’t want you any less in a month than I do today, so don’t completely write me off while I’m gone.”

She smiled, lifted on her toes, and kissed him. “I could never write you off.”

8

She needed another nap.

Caitlyn looked at the spotless refrigerator with pride. In fact, the whole place looked good. Well, as good as it could. The apartment received the benefit of Duke's "I won't want you any less in a month than I do today" playing on a loop in her head while she tried to quiet it by cleaning for hours.

Duke had drained her energy the night before, and Caitlyn was paying for it today. But she reminded herself that last night was last night. And he might say he'd still be interested in her in a month, but a month was a long time, and from talking to Jax and Lexi over the years, she knew a movie set was a great place to find women. Or for women to find Duke. She wasn't under any delusions that he wouldn't be hooking up while he was gone.

Which made her decision to keep things friendly the right call. She wanted things between them to feel good. They'd be seeing each other at all the barbecues and get-togethers Lexi always talked about. Caitlyn desperately wanted to avoid the potential for awkwardness.

The living room door opened to Andi, who froze in the doorway looking shell-shocked. "There's no discount on the rent for cleaning."

"I just thought it would be nice. Trying to keep myself busy. There was some stuff in there that's older than dirt. Hope you don't mind that I threw it out. It wasn't edible."

"God, that accent," Andi griped with a shake of her head before closing the door.

She wore black jeans with horizontal rips in both pant legs from the shin to midthigh, a black sports bra that exposed her flat belly, her belly button piercing, and some kind of tattoo Caitlyn couldn't figure out. Her half-blonde, half-brown hair was still in the spike, but Andi looked tired today.

"I like your belly button piercing," Caitlyn said. "I've always kind of wanted one."

"You didn't touch my room, right?" Andi asked.

"No, not your room. I just moved some stuff around in the fridge and bathroom when I was cleaning."

"Okay, that's cool." Her flat expression made it hard to figure out whether she was being sarcastic or authentic.

"Are you just getting back from work?" Caitlyn asked, trying to warm up the situation.

"Yeah."

"Where do you work?"

"Bougie at night, Top Crop during the day." Andi wandered through the living room, looking around as if searching for something to get pissed about.

"I don't know what those are," Caitlyn said.

Andi opened the fridge and inspected the contents. "I would never have guessed this fridge could get this clean. You got to the grocery store."

"Almost puked over the bill."

Andi laughed. The woman *laughed*. That was a good sign.

"And filling my tank with gas felt like blood draining out my feet."

Andi nodded and closed the fridge door. "Why do you think I've got two jobs? Bougie is a bar, Top Crop is a dispensary."

"That seems hard, the two jobs." She thought of her parents, and guilt snuck in.

"Top Crop's employee discount helps."

Every direction she looked told Caitlyn that living in LA was going to be more difficult than she'd expected. "Guess I'll have to adjust my budget for the prices here."

Maybe Caitlyn would be hitting up Andi for a second job soon. Not a welcome thought.

"Just make sure you've got rent money," Andi said.

"No need to worry, on account of rent will always come first."

Andi seemed satisfied with that. She leaned against the kitchen counter and crossed her arms. "What's your story? Please don't tell me you came from the country to hit it big in Hollywood."

"No. I needed to get out of my small town, and my cousin lives here, so I thought this would be a good place to start."

"What do you do?"

"I'm in PR. The job I start tomorrow has the title of public relations associate, but the job description wasn't exactly clear."

"Probably a fixer, though you don't strike me as fixer material. Too soft."

"What's a fixer?"

"The name is self-explanatory. They fix things. You know, they get rid of problems, sweep things under the rug, pay people off to keep their mouths shut."

Caitlyn shook her head. "I don't understand."

"Fixers make problems go away. Like hiding the toxic work environment on the Ellen DeGeneres show or getting Loughlin's criminal charges lowered. Who do you think trails Britney Spears around, cleaning up all her messes?"

Caitlyn cringed. "That sounds awful."

"Better learn to like it. Food and rent prices aren't going down anytime soon." Andi wandered into her bedroom.

"I really don't think that's what it is, because you're right, I wouldn't be good at that. They had to see that in the interview. I mean, you saw it immediately."

"What did the job description say?"

Her discomfort over the lack of details for the job returned full force. "It was very...generic."

"They can't advertise for a fixer because that would be admitting that they exist. Everyone in Hollywood knows they exist, but they seem to go by the motto *If I don't look at them, they won't see me.*"

A sick feeling sank into Caitlyn's stomach.

Andi walked out of her room dressed in fresh but very similar clothes to the ones she'd come home in. She tossed a few magazines on the coffee table. "I was born and raised here, and I know the dirt. Trust me, PR associate is slang for celebrity fixer. Sorry to burst your bubble, chickie, but you're on cleanup duty."

She tapped a magazine with Reba McEntire on the cover and a headline that read *Love after Heartbreak.* "Good fixer." Then she tapped one with a beautiful brunette on the cover and a headline that read *Demi Lovato's Shocking Overdose. A Life in Danger.* "Bad fixer."

Andi headed to the door before Caitlyn could process the information long enough to form questions. "Later."

The front door closed, and Caitlyn sank onto the sofa, scanning the magazine covers. She didn't recognize any of these people, except for Reba McEntire. Everyone knew Reba McEntire. Caitlyn hadn't considered memorizing celebrity information. She'd never expected to be in a position to need that knowledge.

She pulled out a magazine with the picture of a guy who was on *Friends*. She couldn't remember his name, but at least she recognized his face. The headline read *Bombshell Tell-All. Drugs, Affairs, and Cheating Death.*

And all Caitlyn could think was *bad fixer*.

9

Duke shoved a few more T-shirts into the nooks and crannies of his suitcase. "Did you talk to Celeste today?"

"It's Sunday, and she's out of town for a family reunion. I'll try tomorrow."

Celeste was their attorney, one of the very few available to Kristy. She'd told Peter she wanted a divorce before she'd contacted any attorneys, so Peter went out and consulted with every big and medium shark in the pond.

Then, when Kristy started attorney shopping, none of the good ones would touch her because they'd already spoken to Peter. And even though Peter hired only one, his consults made it illegal for the others he'd consulted to take on Kristy as a client. Lucky for Kristy, Celeste had just relocated from San Diego and wasn't on Peter's radar.

As soon as Duke turned away to pick up something else, Paisley pulled out the shirts he'd just put in and dropped them on the ground with a stomp of her foot and an emphatic "No go."

It started as a game, but slowly turned into meltdown material, and now, Duke was walking on eggshells with her. Scarlett was rolling around the floor with a doll, and Willow toddled around the apartment dancing to the Disney movie on the television.

"Paisley, honey," Kristy said, "do you want to cook? Come help me with dinner."

Paisley dropped to her butt and started wailing.

Duke's heart fell. "Come on, now, turn off the faucet."

He abandoned his suitcase—he should never have even tried to pack while the girls were awake—and carried Paisley to the sofa, where she cuddled into him, clutching her blanket while she latched on to the movie.

"They're all tired," Kristy said. "Dinner, bath, and bed. That goes for me too."

"Where are you going?" Scarlett asked for the tenth time that day.

"Canada."

"Why?"

"Work."

"Where is Canada?"

Duke didn't answer. With his partially packed bag by the door and Paisley clinging to him, he was getting that unsettled feeling about leaving.

"Before you go to bed," Duke told Kristy, "I want to go over all the security with you again."

She groaned.

"This is important. You never think you need it until it's too late. I don't ever want you and the girls in a too-late position." The possibility was unnerving. "Maybe we should have stayed at Mom and Dad's until after the hearing."

But that would mean he wouldn't have met Caitlyn. So...

"He's in Canada, same as you're going to be," Kristy said. They never used Peter's name in front of the girls.

"But his freelancers aren't," Duke reminded her, "and

Canada gives him an alibi. No better time for something to happen."

She stopped stirring the mac and cheese. They ate a lot of mac and cheese these days. Duke was not disappointed he'd be changing up his diet on set.

"Oh, sh—oot." She caught herself before a different word came out. "You're right. I never thought of that."

"And you don't have a restraining order on the freelancers."

"Yeah, okay. We'll go over it all again, but I don't want you feeling guilty for being gone or worrying about us while you're on the set. You need to stay focused while you're scaling mountains."

She returned her attention to the noodles. "I can't lie, it feels good to see you getting back to your life. We've interfered long enough."

"You're not interfering. You're my family."

"Want to tell me about your sleepover?" she asked, grinning. "Are we going to get to meet her?"

"Does Uncle Duke have a *girlfriend*?" Scarlett asked.

Kristy grinned at Duke. "All yours, brother."

"You're such an instigator."

"What's she like?" Scarlett pushed.

"She's not my girlfriend. She's just a friend who happens to be a girl." And after talking to her in the hallway at the restaurant earlier today, he was sure she'd be taken by the time he got around to coming back a month—or more—from now. She was too beautiful, too sweet, and way the hell too sexy not to get snapped up by a man who recognized her as a rare find. The image of her in someone else's arms materialized and yanked on a possessive, protective cord inside him. He hoped he never had to witness that.

"She's very nice," he said, not exactly sure how to appropriately describe her. "Hotter than hell in bed" probably wouldn't be appropriate. "And she has a pretty accent."

"What kind of accent?" Kristy asked.

"Southern. Cutest thing I've ever heard."

"Aww," Kristy said. "I like her already. Been a while since I saw you grin like that over a woman."

He hadn't realized he was smiling until she mentioned it. "Oh, I almost forgot. She offered to help you out while I was gone. Said she could watch the girls or run errands or do laundry." He pulled his phone from his back pocket and texted Caitlyn's phone number to his sister. "Her name is Caitlyn."

"Good God, brother, put a ring on it. You don't find women like that anymore." Kristy transferred the mac and cheese into paper bowls and set them on the table along with milk, juice and Solo and sippy cups. "Come eat, girls."

They gathered at the scarred dining table that had come with the apartment and went quiet as they ate with plastic forks and spoons.

"Where did she come from?" Kristy asked, sipping milk from a Solo.

Duke sat across from her and twirled the macaroni she'd put in a bowl for him. "Kentucky."

"Ah," she said, nodding. "Makes perfect sense now."

"Right?" He shook his head. "So hard to find someone good in this place."

"Then add in your crazy work schedule, your dangerous stunts, and three little girls who look at you like a father..." Kristy shook her head. "Won't be too much longer. Things will get easier soon."

A text pinged on Duke's phone. He hated to admit it, but he hoped it was from Caitlyn.

Unfortunately, it was Cameron, a young guy who'd been with the Renegades a little over a year. "Cam's behind the house. Ready for a dry run?"

Kristy sighed. "Yeah. Girls, finish your noodles. Scarlett watch Willow. We're just going into the other room."

Content with their noodles, the girls barely even acknowledged the shift.

They went into Kristy's room, and Duke pushed the old wooden window frame up, pressed his hands to the sill, and leaned out.

"Ahoy, mateys." Cameron kept his voice down and saluted them.

Duke scoured the yard and the other apartments. It was another perfect California summer night, but despite LA's dense population, no one was out around them. He didn't want anyone seeing anything suspicious in case Fontaine's PIs started knocking on doors.

"You're going," Kristy said, clearly reading his mind. "Don't even think about staying."

"Get the ladder. I'll show you how to attach it to the sill."

The emergency ladder was nothing but a series of metal rods and nylon rope. It wasn't designed to be scaled upward, but Duke knew Cameron would take to it like another limb. The kid was talented. He was about twenty-six, dirty blond, good-looking. Not that he needed help. The job had girls lining up at his hotel room door. Though Cam said he wasn't opening the door to any of them. Something about a bad breakup.

Once she'd secured the top, Kristy let the rope drop straight down. "This is crazy. How is this my life?"

Cameron jumped from the ground with a grunt and grabbed the bottom rung, then climbed the rope like a monkey. Duke and Kristy stepped back from the window, and Cameron gripped the sill, then belly flopped into the house.

"Pretty sloppy, kid," Duke told him.

"I'm here, aren't I?"

"Kristy, pull the rope back up."

"I'll get it," Cam said.

"No, she'll have to do it after we leave for the airport and every morning after you leave. She has to practice."

Kristy messily pulled the rope back into the room.

"Looks like they already found you," Cameron told Duke, barely even breathing hard. "Guy out front in a dark Corolla. Think it's blue."

"Who's that?" Scarlett eased into the room, peeking around the wall. She gasped. "Uncle Cam!"

She ran at Cameron. The other two girls immediately followed, and suddenly, there were six people in a space designed for one, three of them screaming with glee. Cameron dropped into a crouch and tickled the girls until they laughed so hard, they couldn't breathe, then walked all three of them into the living room—one on his back, one in his arms, and one clinging to his leg.

Kristy smirked at Duke. "We probably should have found someone they like more."

They'd returned to town a couple of weeks ago, and Kristy and the girls had been easily welcomed into the Renegade family. The kids had instantly bonded with everyone, but Cam was a favorite.

In the living room, Cam had all the girls clustered around him and a book open on his lap. The guy did amazing impersonations, riveting the girls to the story.

"Let's do this while they're occupied," Duke told her.

They walked through the house, Kristy pointing out the two cans of bear mace and two charged stun guns well out of the girls' reach. They armed and disarmed the security system, checked the cameras, and went through the system's app on her phone.

Back in the living room, Cam was just finishing the story. Kristy took the girls for their bath, and Duke went over all the security information with Cam.

Duke finished packing, gave all the girls good-night kisses, hugged Kristy, and headed out with Cam.

They left the way Cam had entered and waited to leave

until Kristy had the ladder back inside the house. They snuck along the side of the apartments to look across the street, where a blue Toyota Corolla sat beneath a streetlight, one man in the driver's seat, his attention directed toward the vicinity of their apartment.

"Knew they'd figure it out," he told Cam. "Guess I was just hoping..."

"Don't worry. No one's getting near them while I'm here."

They headed back to Cam's truck, and he tapped numbers on his phone before they started toward the airport.

In the silent car, Duke heard the woman on the other end of the phone. "9-1-1, what is the address of your emergency?"

Cam gave her the address of the apartment building, but not the apartment number. "There's a guy in a blue Toyota Corolla sitting outside the apartment, just watching us. He's been out there almost a week, and he's there all night long. It's freaking out my wife."

Cam thanked the operator and disconnected before she could ask more questions, dropped his phone in the center console, and pulled onto the road.

Once they were on the way to the airport, Cam said, "You know, it would be interesting to put a PI on Fontaine's ass."

Duke wasn't used to Peter's last name anymore. Kristy had changed hers and the girls' back to Reid the day she filed for divorce.

"I thought of that, but he's got pretty tight security, and my bank account is running on fumes. I did consider having you come through the front door so the PI knew a man was staying there, but they could easily twist that into saying Kristy was having an affair."

"Yeah, good call." Cam cut a grin toward Duke. "So, Caitlyn. She's something."

Duke laughed. "Yeah, she is. Unfortunately, I'm going to be out of town for the foreseeable future, and as you just said, she's something. Won't be long before she's getting hit on from everywhere."

"This job is incredible," Cam said, "but it definitely interferes with real life. On the upside, you'll be back on the set. You won't even have to look for women."

Duke shrugged. "Where did Taylor come from?" he asked, referencing the woman Cam had brought to the wedding. "She was pretty hot."

"Yeah, she's nice. A paramedic I used to work with. We're just friends."

"Haven't bounced back from your ex yet?"

Cam shrugged, which meant definitely not.

"That sucks." Duke looked at him. "Why do we do this again?"

"The job or women?"

"Both."

Cam laughed. "Have you already forgotten the 'fun' and 'hot' part?"

"Right, right."

Cam pulled into the Departures lane. "Stay safe, and don't worry about Kristy and the girls. I've got it covered."

Duke met Cam's fist bump. "I owe you."

10

Caitlyn was sweating by the time she reached the tenth floor of her office building. She stepped out of the stairwell, and instead of going to the office door, she found the restroom.

Thankfully, it was empty. She pressed her hands against the sink and looked at herself in the mirror. "Who's dadgum idea was it to take the stairs?"

Messy wisps of hair had come loose from her bun, and her face was red. She looked at the time on her phone. Five minutes early. If she'd taken the packed elevator, she would have been late.

She exhaled hard and told herself, "It'll get easier. First days are always hard. You've got this."

She turned on the water and reached for the tie holding her hair up. After wetting her hands, she finger-combed the strands back together and resecured the bun. Then she patted her face with cold hands and sighed.

She was about to head out of the bathroom when her phone rang with Evan's ringtone, "Land of Pirates" by Alexander Nakarada. Evan loved everything pirate.

Caitlyn tapped the Answer button. "Hey, sweetie. Why aren't you in school?"

"I have the flu."

She winced, thinking about how much harder it would be for her parents to handle the boys without her there. "Who's home with you?"

"Cody. He's sick too." Evan's familiar whine started. "He won't let me have the remote, and he keeps turning the channel. He's such an ass."

Caitlyn bit the inside of her lip to keep from laughing. "Give him a break. He feels as lousy as you do."

"When are you coming home?"

Her eyes closed and immediately stung with tears. She hadn't expected to miss them so much. "Why don't you go ahead and watch in Mom and Dad's room?"

"They never let me in there."

"Considering the circumstances, I think it would be okay. Just make sure to leave it as you found it and get out of there before they get home."

"Cody will tell on me."

Yeah. There was that. "Let me holler at him a minute."

Even as Evan handed the phone over to Cody, Caitlyn reminded herself to cut back on the Southern slang. She didn't think she used a lot, until she came here and realized it didn't seem to translate well.

After straightening out her brothers' issue, Caitlyn entered Excel PR's front office, feeling a little more together. More stable. She was really looking forward to having this job to sink into. It would help keep her mind off missing her brothers and wondering what Duke was doing.

The office was everything she'd expected—high-end, sleek, professional. She instantly felt...legit. Validated. Something that made her stand taller.

The receptionist called someone up to the front to meet

Caitlyn. The woman who came around the corner and grabbed Caitlyn's arm was walking and talking quickly. She was thin and had dark circles under her eyes, giving Caitlyn the idea that she didn't get enough sleep.

"I'm Merissa." She pulled Caitlyn along. "The meeting already started."

Caitlyn didn't like the manhandling, and her nerves were on edge. What kind of greeting was this? Especially on a first day. She was missing the Southern hospitality of Kentucky. "I'm on time—"

Merissa turned down a row of cubicles and walked toward the end of the hall, where glass walls framed a conference room. The woman at the head of the table was blonde and wearing a soft pink suit. There was no one aspect of her that labeled her as the boss or as a hard-ass or cutthroat, but Caitlyn knew before she ever entered the room that that was the kind of person she'd be facing. She wasn't sure if the woman was the big boss or not, but she was clearly some type of boss in the company.

Every other chair at the table was occupied by men and women taking notes. Nine other people.

Without any explanation as to what this meeting was or why they were there, Merissa muttered, "Don't say anything unless she speaks directly to you."

She pushed open the conference room door. Not one person looked in their direction, and a decidedly tense atmosphere permeated the room.

"The next time that happens," the boss said, "the person who does it will be fired."

Holy hell. What had Caitlyn walked into?

"Roundtable," she said. "Susan, you start."

Merissa pushed Caitlyn to the back of the room and stood beside her.

"Jansen's she-never-met-him-in-person angle is starting to

take hold," Susan said, her speech sharp and quick. "Press conference scheduled for tomorrow."

The boss nodded, and her gaze moved to the next person, a man, older than Caitlyn, probably in his late thirties.

"My tech wizard permanently deleted Tara's nasty texts from her call log, and I have a guy on set who'll lift Jen's phone today and delete messages from there as well."

The boss waited a beat. "And?"

The man suddenly looked like he'd eaten bad fish. "And?"

"And what about the phone company?"

"I don't understand."

The boss's gaze cut to Merissa, who told the man, "The phone company will have a copy of the messages as well."

"I'll have my guy hack into the phone company's database," he said, frantic, "and erase them there."

"Can 'your guy' do that?" the boss asked.

"If he can't, I'll find someone who can."

She nodded and moved on to the next person at the table. The boss was in her mid to late forties. It was hard to tell because she'd clearly had work done on her face, leaving her austere.

While Caitlyn didn't recognize any client names that were mentioned, she clearly saw the use of illegal and unethical methods for protecting Excel's clients' public faces, including, but not limited to, hacking, lying, stealing, and bribing.

By the time the others filed out of the conference room without being introduced to Caitlyn, she was the one who felt like she'd eaten bad fish.

Once everyone was gone, the boss turned her gaze on Caitlyn. "I see we've hired Mary Poppins."

Caitlyn had never seen Mary Poppins, but she somehow knew she didn't want to.

"I'm throwing you in the deep end," the woman said. "Sink or swim. Maybe your umbrella will help you float. You'll be covering Leo Woods. Merissa will tell you what you need to know."

"Who is Leo Woods?"

The boss exhaled hard. "I'm going to have a come-to-Jesus meeting with HR. This is ridiculous. You'll have your hands full, Merissa. This could earn you a promotion."

"Yes, ma'am. I'll make sure everything goes smoothly."

The woman made a flip gesture, and Merissa took Caitlyn's arm again. But Caitlyn didn't like being dismissed. She'd been underestimated her whole life. She'd come here to be taken seriously.

"What exactly am I doing for this Leo Woods?" she asked, voice level, careful not to add fuel to this fight.

Merissa squeezed her arm. "I'll get you up to speed."

Caitlyn didn't want Merissa getting her up to speed. She wanted to be treated with common courtesy and stubbornly kept her feet planted, her gaze on the boss.

"Come on," Merissa muttered under her breath.

But Caitlyn didn't move. During what felt like minutes of silence, she mentally calculated how many jobs she'd need to make rent after she was fired on her first day.

"You'll be keeping Mr. Woods off drugs and alcohol, and you'll steer him clear of women," the boss said, clearly annoyed Caitlyn had asked. "He's a serial cheater, and his wife is pregnant. Tabloids would have a field day."

"Maybe there's a misunderstanding." Caitlyn was sweating again. She might very well be shaking. "I was hired for the public relations associate position."

"No mistake. You're making sure Leo's relations with the public stay clean." She rested her elbows on the arms of the chair and pressed her fingertips together. "I'd better not see one garish remark about him in the tabloids, or you can go back to Louisiana or Alabama or whatever swamp you came from."

"Kentucky. And it's not a swamp."

"Just so we're clear, if you're not early, you're late. Don't do it again."

Caitlyn had busted her ass to get to the office on time. She'd chosen her apartment partially because it was close to LA Metro, only she discovered she needed a master's in civil engineering to untangle the routes and schedules, so she'd called an Uber a full hour before she thought she needed it. Then she was introduced to the parking lot that was the 405 Freeway.

Merissa got more forceful, and this time, Caitlyn let the other woman pull her from the conference room. Then Merissa slid her arm through Caitlyn's as they continued down the hall and she steered Caitlyn into an office.

"You're feisty," Merissa said. "That will be good for working with Leo, but not Porsha."

"I assume that was Porsha."

"Of course."

Caitlyn dropped into a chair across from the desk, feeling both sick and stupid. She wanted to bolt after she'd been given her first assignment. This had never entered into her imagined worst-case scenario.

Merissa sat at the desk. "I'm your point person. Anytime you need something, you call me, not Porsha. Never call Porsha." She pulled a file from her desk drawer. "You have a passport, right?"

Caitlyn was having an out-of-body experience. "Why would I need a passport?"

"Because you're going to British Columbia tomorrow."

"What? Why?"

"Because that's where they're filming, and where Leo goes, you go."

"This Leo guy is an actor?"

Merissa met Caitlyn's gaze for the first time since she met her in the lobby. "Are you serious?"

"I don't have a passport. No one told me I needed one."

Merissa palmed her forehead. "Jesus, this really is a Monday." She exhaled and tapped a pencil on the desk. "Okay. I'll pull strings to get it overnight."

Caitlyn couldn't imagine how that was possible, but Merissa took her into another room, where she took two headshots of Caitlyn and put them in an envelope.

"Look, Porsha is throwing you into the fire because she really wanted her niece to take this position." She and Merissa returned to the original office. "It would never have happened, because Porsha's sister knows what a cesspool this is, which only pisses Porsha off more."

A swamp. A cesspool. Caitlyn rubbed her temples. "I'm not equipped for this. I was trained to get people into the media, not out of it."

"You'll have to learn fast. Read this." She slid a thick folder across the desk. "Google him, do whatever you have to do to figure him out and keep him out of the papers. Unless of course you get him good press. That will earn you points with Porsha. You're on duty for any of Leo's public relation issues, which could potentially include everything he does."

Merissa snapped a silver credit card on the folder. "Twenty-thousand-dollar limit. If you handle it right, you'll get a higher limit on your next job."

"Heavens." The only time Caitlyn had ever had that kind of money, it had been a scholarship. "What's that for?"

"Anything you need to keep Leo on the straight and narrow, including but not limited to buying damning photos, paying for drugs, picking up his bar tab, bribing women to keep their mouths shut—oh, and I'll email you the form they need to sign if they sleep with him. Print out a few so you have them on hand."

"Form?"

"Consent for sex and a nondisclosure all rolled up in one document."

What in holy hell? "I thought I was supposed to keep him away from all that."

"We all know the reality. And while we're on the topic of other women, he'll sleep with anyone in a skirt, so keep them away from him, and whatever you do don't, don't, absolutely do *not*, sleep with him yourself."

"That would never happen."

"I've heard that before, but he's got a way of charming even the most uninterested women out of their panties. If it happens to you, it won't end well with Porsha. Back to the credit, if it's not enough, and I personally don't think it's enough when it comes to Leo Woods, ping me. I'll see what I can do."

Merissa added a red credit card to the pile. "There's ten thousand on here for your personal expenses. If you don't use it all, you keep it. Judging by your choice of clothes for your first day, I'd say you'd better use all of it. Scrub off that Midwestern film and pick up an LA vibe."

"Kentucky is the South, not the Midwest."

"Whatever."

Caitlyn opened her mouth to argue, but Merissa cut her off. "Do it, because if you don't, no one will take you seriously, and you really should curb that accent. A driver will pick you up for the airport tomorrow at eight a.m. Get out of here and get shopping."

Caitlyn couldn't quite bring herself to quit on the spot, so she picked up the file and the cards and left the office terrified. Terrified what would happen if she quit this job. Terrified what would happen if she didn't.

She slid into an Uber, wishing she had someone to call, but Lexi was in paradise, and anyone back home would shower her with I-told-you-sos and come-home-where-you-belongs. Duke came to mind, but she squashed that idea. She didn't want anyone to think she couldn't handle this.

The drive home took half the time of her trek into work,

and on the trip, she looked up Mary Poppins. Caitlyn was wearing her blue suit. The blazer looked similar—with a darted waist and slight puff to the shoulder. Her white blouse didn't have ruffles, but it was similar as well. And Caitlyn had her hair up in a bun, like Poppins.

"How humiliating."

She moved her thoughts to the information she'd learned in college for her psychology minor. From what she'd heard to this point, she fully expected Leo Woods to turn out to be a narcissist. Luckily, narcissists were pretty straightforward. Some of the advice she'd already heard was good, but not sufficient to successfully handle a narcissist while also keeping her job.

She dragged herself up the stairs to the apartment and found Andi in the kitchen. Her roommate took one look at Caitlyn and said, "Oh, shit." She put down the food she was preparing. "What happened?"

As soon as Caitlyn closed the door, tears burned her eyes. She really didn't want to fall apart. Not in front of her new roommate. But she wasn't sure she had that kind of control.

"You were right." Caitlyn dumped her things on the coffee table and dropped her butt to the sofa. "They hired me to be a fixer."

"Well, that sucks. Why are you home? Did you quit?"

"Not yet."

"Before you do, check the job market. It's not pretty out there."

"They gave me money to buy new clothes, and I'm supposed to leave for British Columbia tomorrow." Caitlyn focused on Andi. "She called me Mary Poppins."

Andi sputtered a laugh, cleaned her hands, and came into the living room, sitting on the edge of a chair. "Who are you fixing?"

"Some guy named Leo Woods."

Andi sat back. "What in God's name did you do to deserve that?"

"Do you know who that is?"

"You don't?"

Caitlyn sighed. "Everyone was right—I should never have come to LA."

"Hey, you got out of your Podunk town and came all the way here, got an apartment, sight unseen, against everyone's advice. If you can do that, you can handle a shithead like Woods."

"He's a narcissist. That's worse than a shithead." Caitlyn might have a minor in psychology, but academia was far different from reality. "I've never had to handle anyone remotely like this. I know nothing about drugs or addiction. I mean nothing. I've never even smoked weed."

"Don't you have brothers?"

"Yeah."

"Men are really just kids in a man's body."

Caitlyn thought about that. Her first and third brothers were constantly in trouble. She guessed narcissists were a lot like kids. "Boundaries," she muttered to herself. "Relationships with narcissists are all about boundaries."

"And Woods may act like he's all that, but narcissists actually have very low self-esteem."

Caitlyn cut a look at Andi, who shrugged. "I've met one or ten. They have wicked imposter's syndrome and live in a perpetual state of fear."

Andi was right. Caitlyn rubbed her forehead. "I'm *so* not up for this."

"If you could get a degree," Andi said, "you can handle an idiot like Woods. And, girl, you're living in LA now. You can't swing a dead cat without hitting a narcissist."

Caitlyn laughed. She rested her elbows on her knees and

her head in her hands. "You're right, I can figure it out. And if I fail, at least I tried, right?"

"That's the spirit." Andi mirrored Caitlyn's posture, leaning in. "You have to let him know you're not intimidated by him; otherwise, he'll try to take advantage of you. He's reportedly a master chameleon, so sharpen all your senses and try to anticipate what will happen next, then you can get ahead of him. There's no place for sweetness, weakness, or indecision in a job like this. Don't believe anything he says. Every word out of his mouth will be a self-serving lie. And don't fall for his charm. He uses it to get whatever he wants. Above all, don't believe he will ever change or fly right. The man has a diseased wing."

Andi held up her hand in a wait gesture, disappeared into her room, and returned with her laptop. After tapping a few keys, she turned the screen toward Caitlyn. "This isn't to scare you, it's just to prepare you."

Caitlyn took the laptop. The title of the article read *The Top Ten Hardest Actors to Work with in Hollywood.* She scrolled through the countdown starting at ten, the least troublesome out of the most troublesome.

Leo's name held spot number two. He was the second worst actor to work with in all of Hollywood. Caitlyn rested the laptop on her thighs and rubbed her face with both hands while she gave herself a silent pep talk.

You can do this. He doesn't have to like you. You just need to keep him out of trouble, like she tried to keep Sam and Cody out of trouble. With her parents both working two jobs, taking care of her younger brothers often fell to Caitlyn. She didn't mind. She adored them. But they weren't exactly easy to manage.

Her youngest brother, Sam, was constantly in the principal's office for fighting or foul language. Her oldest brother, Cody, was returned home by the cops way too often, usually for shoplifting or vandalism. Caitlyn did her best to buffer her exhausted parents from these issues. She knew it would be easier on everyone.

She dropped her hands, took a deep breath, and nodded. "I can be a hard-ass." She didn't like doing it, but she could when necessary. "Yeah, okay. I can do this." She looked at Andi. "What are you doing? Are you going to work soon?"

"Yeah, why?"

"I was going to ask if you wanted to come shopping with me. I was told to get an LA edge. I don't even know what that means."

"Ooo," Andi said, grinning. She was pretty when she smiled. "I do love a shopping spree, especially with someone else's money."

Caitlyn laughed. "You can be my fashion consultant, and I'll pay you in clothes."

Andi popped to her feet. "I'll just go call in sick."

11

Caitlyn felt underdressed.

When she called Merissa for more details on that "LA vibe" yesterday, Merissa told her to stick with business casual. Then added "but keep it light." Whatever that meant.

But Andi seemed to understand. If there was anything good to come out of this, it was that Andi and Caitlyn had bonded yesterday. They'd laughed, ate, drank, talked, and shopped. And Andi had held Caitlyn's hand while she'd gotten her belly button pierced.

Turned out, they really liked each other. Of course, spending someone else's money on clothes helped, but it still made Caitlyn feel a little less alone in this massive urban jungle.

Now, at the airport, looking for a man she didn't know, Caitlyn covered the pierced area with her hand—it was still sensitive—then smoothed the front of her skirt and tugged on the hem of her jacket. The outfit was simple—white tank, taupe-and-white-polka-dot skirt with a midline band of ruffles, knee-high suede boots and a grunge jean jacket to pull it together.

But the skirt felt too short, the boots seemed a little hooker-ish, the jacket was a little too grunge to fit "business" category, and the tank dipped a little too low.

So, basically, Caitlyn hated the entire outfit, but Andi assured her this was LA vibe all the way.

She wasn't sure how she knew Leo when he walked into the gate's seating area. He was wearing sunglasses and a baseball cap, so she couldn't recognize his face. Might have been the quarterback-size man with him—obviously security. A young woman was also in tow, and she was Kylie Jenner gorgeous.

I can do this. I can do this. I can do this.

She pulled in air and brought Andi's suggestions to mind. *Don't let him intimidate you. Sharpen all your edges. No sweetness, weakness, or indecision. Don't believe anything he says.*

Caitlyn had thought a lot about those suggestions while she couldn't sleep last night. She agreed with them, but she planned on implementing them in her own way. The better she and Leo got along, the easier this would be.

Caitlyn approached the group. "Hey, y'all, I'm Caitlyn Winters from Excel PR."

Leo whipped off his glasses and looked Caitlyn up and down. "Porsha didn't tell me how beautiful you are."

She offered her hand. "Nice to meet you."

Leo didn't shake her hand as much as he held it. "Is that a Georgia accent?"

"A mix of Kentucky and Georgia, yes."

"Lovely."

There was something about him that vibrated on a different level. Charisma, probably. And he was good-looking, in that Paul Newman sort of way, but he did less than nothing for Caitlyn.

"This is my assistant, Tara, and one of my bodyguards, Rob."

Caitlyn pulled her hand from Leo's to shake the others'.

When she turned her gaze back to Leo, he was looking at her like she was his next meal.

"Can we talk for a moment?" Caitlyn asked. "Get to know what we expect of each other?"

"Interesting way to put it." He gestured toward seats in the gate area.

When they were seated, Caitlyn looked him directly in the eye. "I am under very specific orders to take care of your public image. I have a few ideas of how to make that happen, but I'd like to get your buy-in before setting any plans into motion."

"Sweetheart, relax. Porsha has always been type A. She worries about every little thing. Whatever she told you, just shake it off. We're going to have a lot of fun together."

"You're as charming as everyone says." Caitlyn earned a warm smile for that comment. Seemed like the perfect time to set some limits. "As far as fun goes, you can have as much as you want as long as it doesn't include drugs, alcohol, or sex with women other than your pregnant wife."

Leo gave a surprised laugh, one that held less humor, more who the hell do you think you are. Caitlyn made sure to hold his gaze, hoping her determination shone through.

Leo leaned back and gave Caitlyn another once-over. She was sure he was going to dress her down right there in the airport lobby, but instead, he hit her with one of those Hollywood smiles. "I like you. We're going to get along just fine."

"Delta Flight 1912 to Vancouver is now boarding..."

Leo stood up and headed toward the gate without waiting for her.

"Well, that was unsatisfying," she muttered to herself.

It was clear Leo didn't take Caitlyn seriously. And if there was one thing that pissed her off, it was being discounted. She was sure she and Leo were on very different pages, but she had to start somewhere. She'd made herself clear. What Leo decided to do with that position was up to him.

She followed the line of people onto the plane and did what they did, hoping she didn't look like a complete novice.

She was seated next to Rob, a few rows back from Leo and Tara—in first class. The seats were leather and roomy. She found the food tray, the outlets, the remote for the television in the back of the seat in front of her.

"You've never flown first class, have you?" Rob asked. He was a big guy, brown hair, brown eyes, and warmer than he seemed on the outside.

"To be honest, I've never flown in any class."

A smile broke across his face, and he turned into an entirely different man. "Bullshit."

She laughed. "Nope."

"Nervous?"

"Not really. I'm just experiencing so many firsts in my life, it's a little overwhelming."

"Good work with Leo," Rob said. "He intimidates most fixers. I'm impressed by the way you stood up to him and held your ground."

She exhaled. "Thank you. I needed to hear that today. This whole fixer thing is alien and not at all what I expected or wanted. He's a grown man with a ton of money and he's addicted to all the things I'm supposed to be keeping him from. He's a class-A narcissist. I don't see how it can be pulled off."

"My suggestion: instead of trying to keep him sober and faithful, focus on keeping him away from the media."

She nodded. "That's so simple, it's brilliant."

"Don't say that until you've tried it. Photographers and journalists are rabid."

"Still, it's nice to have a different way to think about it. Thank you. So," she said, "tell me about this movie."

"It's an American action-war film. *American Valor*. A special forces team goes into Syria to rescue a group of American hostages, but get into shitty situation after shitty situation and have to trek a long way to safety, all while being chased by American-loathing terrorists."

"How...uplifting."

Rob laughed.

"No one told me how long Leo would be here or how long he'd need me here."

"All the filming that could be done in studio has been. The rest will be done in Canada on-site. They estimate the rest of the filming to take about three months."

"*Three months?*"

"Maybe four. I see Porsha is still as forthcoming as always."

All Caitlyn's air left her lungs in a hot stream. "She didn't tell me anything about this job. As in zero."

This was a shock, but when she gave it some thought, as long as she was pulling a paycheck to send rent money back to Andi, there really wasn't much keeping her in LA. Of course, there was Lexi, but Caitlyn had lived apart from Lexi for years. Duke quickly came to mind. He might have claimed to still be interested in her in a month, but three? Four?

"I won't lie, you'll have a lot of long days and annoying delays," Rob said. "You'll be constantly juggling a shifting schedule. But you'll get short breaks. You'll be able to fly back to LA pretty often. They've got a ton of direct flights from Vancouver to LAX, and they're not too expensive."

She closed her eyes and rubbed them.

"On the upside," Rob said, "it's pretty fun. There will be a lot of fight sequences shot in the mountains and valleys, a lot of extras dressed as Syrians, and animals all over the place."

"Animals?"

"Horses—that's how Syrian military get around. Goats—tended by Syrian people. Not sure what else, but there are always a few surprises."

She laughed. "I've had enough surprises, thanks."

"Did you get a script?"

"Of course not. That would require preparation and follow-through."

"I'll email you one."

"Thanks."

"You'll be okay. I'll show you around, give you the lay of the land and show you where you'll be spending most of your time."

"I really appreciate it."

"Of course. Gotta watch out for each other."

That settled her a little. Rob seemed relatively normal. Not skeevy or overly charming. He was also about fifteen years older than her, so sort of like an uncle or older brother.

She and Rob drifted into their own work. Rob opened his laptop, and Caitlyn peeled back the cover of another celebrity magazine. She'd picked up five at the airport, some that looked trashy, a couple that looked semilegit.

During the three-hour flight, Caitlyn learned more about Leo and Hollywood than she ever cared to know. And instead of debunking the negative perception of Leo, it had only confirmed the assumptions.

If these "rags" were to be believed, Leo was fake and manipulative. That said, it appeared as if Leo was in good company with plenty of other A-list actors tagged as similarly problematic. And these magazines didn't stop with celebrities. They trashed or exposed musicians, fashion designers, royalty, even the president and vice president of the United States.

How had she missed all this bull standing in line at the grocery store? She hadn't realized she'd sighed heavily enough to draw Rob's attention until he spoke.

"Don't believe it all. Tabloids print half-truths or downright lies ninety-nine percent of the time."

"So, Leo isn't the second-hardest celebrity to work with in Hollywood?"

Rob smiled. "I didn't say that."

She turned a page in the magazine. "If these things aren't true, how are they able to print them? I mean, why don't these people sue? They have the money."

"To prove libel, they would have to prove that what the tabloid printed caused them to suffer in some way. That can be tricky. There have been celebs who sued and either won or settled. It just doesn't happen very often. Generally, the bullshit these rags print isn't worth the celeb's time or effort, and sometimes, suing only brings attention to something that would have disappeared in the next news cycle if left alone."

Caitlyn shook her head. "It all seems so..."

"Tawdry?"

"I was going to say unethical."

"That too," he agreed.

"Are these stories developed from a grain of truth or just plucked out of thin air?"

"Both. Stories invented by writers are called top-of-the-head. Others are built on what someone else said, for which they couldn't be sued."

"Do they get those quotes from somewhere, or is that all made up too?"

"Both. Celebrity employees can earn a little cash on the side if they share some type of news tidbit—personal trainers, hairstylists, drivers, security, nannies. And—"

"If they say it, the magazine can safely print it."

"Exactly."

Caitlyn thought of the nondisclosure form Merissa had given her. "Don't they have to sign an NDA?"

"Sure. But, again, proving where information came from is nebulous. And if the celeb finds out an employee is talking, they just fire them."

Caitlyn really didn't like all she was learning. She wanted to go back to Lexi's house in Malibu, back to bed with Duke, and forget all the bullshit swirling around Hollywood. She wanted what she'd told Duke she'd probably be doing: creating marketing materials for someone else's client from a small room with no windows.

But that wouldn't be bold or risky, would it?

"Keep in mind," Rob said, "that some celebs and publicists leak information to the tabloid for free publicity. The movie studios often want to spread the word of upcoming movies or TV shows. 'So-and-so's husband is cheating' is less compelling than 'How will so-and-so handle working alongside his cheating wife in their upcoming series X?'"

It sounded like "good fixer" and "bad fixer" was more complicated than she'd thought.

12

With his chest against the granite wall, four hundred feet off the ground, Duke secured his fingers over a small divot in the rock above, wedged the rubber toe of his climbing shoe against another quarter-size indention, looked toward his next position... And sprang.

He pushed with his legs, lifting him off the rock at the same time he let go with his hands. In that moment, he was completely free, no stability, floating through air. He relished moments like this. It was why he always came back to the sport, time and time again. He'd never found anything that gave him the same adrenaline surge, supplied the same sense of power and achievement, or provided the intense, full-body workout. Plain and simple: it was a rush.

Climbing also forced him to be completely in the moment. It pushed everything from his mind but him and the rock. All his problems disappeared for a few hours. He thought moment by moment, with nothing else intruding. It was calming and exhilarating at the same time.

Secured to his new perch, Duke rested his hips against the cool rock and plucked an anchor from his waistband strap, jammed it into a half-inch gap in the rock, then clicked his belay rope into the new anchor.

He rarely scaled virgin rock, and usually didn't have to place the anchors. They were already in place, courtesy of the first climber. But no one had climbed here, and that just made it all the more thrilling.

Caitlyn popped into his mind, and Duke paused before moving on. He needed to keep his mind right here, but his brain paralleled this virgin rock with Caitlyn's lack of sexual experience, and his thoughts veered off the mountain entirely.

While he was already distracted, he took a moment to soak in the setting. Gently swaying trees, blue sky, a creek flowing somewhere nearby, and the challenges this hunk of granite brought him.

He closed his eyes, savoring the tranquility. Times like this helped him realign and settle into whatever life had thrown at him.

But memories of Caitlyn slipped in again.

He opened his eyes, frustrated. "Get with the fucking program, Reid."

He couldn't be thinking about her up here. He shouldn't be thinking about her at all. They had a great night, end of story.

Only, he really didn't want that to be the end of their story. Maybe he'd text her this week, ask how the new job was going. Maybe Duke could fly home once or twice over the length of this job and keep his foot in the door, so to speak.

The problem there was the price of airline tickets. He didn't have any cushion. He needed every penny for attorney's fees.

Now that his thoughts had begun to spiral, it was easier to push them away and refocus.

Looking at the possible handholds above him, Duke reached behind him and pushed one hand into the chalk bag, then the other.

Rest over, he started moving again. The summit was close.

Too close. He wanted to keep climbing, but he had to pace himself. It wasn't as if he'd been climbing every day. The family came first, and they always needed something. Kristy had been good about making sure he got out, away from the girls, but more often than not, it was to help his father with the farm. Climbing had been on the back burner for a long time now.

This rock face was relatively low. A lot lower than the mountain he would be climbing for the film, and a good practice rock face for Leo. He'd supposedly been taking private rock-climbing lessons to prep for the climbing scenes in this movie, but when it came to Woods, Duke would believe it when he saw it.

With three more moves, he pulled himself over the ledge and stood on the peak. It was a gorgeous day. Perfect weather for climbing. Cool but not cold, which kept him from overheating. The sun warmed his skin, and he took a seat on the rocks, appreciating the view of mountains and valleys, forests, and other rock formations. In the valley below, the rock-climbing set evolved as teams arrived.

He swung his feet while he caught his breath. Pulled his phone from the zippered pocket of his shorts and checked his messages. Nothing from Caitlyn, but there was one from Stephanie, a makeup artist who sometimes crossed his path. They'd hooked up a while ago. Like forever ago.

Hey, handsome, heard you're on the set. Let's catch up.

As Cameron said, the job drew a lot of women. Too bad Duke only wanted one.

There was a flurry of messages from his rock-climbing team —Milo, Deon, and Ike—letting each other know when they'd be coming in so they could coordinate the trip from the airport to the set. Sounded like everyone would be here by dinner.

He lay back on the rock and closed his eyes. Now he let Caitlyn's image come to him—back arched, hands fisted in the sheets, skin glistening with sweat. She might think she was inexperienced, but when she let go, she was one of the most passionate women he'd ever known.

Duke sat up and hydrated. He couldn't think about her much longer or he'd have a hard-on, and getting back down the mountain would not be fun or comfortable.

A black Suburban pulled onto the set. Probably one of the lead actors or the producer. Duke wasn't thrilled to be working with Leo Woods, but that was part of the job. Sometimes you won and got to work with actors who were skilled and dedicated and down-to-earth, and sometimes you had to work with pricks. Leo was narcissistic and arrogant. He was also an addict and a total douchebag when it came to women. And there were always plenty of drugs and women on the set.

Duke needed to have a sit-down with Leo and line out the rules of safety he would not be breaking under any circumstances. Managing the safety requirements for certification while working with Leo concerned Duke. He absolutely could not afford to be sidelined for six months—or more—because of a fuckup like Woods.

The SUV pulled to a stop, and four people got out, two men, two women.

He texted the other Renegades to tell them he was on his way back. When he climbed alone, he always let someone know where he was, just in case. Climbing alone was a little more work than having a belay, but it could be done safely by experienced climbers, and sometimes Duke just needed the solitude.

He rappelled down the rock face, packed up his gear, tossed the pack on his back, and hiked toward the set. He had more work to do to loosen up and get into his groove, but that had been a nice warm-up climb.

The temperature on the ground felt ten degrees hotter, but summer in British Columbia was mild. He made his way through the chaos of the congealing set, winding a path around cranes, solar panels, camera equipment, and trailers, greeting people as he passed. He grabbed an apple from the snack table and finally reached what the guys liked to call the stunt bunker, where Wes, Keaton, and Troy were unpacking equipment and setting up very orderly stations for different gear.

American Valor tapped most of Renegades' major talent. They had driving work for Wes, fights for Keaton, and most stunts had to be rigged, which would make Troy a busy boy.

"How was it?" Troy asked.

"Amazing." He dropped the backpack. "I'll put the climbing gear away. Where is it?"

"Blue bags," Wes told him.

"Ready to take on Woods?" Keaton asked with a grin.

"If I can wrangle three little girls into line, I can handle Woods."

"Do *you* do that wrangling?" Troy asked. "Or are you the one *getting* wrangled?"

Duke laughed. "Half the time, I have no idea."

"Sylvia from catering came over," Keaton said. "She heard you were on set. Wants to see you."

"Got a text from Stephanie too," he said. "You remember, the makeup artist?"

They all made a sound of appreciation.

"With all of us off the market," Wes said, "you're going to have to step up and take care of these women."

He just laughed. He knew he wouldn't be entertaining anyone, not while he still had a chance with Caitlyn.

"Incoming." Keaton said, voice lowered.

Duke turned toward a group of people strolling toward the stunt bunker, Leo at the center, the producer on one side, the director on the other, B-list actors and members of the technical team floating around him like suckerfish on a shark.

The group exited one of the temporary buildings holding

makeup and wardrobe on their way toward the stunt team's space.

Duke opened his pack and drew out a T-shirt. When he straightened to put it on, the sight of one of the women in Woods's team made him freeze.

Wes elbowed Duke. "Is that Caitlyn?"

"Did you know she would be here?" Troy asked.

"Yes and no." And while Duke was both shocked and thrilled, the fact that she was part of Woods's entourage didn't sit well.

T-shirt forgotten, he stared at Caitlyn. She looked adorable and sexy in a short skirt and boots, her hair down, soft waves around her face, eyes covered in aviator sunglasses.

She was distracted, holding a notebook, pencil scribbling furiously making notes and looking all around her like she was trying to take it all in.

He saw the moment she recognized him. Her posture changed, her attention focused, her lips parted in surprise. She lifted her hand to the arm of her sunglasses and slid them down just enough to peer overtop, as if she couldn't believe what she was seeing.

13

Caitlyn couldn't swallow. Duke wore shorts and little else. He was sweaty and gorgeous, hands at his hips, gaze narrowed on her. She couldn't tell if he was smiling, glad to see her, or squinting with what the fuck on his mind.

After all she'd been through in the last few days—the new boss, new client, new roommate, new wardrobe, new setting, new sex, and the entirely new world of Hollywood—she was feeling uncertain and defensive, and the attitude she sensed from Duke wasn't helping.

She hugged her notebook and the five tabloid magazines she'd picked up at the airport to her chest, unsure how to act. She didn't feel like having to explain her role with the Renegades to Leo, or her role with Leo to the Renegades.

Leo moved forward, offering his hand to Duke. "Good to see you."

Duke and Leo shook, which was when Caitlyn saw the tape on Duke's fingers and the chalk on his hands. He'd been climbing. Watching the men together also made her realize Duke's hair had recently been cut and resembled Leo's style, short on the sides, long on top. Not a big change, but a change, and it all led to the realization that Duke was Leo's stunt double.

Which also meant she and Duke would be meeting almost every day. If he wasn't looking at her like she was the mastermind of some plot to get under his skin, she would have said that sounded amazing. Like she had another ally.

Only, he clearly didn't feel the same way. Maybe Caitlyn was messing with his plans to hook up while he was here. That would be a hard pill for her to swallow, but, if necessary, she'd do it. They had no commitment. They were both free to do what they pleased.

Still, if there were ever a moment for a hissy fit, this would be it.

"I'm ready to do some climbing," Leo told Duke. "I've been practicing for the last couple of months and working out."

Duke looked skeptical.

Leo turned and introduced his party. "This is Tara. She keeps me on schedule, Rob keeps me safe, and Caitlyn's a new addition to the team. She's supposed to keep me out of trouble, but we all know that's impossible. Pretty little thing, isn't she?"

Anger flashed in Duke's eyes, and he took a deliberate, confrontational step forward. Caitlyn tensed, but Wes put a hand on Duke's arm.

"And you should hear her accent," Leo said, oblivious. "As sweet as sugar."

"I'll get with Tara," Duke said, voice low and rough, "and schedule some training time."

"Great, great. Looking forward to working with you."

The pack moved on, and Tara handed Duke a business card on the way past, but Caitlyn felt like she had lead feet. She also felt the need to explain herself, even though she had no obligation.

"This is a surprise." Duke's voice cleared up any lingering questions about her being here. He was not glad to see her.

"It sure is." She pushed her sunglasses to the top of her head and smiled at the group. "Hey, y'all."

Wes, Troy, and Keaton all offered warm hellos, then went back to their work.

"Looks like you've been climb—" she started, but Duke cut her off.

"What's going on?"

Normally, she preferred direct, but she could use a little fluff today. She closed her eyes to hold on to her shit. "Please don't use that tone. I'm already standing on a tilted floor."

He came closer. "You're way out of your depth."

Her eyes popped open. "Excuse me?"

"Leo is a snake. How did this happen? He's right—you can't keep him out of trouble."

"Wow." That hurt more than she'd expected. More than it should. "Way to support a friend. I didn't get any sleep last night, and this stress is burning a hole in my stomach. The last thing I need is someone else discounting me or my abilities. If you're concerned I'll get in the way of your extracurricular activities, don't be. I don't care who you see or who you hook up with. I won't be interfering."

She started to pass him, and he reached out and put his hand on her arm. The connection pulled all sorts of emotions to the surface. She wanted to lean into him, which was why she pulled away.

"Hey, wait. Hold on," he said, voice soft with apology. "The only thing I'm worried about is you working with Leo. I don't mean it in a bad way. I just—"

"Don't think I'm capable. That came through loud and clear. Not helpful."

She passed him and ignored his apologetic "Caitlyn..."

Her stomach dropped to her feet. She'd been holding herself together with what little hope she could muster, but being here with Duke, whose assumptions dogged her self-confidence, really pulled her down.

He called to her again, and she ignored him, again.

Now, as she continued to follow Leo and his growing entourage, she was both angry and hurt. She shouldn't be. She and Duke could measure the time they'd known each other in hours. What he thought didn't matter. She could—and would—make this work.

She pushed Duke out of her mind and tried to focus on the situation. She'd been dropped into an alternate universe. A city within a city. There were temporary metal buildings dotting the property, trails leading to various areas set up for filming or "sets," and equipment everywhere—cameras, lights, trailers, a lot of things she didn't recognize, food, and people. So many people. All hanging out, talking, laughing. Caitlyn could have used a little camaraderie right about now, but the only thing familiar to her in this world were the Renegades. One of whom had pissed her off already.

She noted all the people Leo spoke with, their names, roles on the set, what kind of reaction they had to Leo, anything that seemed important. It was still early, but Caitlyn wasn't picking up on any of those alleged "hard to work with" vibes.

By the time they returned to the car, all Caitlyn wanted to do was eat, fall into bed, and cry away the stress and disappointment. But this was big-girl Caitlyn, doing big-girl things, so she sucked it up as they arrived at the hotel and received room assignments.

"I'm ready for a break," Leo said, glancing at Caitlyn. "Care to join us?"

"Thank you, but I'm going to pass. I want to work on a comprehensive promotional plan for you. Tara, can you text me Leo's schedule for the rest of the day and tomorrow?"

"Of course."

By the time the elevator stopped on her floor, Caitlyn's belly buzzed with nerves over Leo's possible misbehavior. He had, after all, said she couldn't keep him out of trouble, which meant he was interested in finding trouble.

She stepped off the elevator, then turned and held the door open. "Look, do what you want when the media's not around," Caitlyn told him. "But when they are, I expect you to be the picture of professionalism. Can we agree on that?"

"I think that's reasonable."

"Please tell me when you go out so I can prepare to shield you from the media."

"Of course."

"I can't help you if I'm not there."

"I understand."

At least she could tell when he was lying. Like right now. He wasn't going to tell her when he left. She doubted he'd let Rob or Tara tell her either.

She removed her hand and let the elevator doors close. To Leo, she said, "Be good."

He laughed. The doors closed, and a deep exhale left her lungs. She dropped her forehead against the elevator doors, then banged it a few times.

"I'm so not going to have a job when this is over."

She found her room and opened the door to the sight of her suitcases already waiting. The room was nice. Big, with a king bed and a window with a view of the mountains Duke would be climbing. Caitlyn dropped to a seat on the edge of the mattress and stared out the window, her mind too tired to function.

Her phone pinged with a message, and she closed her eyes. It couldn't be her parents. They would call. She checked the message, hoping it was one of her brothers, but found Duke's name on the display and a message. *I didn't mean for us to start off on the wrong foot. Can we talk? Meet for dinner maybe?*

Instead of engaging, she lay down and opened her laptop to

finish reading an article on surviving Hollywood. She'd developed some sympathy for A-list actors and actresses, reading those articles. Self-doubt and low self-esteem were a real, living, breathing problem. Women, more than men, had very definite shelf lives, and they felt like they were in a race against the clock.

What she found really interesting was what was called Hollywood's scarlet letter—the branding of an actor or actress as "difficult." And if that happened too often, they'd find themselves blacklisted.

She closed her computer and stared at the wall, thinking of this secret high-stress area of acting in Hollywood and how hard that would be to live with, day in and day out.

She let her heavy lids fall and almost instantly drifted off.

14

Caitlyn's ringing phone kicked her upright. Her brain was fuzzy. She looked around and oriented herself. It was growing dark outside, telling Caitlyn she'd slept far longer than she'd intended.

Her phone display showed Rob's name.

She answered, trying to keep the fatigue from her voice. "Hello?"

"It's Rob. Leo is sending me home. Says they have enough security on the set, but I'm not a yes-man and I think he just doesn't want to hear what he doesn't want to hear."

"I'm sorry."

"Don't be, I get paid whether I work or not."

"That's a great gig, but I'm bummed because you're the only person I had in my corner."

"You're smart. You'll be okay. You've already proven you're not intimidated by him—a big difference between you and others in your position. It still surprises me that Porsha would send you here for your first job. She knows how sneaky and manipulative Leo can be."

"That's exactly why. She wants me to fail." She sighed and rubbed her eyes. "I hate people. I went into the wrong field."

Rob laughed. "Hang in there. Last I heard, they were planning drinks downstairs before going out. No one mentioned calling you, so I'm betting they won't."

"He acts like he *wants* to get caught."

"He doesn't think anything can touch him. He's just that arrogant."

She sighed. "Right."

"Call if you need to hide the body," Rob said.

Caitlyn burst out laughing. "Now there's a real friend."

She disconnected and stared out the window. This job was really a nightmare in a dream's clothing.

Caitlyn decided to wait in the lobby. That way, if he decided to leave without telling her, she wouldn't be out of the loop.

She slipped into one of her new dresses, washed her face, and reapplied a little makeup. Then she added a couple of curls to her hair and headed downstairs.

Rob was right, Leo was at the bar with Tara and a handful of other people Caitlyn didn't know. Most of them women.

She walked toward the back of the bar and paused at Leo's table.

"Told you it's impossible for me to be good," he said.

"I see you don't live up to your word either. Guess I'll have to stick extra close."

"I'm all for that, sugar."

"Not the way I mean it." She earned a smirk and wandered to the bar to get a drink. "A soda and lime, please?"

She chose a table near a window where she could see the people coming and going from the building. She needed to eat something, but the stress was doing a number on her stomach, so she went for a fruit bowl when she wanted a platter of potato skins.

A group of people entered the bar right as the waitress

delivered her fruit, which looked incredible—oranges as big as cantaloupe. Every apple under the sun. Fat watermelons.

But the fruit lost its appeal when she saw Duke strolling in with the happy, rowdy bunch, including his Renegade brothers and several beautiful women. He'd showered and changed at some point, back into the jeans and T-shirt she was used to seeing him wearing.

Caitlyn hoped he didn't notice her in the shadows. He looked carefree and handsome, his stride lazy and confident, his posture sure and sexy. But when he saw Leo, Duke scoured the restaurant until he found Caitlyn.

"Dadgumit," she muttered.

He said something to the other guys, then headed toward her. The other Renegades hovered by the hostess stand with menus, probably ordering takeout. The women in the group took a table in the bar.

Duke paused at Leo's table and spoke to him for a couple of minutes. She couldn't guess the content of their conversation. They both had poker faces.

When Duke turned in her direction, Caitlyn's stomach fluttered. At her table, he sat on the edge of a chair. God, she wanted him. Wanted him to lean in and kiss her. Wanted him to rush her onto the elevator where he sexily mauled her before taking her to the room, stripped her, and repeated every single thing he'd done during their night together.

Just the idea made her wet.

"You look incredible," he said. "What's the occasion?"

"Just prepared for the inevitable."

"Which would be...?"

"Leo leaving the hotel without telling me."

"Ah." He tapped the table in a restless gesture. "About earlier—"

"This is probably a subject better left undiscussed. You've

done an amazing job of pissing me off in what little time I've seen you today."

"I'm good like that."

"Be good somewhere else."

"Look, it's just that after decades in this industry, I know Leo is way out of your wheelhouse."

"You've known me a day. How could you possibly decide that?"

"Okay." He lifted his brows. "Is he in or out of your wheelhouse?"

"Maybe I just need to retool my wheelhouse. I'm a quick study."

"Study isn't going to work here. You need experience."

"I guess that's what I'm getting, isn't it?"

He sighed, reached for the fruit bowl, and picked up a watermelon ball. She slapped his hand. "That's mine. I haven't eaten all day."

He lifted it to her lips. "All yours. I just want to watch you eat it."

Okay, yeah, that was sexy but... "Are you completely oblivious to how irritated I am with you?"

"No, but I think I can turn that around in, say, thirty, forty minutes alone with you. Maybe erase it entirely with a couple of hours. For the record, I vote for the hours."

"What makes you think I even want to sleep with you again?"

He chuckled. Then laughed some more. The sound was deep and smooth and slid through her in a warm wave. "You're adorable."

"Looks like you've already got your hands full. Go back to your friends."

"I'd drop them in a heartbeat for time with you."

Leo and the rest of the people at his table collected their things and headed toward the lobby.

She grabbed a couple of pieces of fruit. “Gotta go.”

She followed the group toward the entry, wishing she had someone to call for support. Wishing she didn't feel like she was alone in this, even with the Renegades family here. This wasn't their mess.

She tucked her phone away in her purse and passed through the lobby doors—just as Leo's group slipped into a taxi and drove away.

“Hey—” She panicked as she watched their taxi turn onto the main street. “Are you freaking kidding me?” She turned toward the valet. “I need a taxi.”

He hailed one sitting at the corner waiting for the next fare, and she slid in and said something that felt stupid and melodramatic. “Follow that taxi.”

She only relaxed when Leo's taxi was within sight again.

She felt inexperienced and inept. Naive. She was oddly hurt by the evasion tactic. It made her feel like she was in high school again, and all the popular kids were off having sex or doing drugs. While they might have befriended Caitlyn during school hours when they needed a paper written or a math tutor, they couldn't wait to ditch her when the real fun started.

She arrived at what could only be a club, where Leo collected a handful of women and passed the line, ushered in by a bouncer. From the crowd, a series of white flashes pulled Caitlyn's attention to a young man with a very professional camera. She rushed toward him and covered the lens with her hand, gripping it when the photographer tried to pull it away.

“Get your hands off my camera.” He jerked her around until she saw Leo was inside, then let go. “What the fuck is wrong with you?”

“No photos tonight.”

The guy was looking at the screen of his camera and a slow smile replaced the scowl. “Too late. I've already got some good ones.”

He turned the camera to show a shot of Leo, grinning, surrounded by beautiful women he was corralling into a club.

The first night and she'd already been played. She dropped her head back, eyes closed. "I'm going to lose my job if you print those."

"And I'll lose my apartment if I don't."

"You realize he has a wife who's pregnant. Those pictures will kill her."

"I'm not the guy cheating on my pregnant wife. Put the blame where it belongs."

"I did *not* say he was cheating on his wife."

He just shrugged.

She pinched the bridge of her nose. "How much?"

"A grand."

She broke out laughing. "I know I've got an accent and all, but I really didn't just fall off the turnip truck."

It was true. She hadn't fallen. She'd been kicked out.

"Seven hundred," he offered.

"Three."

"Five."

"Fine." She sighed like it was a huge concession. "Let me see them again."

He turned his camera and toggled through. She took an image with her cell phone then told the guy, "Don't move."

Caitlyn started toward the huge man at the front of the line, clearly in charge of letting people in. He was at least six foot four and probably two hundred and fifty pounds. His hair was blond and spiked, a lot like Andi's.

She smiled politely at the bouncer. "I'm with Leo Woods."

Instead of stepping aside to let her in, he crossed meaty arms. His scowl was rather intimidating. "Back of the line."

"I'm sorry, I wasn't clear. I'm with Excel PR, and I'm the public relations assistant to Leo Woods. He just came in, with, like, half a dozen women."

"He did, but you weren't one of them."

"No, really. I need to get in. There's no telling what damage he'll do to himself in there."

"He's a big boy and he's been doing this a long time. He'll be just fine. Back of the line."

She glanced that direction, experiencing the second ego hit in half an hour. "How long is the line—"

"Two hours."

"Oh no." She faced the man again, panic rising, ready to throw herself to the wolves. "Please. If he does something stupid and it reaches the media, I'll lose my job." She put her hand to her chest. "Cross my heart, I'm not lying."

"If you only knew how often I've heard that." But his gaze stayed on her now instead of straying toward the line. "Where you from? Georgia?"

"No. I did go to college in Atlanta, but I was only there two years."

"Louisiana."

She patiently played his game because it was the most attention he'd shown her since she'd walked up. "No. They have a much thicker creole accent."

"Hmm. Kansas. You've got that Midwest sun-kissed look about you."

"Well, thank you, but, no."

"I give up."

"Kentucky. Ever been?"

"Nope."

"A lot of people think it's flat and boring like a few other fly-over states, but it's not. Let me tell you about my last few days. It's so miserable, it's funny."

She didn't wait for permission, she just took a breath and started recounting her week, including how no one supported her coming here, how she was striking out on her own for the first time, against everything her family wanted.

Then she moved on to the job, while he remained riveted. And she cathartically unloaded on this poor man.

"I had never even heard Leo's name before yesterday. I'm not much of a movie girl, more of a TV series or reading girl. My boss purposely gave me Leo—currently in second place for the actor no one wants to work with in all of Hollywood—hoping I'll mess up. There was some story about my boss wanting to give my job to her niece, but her sister knew that would be a bad idea. Right now, I'm wishing I had a woman like my boss's sister in my corner."

"Sounds like you need one."

"Right? This is the worst first assignment ever, and I really don't want to mess up. I'm dead serious when I say I'll lose my job if Leo gets banged up by the media." She pulled cash out of her pocket. "See? This is for buying photos. Ask the shark photographer right there."

"Just making a living," the shark said.

"Aw." She softened her voice for maximum effect. "Bless your heart."

The bouncer laughed his ass off. He obviously understood the many meanings of the phrase.

"You're not the only one trying to make a living," she told the shark. "We're all just trying to keep our heads above water." She faced the bouncer again. "How do you stand out here all night and *not* swat those guys like flies?"

That made the bouncer laugh again. "Okay, okay." He lifted the rope leading into the club. "But I'm only letting you in because one, I love that accent; two, your story, if true, is pathetic, if not very imaginative; and three, you're smokin' hot, not to mention funny."

Caitlyn felt a smile break out. "That's the nicest thing anyone's said to me today."

"If you're not back out here in twenty minutes, I'll send

people in to get you. And you don't want me to send people in to get you."

"Twenty minutes? Will I be able to find him in twenty minutes?"

"Try the far side of the bar. He likes the tables in the back."

"You seriously just saved my job." She offered her hand. "I'm Caitlyn."

They shook. "Donny. That job doesn't exactly sound like a keeper."

"True, but a girl has to eat." She lowered her voice and added, "I'm going to quit as soon as I can, but no one can know that."

"Your secret's safe with me."

She pushed the money back into her pocket, then said, "I don't want to insult you, but I'd like to offer you a tip for helping me out. I've never done this. Is that an okay thing to do?"

"It's okay with me."

She grinned, happy she could do something nice for him, and pulled out two hundreds.

The bouncer took the tip, shaking his head. "Try not to change, sweetheart. You're a real sparkle in this smog."

"I'll do my best." She took a deep breath. "Wish me luck."

"You'll need it, little country girl."

Caitlyn stepped into the club and was sucked into a dark void of ear-piercing music. She followed the hallway to where it opened into one huge space, and she stopped, staring at the enormity of it.

She'd been expecting something closer to a bar with a dance floor. This was not that. This was an endless writhing mob, lit in colored strobes. The club was so loud, she couldn't think, and she had no idea how she would ever find one man in this jungle.

Caitlyn did a quick Google search, pulled up a picture of

Leo, took a deep breath, and set out. She tapped a lot of shoulders, followed a lot of pointing fingers, endured a lot of butt slaps and chest rubs, and, to her surprise, found Leo at a table with half a dozen new women.

He caught sight of her. "Uh-oh, the reputation police are here."

She changed the photo back to the one from the photographer and showed it to Leo. He made a gesture, dismissing it.

"Buy it," he yelled over the crowd. "That's your job. Get rid of it."

She was beginning to see Leo's difficult-to-work-with side.

"I didn't sign up for this," she yelled back. She pulled cash out of her wallet, grabbed Leo's hand, and slapped five hundred dollars into his palm. "Your stupidity, your problem. Go buy it yourself, or let your wife see it in the tabloids tomorrow."

15

It was a beautiful night, midsixties, black sky smothered in stars.

Duke leaned against a parked car and crossed his arms as he watched the club door for Caitlyn. He'd been in clubs enough to know she wouldn't get out of there without having hands all over her, and that really, really, *really* annoyed him. But he had to admit, watching her badger the bouncer had been entertaining.

Her accent deepened when she was angry, her face flushed with color. She tried telling the bouncer she was with Leo. When that didn't work, she attempted to convince him by telling him the whole sordid story about what was happening, including how shitty she felt over being disrespected by Leo.

Chatty, chatty, chatty.

The bouncer said something to the effect of she was only getting in because her story was imaginative, and she was smokin' hot.

Duke couldn't argue there.

He shifted on his feet. Checked his watch. This protective streak was annoying. He really would rather not care whether she was getting herself into trouble or not. He didn't like having to track her down everywhere she went or follow her on a fool's errand, like this one. What he really needed was some extra sleep. But that too brought his mind back around to Caitlyn. He'd sleep so much better with that woman in his bed.

While he waited, his eyes on the door, he wondered if she'd ever been in a club before. Wondered what kind of trouble she was getting into in there. Hoped he wouldn't have to go in there after her, because if he saw someone touching her, it wouldn't end well—for them.

He grew antsy and walked in a circle. How long should he give her? Five minutes? Ten? Thirty?

Turned out, he didn't have to decide after all, because she finally emerged, disheveled but intact. Duke breathed a little easier, but grew confused when she didn't return to the photographer, just stood on the sidelines, catching her breath, staring at the club, chatting with the bouncer, while checking her clothes and hair to make sure she was together.

Duke pushed off the car to move toward her, but Leo came out, so he stopped. Duke couldn't figure out what in the hell was going on. Leo looked around, found the photographer, and approached the guy. After an angry conversation, Leo handed the photographer the money. Caitlyn stepped in and took the camera from the photographer, then manipulated it while the photographer tried to get it back and Leo blocked him. Once she was done whatever she was doing, she turned and handed it back to him, and the angry photographer called it a night.

Then she turned on Leo. "We can do this as many times as necessary for you to get it through your head—your picture in the tabloids would hurt your marriage and your career. So, unless you're on a kamikaze mission and plan to take me down with you, you need to think about what you're doing. Every action has a consequence. I may be here to mitigate those consequences—which I resent, for the record—but I can't be everywhere all the time."

This time when Leo returned to the club, she exhaled and looked at her phone.

Before she could call a ride, Duke strolled up to her. "Hey."

She looked up, rolled her eyes, and muttered, "Dadgumit."

The Southern saying in that beautiful drawl of hers made Duke grin.

"What are you doing here?" she wanted to know.

"Watching a little spitfire lay down the law."

"Amen," the bouncer agreed.

"Stop following me," she told Duke.

"Stop going places you shouldn't."

"There are stalker laws, you know."

He laughed. As did the bouncer. "Are you staying or going back to the hotel?"

"Depends on what Leo does. You?"

"Depends on what you do."

She exhaled and closed her eyes. "*Stop. It.*" She opened her eyes with a ready glare. "How much clearer can I say it? Don't you have a bridge to jump off somewhere?"

"Why did Leo pay for the pictures?"

"His mess, his fix." She looked at her phone again. "Worked on my brothers when they stole from the corner store. Apologize and return—fastest cure to stealing ever."

At least until the embarrassment had faded, and Cody did it again. But that's all she had up her sleeve to throw at Leo right now. She'd worry about it happening again when it happened again.

Leo emerged from the club, clearly annoyed and subdued, a kid being sent to his room. "Order me an Uber, will you?"

"I'll consider it if you tell me where you're going."

"Relax, Mom. I'm going back to the hotel."

"Hallelujah," she said, her drawl thick on the word. "Order this man an Uber."

"She sounds a little like McConaughey, doesn't she?" the bouncer asked no one in particular.

She returned to the bouncer with a smile and a soft "All right, all right, all right," making everyone laugh at a damn good impression of a McConaughey signature saying.

The fact that she wasn't surprised at the comment and had the retort ready made it clear she'd been referenced to McConaughey before.

"Thank you for your help. Looks like I'll live to crash another party." She pushed up on her toes to kiss Donny's cheek. The guy lit up like a spotlight.

"Don't change, girl."

"Sparkle in the smog."

"Damn right."

When Caitlyn returned, Duke opened the app and ordered a ride. "What was that sparkle in the smog about?"

"Just a creative compliment from Donny."

"Donny?"

"The bouncer."

He looked up from his phone. "You're on a first-name basis already?"

Leo offered her what looked like a business card. "Hold this a second."

She took it while Leo shook out his light jacket and slid his arms in, then straightened the collar.

There was an Uber right around the corner, and within minutes, Caitlyn was seated in the front and Duke and Leo sat in the back.

"Are you going to be a menace the entire time you're here?" Leo wanted to know.

"You betcha. Menace, wet blanket..."

"Drag," Duke offered, pleased when he got a smirk out of Caitlyn.

"Downer," she added.

"Sourpuss," he said. "Come on, you've got to have a few Southern ones up your sleeve."

"Don't know if they're officially Southern, but curmudgeon, crash queen, whinger..."

"Whinger?"

The way Caitlyn smiled at Duke made him feel like they were on the same page again.

"You having hearing problems now?" she asked.

"A better question," Leo interrupted, "is are you two finished?"

"Look," Caitlyn said with admirable patience, "we're on the same side here. We both want the same thing for you—a successful career, a great marriage, and a child who can look up to you, right?"

Leo looked away, his jaw shifting.

"We don't have to be at odds the whole time we're here. If you're really going to be difficult, I'm going to have to hire a security detail, because I obviously can't watch you twenty-four seven, and I really need to sleep."

"Are you serious right now?"

"My beauty rest is no joke. But to ease the sting of rules, I would be willing to play board games until your bedtime."

Duke laughed. Hard.

Leo shook his head, looked out the window. "This is ridiculous."

"Ludicrous," she agreed.

"It's the first night. We always go out the first night."

"Next thing you're going to tell me is it was one of those team-building thangs."

Now both Duke and Leo were laughing. Leo looked out the

side window. “Scrabble. I’ll wipe the floor with you in Scrabble.”

“I don’t mind losing at Scrabble, because I will kick your tuchus in Battleship.”

“Oh, I hate Battleship.” He snapped his fingers and pointed at her. “Cards Against Humanity.”

“With you? Never.”

“Speaking of never, how about Never Have I Ever?”

“Not on your life.”

“Okay, Pictionary.”

“We don’t have enough people.”

They pulled up to the hotel. Duke and Caitlyn thanked the driver, but Leo exited without a word. He started for the hotel. He was on the second stair to the entry when he snapped and turned back toward Caitlyn. “Oh, that card.”

Caitlyn looked at her hand like she’d forgotten she was holding it and offered it to Leo.

All the hairs on the back of Duke’s neck stood up, and he grabbed the card before Leo could.

“Hey, that’s mine.” Leo’s clear anger confirmed Duke’s suspicion. It wasn’t a business card—at least not a real one. It was too thick.

He pulled the tiny bag of white powder from a compartment inside the card. It was so small, Caitlyn couldn’t get a good look at it, covered with Duke’s fingers. “You fucking sonofabitch.”

“What—” Caitlyn started.

“It’s coke,” Duke almost yelled at Caitlyn.

Her eyes latched onto the bag and grew wide. “You mean...cocaine?”

“And he was using you to hide it,” he told her.

The color drained from her face.

“It’s barely enough to get a buzz,” Leo said.

Duke turned toward Leo, who still thought he was going to

get it back, gripped the front of his jacket, and slammed him up against the nearest wall. An *umph* bolted from Leo.

"Duke," Caitlyn said, "don't. I'm sure it was just a miscommunication."

"It wasn't. Tell her why you gave her the coke," Duke demanded.

"Really, I forgot about—"

Duke pulled him forward and shoved him back again.

"Stop," Caitlyn yelled. "*Stop.*"

"Okay, okay," Leo said. "I gave it to her."

"Tell her why."

"I just needed an extra hand. I forgot—"

Duke slammed Leo again. "Let me help you out. You thought that if the police stopped us after coming out of the club, which often happens..."

He left the sentence open for Leo.

"They'd find it on her."

"Instead of..."

"Instead of me. But seriously, the penalty is so low for a first-time offender, she'd probably only get community service."

"And a rap sheet," Duke said. "Don't fucking minimize what you did. You threw her under the bus. The person who is looking out for your career. Damn, addicts do the most idiotic, selfish things."

Caitlyn's jaw dropped.

"It's just to relax," Leo insisted. "I'm not an addict."

"Tell that to someone who doesn't know you." Duke gave Leo another slam against the wall. "You don't touch her, you understand? You do one more thing to compromise her, and you'll regret it."

"Yeah, fine, whatever."

"Fucking bastard." Duke released him with a shove, opened the bag, and let the breeze take the coke.

"Nooo," Leo whined.

Duke refocused to find Caitlyn yelling at someone with a camera shooting images of the argument. The guy looked at his camera screen and smiled. Duke turned and lunged for him.

Caitlyn fisted the back of Duke's shirt, catching him inches from getting his hands on the guy. "*Stop*, damn it."

She got between Duke and the photographer and yelled at Leo. "Get back in the hotel and stay there."

Leo disappeared. Duke was still glaring at the photographer when she lifted Duke's hand and pushed cash into it. "Your mess, your fix."

16

Caitlyn walked straight to the elevators. Her skin felt too small, her thoughts too big.

She didn't know how to process all this. The self-destructive behavior, the laws broken without any concern for the repercussions, the brazenness of Leo's actions, the general perception that he was above the law and more important than the average person.

She may have seen the opulent, civilized side of LA while she'd stayed with Lexi and Jax, but since she'd pulled her car into the parking lot of her apartment building, then shaken Leo's hand at the airport, she'd gotten an up-close-and-personal look at the grungy, demanding, self-absorbed side of Hollywood.

The elevator pinged, and she stepped on, praying no one else did. When the doors closed and she was alone, she covered her face with both hands. "This is a clusterfuck."

She rarely swore, but if there was ever a time for it, this was that time. Her breathing stuttered, and emotions rose inside her, swelling her gut and rising like the tide, slowly filling her to the brim with anger, regret, fear, and some emotions she couldn't even untangle.

With tears pushing at her eyes, Caitlyn called Merissa.

She picked up on the second ring. "Please don't quit."

"If I could, I would."

"Talk to me."

Caitlyn pulled in a breath and gave Merissa the rundown of the day with Leo. "If he doesn't even want to keep his life intact, how am I supposed to do it? I don't know what the hell I'm doing."

"Sounds to me like you're doing an amazing job," Merissa said, voice compassionate.

"I don't know that I want to be good at this. I feel like my integrity is draining out of me."

"Sweetie, no one cares about integrity around here. They care about money, power, and image. Leo's being a shit because he can. Because he doesn't like having a babysitter. Much like Porsha, he's testing you. Once he sees you won't bend, he'll lighten up."

Caitlyn's breath leaked out, her shoulders dropped, and tears blurred her vision. She hated the fact that everyone back home had been right about LA. She loathed the idea of going home a failure. She'd be the butt of town jokes for years. Maybe decades. She was embarrassed that she'd looked at this opportunity with rose-colored glasses and now felt naive.

Maybe she could find another job. If not in public relations, something that paid enough to stay here. She could always lie to her friends and family. It wasn't as if they'd ever come to visit her. They'd never know what she was telling them wasn't the truth.

She'd just fallen another notch—considering lies to save face. "I don't think I can do this."

"You're already doing it, and from what I've heard, you've saved his ass at least a couple of times in the last few hours. The middle of anything is always messy. The only thing that matters is how things turn out in the end. Stay this course, and you'll knock Porsha's socks off. One year with Porsha and you'll be getting recruited by headhunters for top jobs, making more money than you ever imagined."

The elevator stopped on her floor and Caitlyn headed to her room. "I'll do what I can, I guess."

"Call to bitch to me anytime. Some celebs can make a person crazy."

"No joke." Caitlyn thanked Merissa and disconnected. She flipped on the lights and just stared at the room. The room that would be her home for the next few months. God, what a departure from her normal life.

But that was what she'd wanted. And that was what she'd gotten.

"Be careful what you wish for, missy."

Caitlyn changed out of her dress and into a tank top and shorts. She scrubbed the makeup off her face, making her look sixteen instead of twenty-six. Then just stared at herself.

"Who the hell *are* you?" She'd never experienced disassociation, but right now, she was the poster child for losing her sense of self under stress. And she didn't like the person looking back at her, which dragged her heart farther toward her feet.

A knock at the door made her jump. She pressed a hand to her chest. "Jesus Christ."

"Caitlyn." Duke's voice was muffled from the door between them. "Come on. Let's talk."

She came out of the bathroom and rested a shoulder against the wall. Even after all the bullshit she'd been through, she wanted him. Maybe even more now. She was feeling so shitty, and there was no doubt he could make her feel better, at least physically.

Maybe a distraction would be good. Then again, her other decisions had gotten her here, so...

He knocked again. "Caitlyn."

She pressed her eyes shut. "Not interested in talking."

"I'm up for other activities too."

She laughed. Despite the misery, he could still make her laugh, but the humor didn't last long. "I'm not good company right now."

"Caitlyn."

The tone of Duke's voice made her close her eyes. It shot her straight back to the bedroom and his coaxing instruction in bed. *"Lift into me. Perfect. Just like that. Fuck, that's good." "Slow down, sugar, enjoy the ride." "Spread those sexy thighs. Make room for me, I'm gonna be here awhile."*

"Come on." His voice dragged her back.

She was so out of control, in so many ways. Growling, she swung the door open with a sharp "What?"

"You should check who it is before you open the door."

"That's a stupid thing to say when I knew it was you. But let me appease you." She stepped back and shut the door in his face, a little harder than necessary.

He started laughing. *Laughing.* What guy laughs when he gets a door slammed in his face?

"Let's try that again," he said.

"No one's home. The woman in this room skipped town, said something about the Cayman Islands. She looked catty-wampus, like she was ready to fly off the handle. I'd stay away from her if I were you."

"Caitlyn."

"Go away, or I'll call security."

He laughed again.

She swung the door open. "Would you stop laughing?"

"Would you stop being funny?"

She groaned, dropped her head back, and walked away

from the door. Duke entered, closing the door behind him, and followed her, sauntering through the hall and into the room.

"This is nice," he said. "Lots of space. I'm in a cracker box with two beds. Can barely move around, but since I don't do anything but sleep there, I can't complain."

"Say what you came to say. I'm tired. I want to go to bed."

He held her gaze with a smolder that told her he wanted to accompany her to bed. She shouldn't have let him in. She should have known she needed a locked door between them to stay apart.

"Sugar, you don't have the first idea of how to deal with a man like Leo."

"Stop assuming what I can or can't do. I've got a degree that says I can do this job. And I've handled it pretty damn good already, considering I got him to pay for his photos and leave the club early, thank you very much."

He had his hand pressed to the back of a chair at a small table. He was so still, it was unnerving.

"I mean, is anything in life what you expect it to be?" she asked, desperately needing to fill the silence. "This might not have turned out to be what I thought, but I'm not a quitter. I'm not going to run away because things get a little sticky. I'm here and I'm staying, so I've got to make it work. I'll have to learn as I go."

He stayed quiet, gaze fully attentive and on her.

"You must have been in that position before. Maybe you ended up in a tough spot while climbing or in your stunts or even with your family and had to figure out how to make it work."

He didn't respond.

"Did you know anything about abusive men before you learned about Kristy's husband? Did you know anything about a no-contact order before Kristy needed to get one? Did you know how to take care of a little girl before you took on your nieces?" She paused, but he didn't speak. "Why aren't you saying anything? You're like a sexy mannequin or something."

That got her a laugh.

"Good to know you're still alive."

"Don't take this wrong, but it's kinda fun seeing you mad."

"What? *What?*"

"It's just the way you get all huffy and chatty. It's so...cute isn't quite the right word, but..." He shrugged. "It's cute."

She pressed one hand to her forehead and used the other to gesture behind him. "The door's right there. Get out."

"Look, this situation with Leo is a slippery slope, and once you start sliding, it's nearly impossible to get your footing again."

"You're getting dangerously close to stepping over a line."

"Sugar"—his grin made her want to forget all about his doubt—"we crossed that line—several times—already."

She squeezed her eyes shut, but that didn't banish the thoughts. It just gave them a black screen to play against. Duke's hands learning her body. Duke's mouth tasting every inch of her skin. She'd known even before she'd fallen asleep that night that she would never be the woman she'd been before Duke Reid came into her life. Would never look at sex or hookups or men the same way.

"What's this?"

She opened her eyes and found Duke holding a handful of tags hanging from her new clothes where they lay over an ottoman.

"I thought you were cash-strapped."

"I am. My boss gave me ten grand to update my wardrobe."

"*What?*"

"What?"

"Money like that comes with strings. It's like a signing bonus. If you leave before a predetermined length of time, you have to pay it back."

Her eyes went wide. "Pay it back? I didn't sign anything. I think my boss was concerned about the company's image. She called me Mary Poppins."

Duke grinned.

"Don't even think about running with that. It was humiliating, a hard blow to my already damaged self-esteem."

His gaze drifted to her tank and shorts. "You don't look like a Mary, but the pop fits you. Yeah. Sugar pop."

"*Sugar pop?* Go jump off a mountain somewhere."

He sighed and sat on the edge of the bed. "Why are you so defensive?"

"Because everyone underestimates me, and it pisses me off. University is harder than junior college, Caitlyn. You'll never earn any money in public relations, Caitlyn. You'll never move away, Caitlyn. Why go to college, Caitlyn? Brett will take care of you. And now I get you're in over your head, Caitlyn. You can't handle a guy like Leo, Caitlyn."

She paced in what little space she had. She could feel herself coming apart at the seams, muscles tight and shaky, voice thick and broken, hot face, wet eyes.

"Just because I'm small, everyone thinks I'm weak. Just because I have a Southern accent, everyone thinks I'm either stupid or too sweet to handle anything difficult. Fuck them. Fuck you. I don't need—"

Duke stepped into her path. He stopped her with his hands on her waist and she felt the first tears fall. Thin warm trails down her cheeks. Perfect. This would only perpetuate the problem.

She covered her face with both hands, and Duke wrapped her in his arms, against his body, one arm at her waist, the other hand in her hair. He had a way of making her feel so safe, so cared for, and the emotions made her break. She tried to keep it in, but she'd been holding so much in for so long.

"I'm sorry," he said against her hair. "I never meant to make you feel that way. I only wanted to make sure you were safe. This industry really is its own animal, and it takes time to train that animal to become what you want. And, if I'm being completely honest, I agree you're a sparkle in the smog. I didn't want LA to ruin all the good in you."

She could already see those changes happening, and she didn't like it either.

"Truthfully," he said, "you impress the hell out of me."

His words eased the sting and settled her a little. But she still felt raw—lost and confused and hurting, and she leaned into him, using his support, enjoying the feel of his body, and he felt so damn good.

"I assume Brett is the ex?"

"Yeah."

"How long were you together?"

"Seven years."

"Jesus."

She wanted to forget. Wanted to escape. As much as she wanted to use Duke to do that, she knew that would be both wrong and futile.

She pushed away, moved to the door, and opened it. "I need room to think. Please."

17

The high-top table was covered with plates of food from the breakfast buffet, rim to rim.

"Why aren't you eating?" Keaton pulled Duke's attention from the lobby.

"I'm eating."

"You're picking," Troy said. "You need that protein for the climb today."

The hotel restaurant was overrun with crew, support staff, and a few secondary cast members. Duke, Wes, and Troy were climbing the mountain that would be used for the dramatic shots today, placing anchors for Duke's path as well as two other paths for cameramen. Keaton would be working with another actor, mapping out fighting sketches.

"I hate that you get to work with Cavill," Duke said, "and I'm stuck with Woods."

Keaton grinned. "Don't hate me because I'm beautiful."

"He's not eating because he's waiting for Caitlyn to show up," Wes said.

"Shut up." Duke speared a forkful of eggs, stuffed them into his mouth, and gave them all a look-I'm-eating glare, making Wes laugh.

But Wes was right. Duke purposely sat facing the lobby from the dining room so he would see Caitlyn when she got off the elevator. Knowing she was in the same hotel, a few floors away, made it next to impossible to sleep.

"Hey, guys." Sissy, a woman from Sets they'd all worked with in the past, stopped at the table, her hand on Duke's shoulder.

Sissy wasn't her real name. It was her nickname, referencing a young Sissy Spacek—cute face, lots of freckles, and a bit of a temper to go with that auburn hair. In fact, Duke didn't even know her real name.

"I heard Jax finally got Lexi to the alter."

"Good things come to those who wait," Keaton said.

"You know the entire female population goes into mourning when any of you find The One." She swayed to press her hip against Duke's and smiled at him. "Are you the only single guy in this tribe now?"

"Cameron's single." He hoped the mention of a younger guy would give her attention somewhere else to land.

"Haven't met him yet. Is he as hot as the rest of you?"

"Of course," Troy said, grinning. "It's a job requirement."

Caitlyn stepped out of the elevator, and Duke lost track of the conversation. She paused to look at herself in the mirror covering a wall in reception and tugged at the bottom edge of her top, one that didn't quite cover her abdomen. Everything inside Duke tightened up and tugged.

Sissy left the table, but Duke barely noticed.

Caitlyn's skirt was yellow with a white pattern. It ended just below her knees and had a long slit up the side, showing her gorgeous thigh when she moved. Her sandals and her top were the same white as the pattern, but the top was way too revealing for Duke's taste—at least when she was going to be surrounded by other men. Thin straps, cropped to show her flat belly, fitted to expose her shape, and gathered across her breasts to reveal the kind of cleavage that made Duke almost drop his fork.

The fumble made the guys look at Duke. Wes and Keaton followed his gaze, and both lit up with smiles. Keaton gave a low whistle through his teeth. Wes shook his head.

"What?" Troy twisted to look over his shoulder and turned back laughing. "Good luck concentrating, brother." To Keaton, Troy said, "Maybe you ought to climb with us today. I'm not sure this guy's head will stay in the right place."

"Sorry," Keaton said. "I'm going to play in the mud with Syrian fighters. I'm lucky that way."

"Fuck me." Duke exhaled and rested the tines of his fork on his plate. "She's going to be hit on every minute of every day."

"Welcome to our world, buddy," Keaton said.

"You're all solid. It wouldn't matter who hit on Rubi, Ellie, or Brook. God only knows why, but they're in it for the long haul. And none of you would be kicking back if you had to watch guys hitting on them."

Duke finally put his fork down, his appetite gone. She looked mouthwatering. These feelings of inadequacy were new and uncomfortable. He wanted to wrap her up and hold on to her. He was already jealous as hell, and no one had even looked at her yet.

She disappeared into the hotel's gift shop on her path toward breakfast.

"Caitlyn is like a baby deer. She's only been with one guy—"

"Two now," Wes added with a smirk.

"—and she's going to have men falling at her feet here."

On cue, Caitlyn left the store and strolled into the restaurant, and heads turned.

"We all know what happens to ninety-nine percent of women who come here from small towns."

"When did you become such a pussy?" Troy asked.

"Two years living with four females," Keaton said. "What do you expect?"

"Weird to see you jealous," Wes said.

"Never had anything to be jealous of before," Duke said.

"You aren't giving her enough credit," Wes said.

"She's smart," Troy said, "And anyone who can leave a small town where she knows everyone to come to a city where she knows one person is strong. If you think you're going to be able to treat her like she's fragile, you can kiss her goodbye right now."

Keaton grinned. "Can you imagine any of us treating *any* of our women like they're fragile?"

"They'd kick our asses," Wes said. "For real. Have her sit with us. Showing a hint of ownership will keep the less confident away."

That was a good idea. Duke pressed his hands to the table, preparing to stand, but Caitlyn got a phone call, so he sank back into his seat. "She's on the phone."

He watched her pick up a banana and an orange and drop them into her bag. Then, with the phone positioned between her ear and shoulder, she made herself a bowl of oatmeal.

Duke shook his head. "I'm not going to do this to myself. Troy's right. My attention needs to be on climbing, and I can't do that if I'm thinking about her."

"Chicken," Keaton said.

"Shut up," Troy told Keaton. "*We're* climbing with him."

"It's a pipe dream, anyway." He shook his head. "Between my sister and the girls and work..."

"If you really want her, you'll make it happen," Wes said.

Duke pushed his food around some more, watching at least a dozen men watch Caitlyn. He couldn't just sit by like he didn't care, like he didn't want her. Wes was right. Duke had to make this happen.

He pushed to his feet and ignored the guys' parting jibes. Caitlyn wandered into the lobby and sat on one of the sofas there, her back to Duke, talking on the phone between bites of oatmeal. Duke stood off to the side, waiting for her to finish her call.

"I've been really busy," she said into the phone while turning pages of a magazine. "It's a new job. They're always demanding in the beginning."

She went quiet before saying, "Look, I know this is hard on everyone, but at the end of the day, this is my life, and this is how I want to live it. That doesn't make me love any of you less, and I'm sorry this is putting more pressure on you. I'll eventually find a job that pays well enough for me to send money home. Then maybe one of you could quit your second job, spend more time with the boys."

She listened to the person on the other end—clearly one of her parents—before closing the magazine—*Star*, a trashy tabloid—with a snap.

"Stop it. You have no right to talk to me that way. I've spent years helping with the boys, and I gave everyone plenty of notice. Months, in fact. It's not my fault it took y'all so long to realize I was serious. I know how ridiculous this looks to you, but I'm twenty-six. I don't need anyone else's approval. This is what I need to do now. This is where I need to be. I don't expect anyone else to accept it, but I do expect everyone to respect it. I've given you plenty of opportunity to do that, but all I get is this—anger, disapproval, judgment. I don't want it, and I don't deserve it. Please don't call me if you don't have something nice to say."

She disconnected and set her phone down with a sigh, then pressed her fingers against her closed eyes.

Wow. Duke blinked hard a few times. Seeing her put

someone in their place so smoothly, so accurately—and one of her parents, no less—made him both scared and excited.

He approached as she set her bowl down on a side table. "Hey."

She stood. "Hey."

Duke could see the wetness in her eyes, but something sparkly drew his gaze to her middle.

"Is that..." Jesus fucking Christ, he knew exactly what that was—a belly button piercing, complete with a sparkling stone. His mouth watered. "When did you get that? You didn't have it when we were together."

"When I went shopping with Andi."

"Andi?"

"My roommate."

He forced his gaze off the piercing and reordered his thoughts. "Are you okay? That phone call seemed rough."

"I was just reminded of how selfish I am. Good times."

He gestured to the magazine she held on her iPad. "Reading trashy tabloids now?"

"Gotta stay in the know."

He scanned her head to toe again, and his gaze held on that piercing. "Well, I know you don't feel incredible, but you sure look incredible."

A smile stuttered on her lips before they fell again. "Thanks." She looked down at herself. "Mary Poppins is still getting used to this LA vibe. I'm worried it's a little too...I don't know...something, but my roommate swore up and down it was perfect."

"I like your roommate."

She smirked.

"Fair warning," he said, "it will have every male between the ages of five and ninety-five hitting on you."

She gave a one-shouldered shrug and changed the subject. "I'm sorry about last night. None of this is your fault, and I shouldn't take it out on you. I'm just on edge and not great company right now."

"You would be great company"—he grinned at her—"if you stopped throwing me out of your room." When she made no reference to having him in her room, as in, inviting him there, he moved on. "What are you doing today?"

"I'm going through as much of Leo's day with him as I can stand. I want to see where the potential problem areas are. You?"

"I'm climbing with Troy and Wes to place anchors and scout for photo ops, then training Leo. You should join us. I've had the director set up a practice wall. It's really fun."

She looked down at herself. "I don't think this LA vibe would accommodate."

"I can get you some shorts or leggings from wardrobe."

"Let's play it by ear. It'll depend on whether I can get publicity puzzle pieces in place or if I'm scrounging to put things together." She pulled a printed schedule from her notebook and scanned it. "The wall isn't on his schedule."

"I saw Tara in the elevator on my way down for breakfast. She said he'd be there at noon."

"This shows he's in wardrobe at noon." She sighed. "Sure is hard to do a good job when everyone is plotting for you to fail."

She really did have a lot coming at her from every direction. Duke should be in her corner, and he was ashamed for being so selfish and wanting her all to himself.

"I'm sorry about last night too. I've become overly protective in the last couple of years, I guess. I know you'll find your own way to manage Leo. I just... I worry."

Her gaze went soft, and she opened her mouth to say something, but Wes's whistle broke across the lobby.

"Warm up, dude. Let's hit it."

18

While Duke returned to the guys, Caitlyn made her way toward the vans that shuttled crew between the hotel and the site and boarded one that was still empty.

When her phone rang again, she closed her eyes and dropped her head back. "It's temporary," she told herself, sure it was Brett or her mother, calling to chide her for hanging up so abruptly. "They'll adjust...eventually."

She dropped onto the bench seat and leaned against the wall before glancing at the screen. It was someone from the office, probably Merissa.

She answered, rubbing her temple. "This is Caitlyn."

"I hear you think on your feet."

It was Porsha herself. And she sounded...*not* mad. Not an attitude Caitlyn expected from Porsha. Everything in Caitlyn's world was backward. The people who should be nice to her were mean, the people who should be mean to her were nice. She felt upside down and didn't know what to expect next.

"I try."

"Still want the job?"

"Highly questionable," she said truthfully. Caitlyn was tired of pretending.

"That's fair. There've been a couple of developments. First: *Entertainment Daily* got ahold of the club pics with Leo."

Her stomach dropped. "No. I paid off the photographer. Deleted the images from his camera and took the SD card."

"Oh, dear, you have so much to learn. They transfer photos by Wi-Fi now. The instant they're taken, they're in the cloud."

She pinched the bridge of her nose. "What do you want me to do?"

"As a crisis rep, you determine that answer."

She dropped her hand. "A crisis rep? Does that title come with a raise?"

Porsha gave her a silly-little-girl laugh. "If it were me, I'd draw everyone's attention away from the club news with other news. Something bigger, flashier."

There wasn't anything bigger or flashier to focus on. Other than the whole business-card-drug thing—not exactly a positive swap. "I don't—"

"You think on your feet. Figure it out."

Caitlyn exhaled, growing angrier. "And two?"

"Tara had to go home because of an emergency with her mother. So, you are now Leo's assistant in addition to being his crisis rep."

Her mind swam in confusion and alarm. "You can't be serious."

"As a heart attack," Porsha said. "Get it done." She disconnected.

Anger steamed inside Caitlyn. This might be the film industry, but most people still showed common decency, like saying goodbye before they hung up and not hijacking her every move. She was swimming in anger. Now she was doing two shitty jobs and only getting paid for one. And not paid well.

She stewed while a few members of the crew wandered

onto the van and took seats. Caitlyn dreaded hearing what Leo would require of her. But she couldn't quit, not until she had another job, and she couldn't very well go on interviews while she was in Canada. She'd just have to spin this situation for the good.

She decided to pull a publicity idea from up her sleeve. One she'd been saving for good press when Leo needed it. He just needed it sooner than she expected.

Caitlyn prepared for more Porsha-like behavior and called Leo's wife, Kendra. She took a deep breath, slid her walls up, and dialed the number.

"Yes?" Kendra answered.

"Hello, Mrs. Woods, my name is Caitlyn, and I work for your husband's publicity firm."

"What has he done? Lord, he's only been gone little more than a day."

Caitlyn would have to think about the odd statement later. "I'm wondering if you'd be willing to come up for a short visit. We'd love to get some images of your beautiful pregnant self with your husband. The entire country is wondering how you make it work, with the distance and all. I know they'd breathe a sigh of relief to see you healthy and happy."

Silence filled the line for an extended moment. Caitlyn held her breath. She had no clue what she'd do if his wife wasn't willing to help out.

"When?" Kendra finally asked.

Caitlyn released her breath. "Today, if possible."

"I could use some publicity for my maternity fashions rolling out this fall," she murmured as if the words were a private thought. Then she spoke to Caitlyn again, clipped and assertive. "I'll be on the next flight with a new ultrasound photo of the baby, but we talk about my business, not Leo's movie."

So relieved, Caitlyn sputtered a "Yes, of course," even though she didn't know how she'd do that.

Caitlyn got off the phone and pulled in a deep breath. As other crew members filled the van, Caitlyn booked a flight for Kendra and sent her the information.

The ride was short, and the crew was friendly. It was oddly comforting after her hometown had turned on her. And her employer screwed her.

By the time they reached the set, Caitlyn had been asked out twice and stared at by one guy who rated an eight out of ten on the creepy scale. Duke's protectiveness might not be as misplaced as it seemed, but she could handle herself. That was what she came here to do.

Her phone pinged with another message. Before she could look at it, two more came in.

I need organic Brazilian nuts in my suite at all times, and I'm out.

It was from Leo. Caitlyn didn't know whether to laugh or fume. Then read the others.

I take two showers a day—first thing in the morning and last thing at night. The water temperature must be exactly 102 degrees.

She sputtered an absurd laugh. This had to be a joke. She'd bet one of the Renegades had picked up Leo's phone and was having some fun.

I keep cold sparkling water on the set. Since we're in British Columbia, I'm drinking 10 Thousand BC. Make sure every refrigerator on the set is stocked. Oh, and get some publicity photos with me drinking it.

While Caitlyn's mouth hung open, she received an email from Tara. The contents read *Good Luck* with a pdf attachment listing everything Tara did for Leo and all Leo's preferences.

Tara will email you the rest. Come to building K and follow me from there.

"Oh, hell no." Caitlyn shook her head. "Mmm-mmm, no way, not happening."

Caitlyn dialed Merissa, who answered with "I've upped the

limit on your card to forty thousand. Let me know what I can do from here. You want me to find a temporary assistant for him? Free you up?"

"Oh God, yes."

"Got it. I'm really sorry this is happening on your first job."

Caitlyn exhaled and rubbed her forehead. "Thanks. I'll call you in a bit." She disconnected and muttered, "This just keeps getting better and better."

The van parked near the stunt area where all four Renegades were warming up with some fancy rope jumping. The crew disembarked from the van but didn't get far. They huddled around the guys to watch them show off. The music was loud, and the crowd clapped to the beat. It seemed this was a morning ritual.

Caitlyn could see why. The guys had some fancy moves, and they were damn fun to watch. Not to mention sexy and wearing nothing but shorts and shoes. Each Renegade took a turn determining the jump, and they shifted between styles effortlessly.

Duke was intensely absorbed in the work. He seemed hyperfocused. She supposed there was nothing more important in rock climbing than staying in the moment.

Then the music ended along with the warm-up. Duke came out of a trance to accept the applause and bowed with the others.

He was grinning and breathing quickly when he straightened, clearly in his groove. He fit so seamlessly with the other men, and it made Caitlyn a little jealous. She wished she had that kind of connection with someone. But right now, she felt completely misunderstood—even by herself.

His gaze found hers and held. Caitlyn felt his smile deep in her gut, and she let herself absorb the warmth. Then the crew drifted away, and Caitlyn went in search of Leo.

The set was a maze of people and equipment all nestled

into a valley surrounded by monstrous mountains and cliff faces. When she thought of Duke on those vertical slabs of granite, her stomach took a roller-coaster drop, so she concentrated on getting her bearings. She'd rather not be asking everyone for directions all the time.

She trekked past pop-up tents and equipment storage, clothing and heavy equipment, scaffolding and a couple of drink and snack carts. She wasn't completely oblivious to the heads turning and wondered if that was because she'd gotten the LA vibe right or because, somehow, they all knew she was in over her head.

Leo's laugh finally directed Caitlyn to him. He was bullshitting with a guy a decade or so older than Leo.

Caitlyn pulled a folding chair from rows and rows of them and set it up under a tree where she texted Merissa for information on the major media outlets and the firm's contacts at each. Then she texted all three of her brothers and both her parents. Nothing specific, nothing glowing, just the basics, and that she missed them. Telling them the upside of the job would only frustrate them.

She let Leo carry on for thirty minutes while she worked up a script to use when contacting those companies and finished a draft of the press release. Then she opened the document from Tara and nearly had a coronary over the list of petty, meaningless bullshit Tara did for Leo on a daily basis.

This bone fide narcissist needed new boundaries.

"Is this pretty little thing with you?" the man asked, bringing Caitlyn's head up.

"Unfortunately," Leo said on an exhale.

"So nice to be appreciated." She stood and offered her hand to the man she didn't know. "Caitlyn Winters. Excel PR."

He took her hand, expression on the stony side. He was in his late forties with strong features and a full head of dark hair. "Tom Hadley, director."

"Nice to meet you."

"You're a firecracker, aren't you? Lots of explosives packed into a little box."

She didn't need a reminder of how easily everyone could underestimate her.

She released his hand and told Leo, "We need to go. You have a meeting with..." She read from the schedule, "Matt Forge and Tom Easton in ten minutes."

Hadley glanced at Leo. "She doesn't know who they are, does she?"

"Probably not. Kentucky."

"If you're going to talk about me," she said, "at least do it behind my back. Let's go, Leo."

A smile broke across Hadley's face. "It's good to see someone talk back to you for a change, Woods."

When Hadley was out of earshot, Caitlyn stopped and turned toward Leo. "We need some ground rules."

"Actually, I need to be on my way if I'm going to make the meeting with Forge and Easton."

Leo turned, and Caitlyn stepped into his path. She wanted to handle this with less anger and more control, but she was overwhelmed at the moment.

"I'm already at my limit," she told Leo. "Don't push me, or this little firecracker will blow. I don't know if you're trying to piss me off or not, but don't pull an attitude with me. I have the power to turn you into a leper or a hero in the media. Which would you prefer?"

"You have no idea how beyond the scope you are right now. You're overselling yourself. You haven't been here long enough to know how little control you really have—"

"Kendra is on an afternoon flight with a new picture of the baby. I've arranged exclusive images with *People Magazine* and a press conference to put a spotlight on her maternity line. And you're going to be the lovesick husband and thrilled soon-to-be father, supporting your wife every step of the way.

"And, before you ask, no, it's not something we can cancel, because the photos from the club last night leaked despite my attempts to keep that from happening, and we need bigger news to knock down the weight of the images of you living the high life with other women on the set while your wife is home incubating your child. Try telling me I'm overselling myself now. Tell me exactly how little control I have."

Now that she was on a roll and had all her anger, frustration, and disappointment at the forefront, she let herself rail. "As far as taking over Tara's job—no. Just no. I will not be fielding your ridiculous, petty requests for organic anything or twenty-dollar bottles of water. And I sure as hell won't be stepping foot in your suite, let alone your bathroom. Merissa is hiring you a temporary assistant, and if I hear one word about you being inappropriate with her, I'll pull her, and you can handle your petty needs yourself, like a big boy."

Leo's expression turned from angry to...it was hard to decipher. Cunning, maybe?

"Kendra's coming?"

Caitlyn tilted her head. "Is that all you heard?"

"I've been asking her to visit me on set for over a year, but she's always too busy with her clothing line. Then she got pregnant, after we agreed to no kids and turned the stylish clothing line she'd planned into a maternity line. Surprisingly, it's gotten lots of press and lifted my public image."

Caitlyn's lips parted, though she wasn't sure what she'd planned on saying. This man confounded her.

"This could work," he decided. "When? I want to meet her at the airport. Leak this to the media. I've got my eye on a couple of parts that will be cast soon. It wouldn't hurt to get some positive press."

There he was: the blatant narcissist.

"You go on and work on that," he told her as if she were twelve and he was telling her to work on her science fair project. "I won't need you at the meeting."

She watched Leo walk down the path toward the epicenter of the site and disappear. And her faith in the human race fell another notch.

19

The first chords of "Sweet Home Alabama" played through the portable speaker Duke had attached to his harness.

He pushed his thumb into a hole in the rock, dug the tip of his climbing shoe onto the edge of a fist-sized crag, and paused. "This climb isn't an eight."

The difficulty levels of mountain climbing routes were defined with the Yosemite Decimal System, from one to fifteen within level five. Level five was where true rock climbing began. The simplest was 5.1. The highest and most difficult level was 5.15. At the height of his climbing career, Duke had been close to conquering the 5.15 multiple times.

"I told you," Troy said, climbing to Duke's right. "This is way closer to a 12."

"It's no more than a 10," Duke said. "Your skills are just rusty."

"Well, someone went and blew up our climbing club by falling off the map for two damn years," Wes said, climbing to Troy's right.

"You're both good enough to climb on your own. You don't need me."

"But then there'd be no one to beat," Troy said. "Lawson's no fun. He's still at the toddler stage."

"Hello, dumbshit," Wes said. "Look to your right."

Troy didn't, but he didn't need to, they all knew they were shoulder to shoulder with each other. Duke could climb a lot faster and more efficiently, but this climb was about securing a path for both Duke and the cameramen who would be scaling the mountain at the same time.

"There's a really annoying buzz up here," Troy said, using his free hand to pretend to swat something away from his head.

"Keep your hands on the rock, dude," Duke said. "An accident is the last thing I need."

"Not to mention facing Ellie if he hurt his stupid self," Wes added.

Troy chuckled. "She's a fierce one, but no fiercer than Rubi."

"Which is why my hands are on the rock," Wes said. "But you may not reach Ellie if Beau gets ahold of you first."

"He's a stickler," Troy agreed. Their set medic, Beau, took his job very seriously. "He's going to bitch at us for playing music."

They all advanced to the next pause, found comfortable positions, and placed anchors. And sang. Who *wouldn't* sing along with "Sweet Home Alabama"?

They each sang a line, and continued rotating through the song, but all of them sang the chorus at the top of their lungs and their voices echoed off mountains and through the canyon.

Duke used his thigh and butt muscles to push himself up so he could grab the next ledge. The three of them stayed side by side for the next few minutes, singing, placing anchors, and moving on.

"Sweet Home Alabama" transitioned into the Eagles' "One of These Nights."

"Good music today," Wes said.

They all picked up the lyrics of the new song, continuing to climb. Duke gripped a one-inch ledge and wedged his other hand into a two-inch gap. He pushed with his legs and released the rock to grab more.

"Keaton missed out," Troy said. "I'd forgotten how much fun this is."

"He's having his own fun," Wes said. "Whenever he's with Cavill, there's a lot more laughing than fighting going on."

Duke found a spot where he could rest. He planted his feet and straightened his arms, leaning away from the rock. His muscles took a deep breath of oxygen, and the fatigue started to fall away.

He repositioned himself to look out at the view and got that familiar rush. Freedom? Excitement? Accomplishment? All he knew was that when he was up here, looking at all this, his problems seemed so damned small.

That was until five days ago, when he added a new, surprisingly complex problem to his life. But now that he and Caitlyn were in the same place for the foreseeable future, he had time to iron out the issues between them and get close again. He really wanted to be close to her—in every way.

Duke paused on a four-inch ledge, running horizontal across the boulder all the way past Wes, almost reaching Troy. It also crossed a cavern. No boulders, no ground. Just air. And darkness.

It was the perfect training activity. Not that they were training today, but Duke loved to push himself. This was the kind of thing Duke's self-devised training climbs were made of.

"Who's ready for a challenge?" he asked.

"I've been waitin' to kick your ass all day," Troy said.

"Leave your anchors for now, and get to this ledge," Duke told them, gesturing to it.

It took a few minutes for the guys to reach their portion of the ledge.

Wes and Troy looked down.

"You mind fucker, you," Wes said.

They each had dozens of anchors in place to catch them if they fell, not to mention the best belays Duke knew, watching over them from the ground, prepared to lock them down at the first tug of the rope.

This was all about mastering the mind.

"This is perfect for those amazing shots Hadley wants," Troy said. "Imagine this viewed from every angle. It truly is a mind fuck, one that would transfer perfectly to the screen."

They all agreed.

"We all crawl the ledge to the left until you reach the next person's last anchor," Duke said. "Troy will go to Wes's anchor, Wes will come to my anchor, and I'll…" He looked to his left and saw the ledge ended at about the same distance. "Go to the end, I guess."

"I need a minute," Troy said. Wes seconded that.

"Are you going to get back into climbing?" Wes asked. "It really sucks that you couldn't take that spot for the World Cup last year."

"You've got us now," Troy said. "We'll all take over with Kristy and the kids so you can get away."

"That takes a lot of weight off my shoulders."

"Funny to say that here and now," Wes said, looking at the behemoth skyrocketing into the field of blue sky overhead.

"Okay," Troy said. "Ready."

Wes agreed.

"On three, we start," Duke said. "First one to the anchor and back wins."

They all knew the prize was nothing but bragging rights. It was the thrill of the challenge that pushed them.

Lynyrd Skynyrd's "Free Bird" belted from the speaker and echoed in the canyon.

"Did you plan that?" Troy asked.

"If I could plan something like that, I would be in an entirely different place in life."

"Are we going *on* three?" Wes asked. "Or—"

"The beat *after* three?" Troy finished Wes's thought.

Duke laughed. "*On* three."

Everyone chalked their hands, and Duke counted down.

They prepped themselves to take the ledge. Dropping the last toehold was the hardest part. It meant gripping the ledge with both hands, willingly and literally walking off the edge of a cliff with nothing but blackness beneath them.

"Who masterminded this?" Troy asked.

"You're the one who jumped at it," Wes said. "Your eyes are always bigger than your stomach."

"It was his idea," Troy said, lifting his chin toward Duke. "I should have known to blow it off. His mind's not right after living with all those girls."

"Oh, you have no idea how right you are, my friend," he told Troy. "Ready?"

Duke's question was rhetorical, and no one answered. Anticipation, possibility, energy, they all electrified the air.

"One." They all repositioned their weight in preparation for taking the ledge. "Two." They all moved just a little closer to the edge of their respective ridges. "Three."

No one moved. After an extended moment, filled with nothing but "Free Bird," they all broke into laughter. In fact, they were laughing so hard, they almost lost their balance and dropped by accident.

When they caught their breath, Duke said, "Take two. One, two, three."

They all released their foothold on the boulders and swung

into thin air, the only thing keeping them on the cliff face, their fingers on a barely there ledge.

"*Holy. Fuck,*" Wes said, his voice somewhere between exhilaration and terror.

"Don't forget to use your bodies for balance," Duke told them, taking the ledge hand over hand, swinging his legs just enough to keep up momentum, but not mess with his hold.

"Fuck balance," Troy said. "I'm getting to that anchor and back as fast as fucking possible."

"You could just go back now," Duke said.

"Fuck that. I'm no pussy."

They all laughed, again having to stop where they were so they didn't lose their grip. They all knew they only had the luxury of laughter because they were as safe now as they had been with their feet on the boulders. It just didn't feel like it.

Duke caught his breath and continued along the shelf. He loved this feeling. Playing chicken with Mother Nature, pushing himself physically and mentally. And it was so much more fun with friends.

"This is taking way too long," Wes said.

"We've only been on the shelf for two minutes," Duke told him.

"Like I said, way too long."

"If you fall," Duke said, "curl up before you hit the wall."

"Bad juju, dude," Troy said. "Don't say the F word here."

After another two minutes, they'd all reached their end point and started back toward their footholds.

"I suppose it goes without saying," Wes said in short bursts, "this stays between us. The girls don't…need to know how—"

"Idiotic," Troy offered.

"Impulsive," Duke said.

"We are," Wes finished.

"They already know, dude," Troy said. "They already know."

They returned to their holds and caught their breath. Wes and Troy were too traumatized to care who'd won.

"Let's not ever do that again," Troy said.

"You were just saying how fun it was," Duke said.

"Not climbing." He gestured toward the abyss. "That."

Wes and Duke laughed.

"Let's get to the top and head back," Wes said.

Troy agreed. "I'm starving."

Duke wasn't all that interested in food. He hoped Caitlyn would be at the base camp by now. And despite dreading the climbing wall with Leo, he was really looking forward to seeing Caitlyn. He only hoped her day had improved since he'd seen her this morning.

20

Caitlyn couldn't have felt more out of place.

The crew at the climbing base camp talked about places and people she didn't know. Laughed about things she didn't understand. All wearing jeans or shorts and T-shirts.

Merissa made a good call about how Caitlyn should dress. Others looked at her differently, took her seriously. At least more seriously than they would have if she'd been wandering around in jeans and tees like everyone else.

The rock-climbing base camp consisted of a couple of pop-up tents, tables and chairs and a bunch of equipment—climbing equipment, filming equipment, medical equipment, and mystery equipment. She couldn't imagine how all this worked, and she really didn't want to know. Her brain was already working at maximum capacity.

She tucked the field binoculars she'd been given under her arm and used her cell phone to grab a short video showing the guys on the mountain first, then all the equipment and setup. She'd send it to her brothers.

She offered the binoculars back to Jarred, the man who managed the climbing set and made sure everything was where it should be, everyone had the equipment they needed, and everyone was doing what they were supposed to be doing.

He was probably midthirties, carrot orange hair and brows, freckles, thick around the middle.

"How do they keep from falling?" she asked.

He looked in that direction. "They secure themselves at each anchor as they place it. So, if they fall, they only fall as far as the anchor below them will allow."

"That's...unnerving." Somehow that one little rope didn't give her any reassurance.

"They're all expert climbers, and they've got really experienced belays. Beau, our set medic, is a former air force pararescue specialist, and Duke's won a bunch of competitions. He taught all the other guys how to climb."

"Competitions?"

"Yeah—local, regional, national, international."

"Really."

"He earned a spot in the World Cup competition, but he didn't take it."

"Why not?"

Jarred shrugged. "Family stuff, I guess."

Duke had sacrificed even more than Caitlyn realized.

Behind Jarred, on the edge of the clearing, Caitlyn noticed someone new. He was handsome and in his fifties. When he caught her eye, she walked toward him and offered her hand.

"Caitlyn Winters, Excel PR."

"Ben Kingsley."

"Producer," she confirmed.

"Guilty."

"Good to meet you."

"I heard you're shadowing Woods."

"That information traveled fast," she said, then confirmed, "I am."

"I also heard you're new to this animal—LA promotion, not Woods, though Woods himself is a beast all his own."

She smiled, forcing herself not to show the frustration these assumptions caused or the fear they instilled. "You sure have your ear to the ground."

"I like to know what's happening on my sets. What have you got planned for him?"

"Well, I've been told to keep him out of trouble, but since it's clear that's not possible, I thought I'd try to get him some good press. I'm here anyway, right? Maybe I'll be able to outweigh the bad press with some good. Put some spin on things."

"I like that plan."

"That means a lot coming from you. His wife is coming in tonight. We're having a press conference on the set to play up the baby angle and talk about Kendra's maternity line. Thought it would be fun and different. Better than a boring conference room, right?"

"That's..."

"That's?" she said when he didn't finish.

"Bold. Risky."

Apprehension evaporated, and she grinned. "Perfect."

"How do you know which journalists to invite? There are more than a few assholes out there who love nothing more than to start a feeding frenzy and get the others to join in. And Leo's not exactly well liked. He's a prime target for twisting the truth. Or in his case, reporting a little more than the truth."

"I'm working with contacts provided by Excel, and I have a few other tricks up my sleeve." She didn't, but she would. Now that she knew that was what could happen, she'd have to add a little more security into the plan.

The music preceded the guys as they headed toward the set. More Lynyrd Skynyrd, this time "Gimme Three Steps," turned up loud, the guys singing along the way they had on the side of the mountain—sound traveled well outdoors. Only this time, the crew started singing too.

Carrying their gear, Duke, Wes, Troy, and their belays danced their equipment to the gear area and dropped everything into the appropriate pile. Caitlyn laughed at their sexy, fun blend of street dance styles. Duke's dirty skin shimmered with a sun-kissed, sweaty glow, and his hair was wet around the edges.

The song ended, and everyone cheered. Then cheered again as the lunch truck showed up.

Caitlyn had the biggest smile on her face when Duke's high-wattage smile met hers, and her heart took an extra hard beat.

Then his gaze clicked to Kingsley, and a seriousness edged his expression. He shut off the music as the crew headed toward the lunch truck, and Duke and the team approached Kingsley.

"Looking good up there," Kingsley told the guys.

They all shook hands with Kingsley, and Duke introduced their belays as the most experienced in the business, which seemed to please the producer. When the others drifted toward the equipment area, Caitlyn followed, keeping one ear to Duke's conversation.

He explained his plan to Kingsley, pointing at different areas of the rock face. They used a language Caitlyn barely understood, but in the end, Kingsley was clearly impressed. He shook Duke's hand and waved to the others before he headed toward the set parking lot.

Duke turned toward her, pulled a rag from the pocket of his shorts, and wiped his face, neck, and chest. "Have you killed Leo yet?"

Before she could open her mouth, Leo approached.

"I guess not," Duke said.

To Caitlyn, Leo said, "Did you reschedule the climbing wall with him?"

"I'm right here," Duke said. "Why do you have to reschedule the climbing wall? Let me just tell you now, I'm not on board with that idea if it means you're hitting the clubs earlier."

"No. Caitlyn's got Kendra coming."

His gaze jumped to Caitlyn. "Does she? Well, I'm not the kind of man to stand between a guy and his girl. We'll reschedule, but it's got to be tomorrow because we start filming the day after, and I still have to drill your handholds into the rock. I need to watch you climb before I can do that."

"Tomorrow, for sure." To Caitlyn, he said, "Add that and send me an updated schedule."

"Didn't your mother teach you how to ask for something?"

"*Please,*" he added before he headed off the climbing set.

Duke sauntered closer to Caitlyn, frowning at Leo's back until he disappeared. "What's going on with him?"

"He's excited to pick up some good press, courtesy of his pregnant wife and her maternity fashion line."

"Huh. Where's Tara? Why is he asking you to change his schedule?"

"She had to go home for a family emergency. I've been assigned to that job in addition to my own."

He winced. "Girl, you are getting hammered."

"Right?"

"How's that going to work?"

She heaved a sigh. "Probably with quite a bit of arguing and arm twisting, with the threat of losing my job every day. I told him my office point person will hire someone to handle the small things, I'll handle his promotional things, and he's SOL for the rest. Guess he'll just have to do it himself. For the moment, he's happy with me, but wait, that will probably change any moment."

He reached out and brushed hair out of her eyes. It was one

of those sweet gestures that made her want to wrap her arms around him.

"I hate your boss," he said, voice soft, "just for the record."

"Yeah. I hated her the minute I saw her."

"I know you don't think I believe in you, but I do. I really do. You're smart and tough." He skimmed her jaw with his knuckles, but it was the look in his eyes that softened all her rough edges. It was sweet and real. "I really care what happens with you, so I worry. Will you tell me if you need help? You're doing two jobs for the hardest man to work with in Hollywood."

"Second hardest," she said with a laugh. "And maybe on the help. I'm realizing that's harder for me to ask for than I realized."

"When you're used to being the one everyone leans on, asking for help doesn't come easily."

She nodded. "Maybe we're a lot more alike than I thought."

He tilted his head and chuckled. "Maybe we are." He glanced toward the lunch truck. "Are you hungry? Catering is pretty good on these jobs, and you didn't eat much this morning."

She wasn't used to someone caring about her like this, let alone paying attention to how much she ate.

She pressed a hand to her stomach. "I was until I watched you on that mountain."

He looked over his shoulder. "Can't see much from here."

"Jarred gave me binoculars. I saw enough to scare the hell out of me."

He returned his gaze to hers. "Guess it takes some getting used to."

"Hard to believe I'd get used to seeing that."

His gaze slid over her again, and her skin tingled as if he'd touched her. He smiled. "That piercing..."

She looked down. "What about it?"

"It's, wow, just really sexy."

She smiled, proud of herself for doing it. "I like the sparkle."

"Like your dress at the wedding."

And just like that, they were talking on the beach, walking hand in hand. "Was that night magical, or is that the naive country girl talking?"

"Magical. From the moment I saw you. And it's not just the piercing that's so sexy. It's the thought process that went on for you to go through with it. I love seeing you shed the rules and expectations smothering you."

Tension slid out of her shoulders. "Sometimes I feel like you really get me. Then you go and do something to piss me off."

He laughed and looked at the ground. "I'm working on that last part."

"After all the shit I've taken from my parents and Brett, it feels good to have someone see value in my decisions."

He lifted her chin with two fingers, and his gaze lowered to her mouth. "Think anyone would notice if I kissed you?"

"I'm sure there will be rumors swirling either way."

"You know, I've got a climbing wall that's not being used. Want to see it? Maybe give it a try?"

"We're not talking about climbing anymore, are we?"

His face broke into a smile that made her knees weak. "We can be talking about anything you want."

She leaned into him and curled her fingers around his. "Show me."

He tightened his hold on her hand and started down another path on the opposite side of the clearing.

"I hear you've won quite a few competitions."

"Talking to the crew, huh?"

"Pretty impressive."

He gave a one-shouldered shrug. "It's cool, but little else. I mean, sometimes the wins come with prizes, and sometimes the winners get short-term sponsorships, but not enough to move the needle on a regular basis. Certainly not enough to take care of a family. But, yeah, it's fun. What's going on with your parents and Brett?"

"Just phone calls and texts to the effect of 'stop being dramatic and come home.' I've gotten a lot of 'this is silly' from Brett and a lot of guilt from my parents. They both work two jobs, and my brothers are handfuls. It was really hard to decide to leave them."

"I can imagine. It was hard for me to leave Kristy and the girls to come here, and I'm only gone a month. I mean, Kristy really wanted me to come. She feels like she's become a roadblock to my life no matter how often I tell her I'm where I want to be. But not being on the front lines to protect them is nerve-racking."

"We're a pair."

"That we are. What were you talking to Kingsley about?"

"I just introduced myself. Small talk."

"I love the way you treat everyone the same, from the biggest stars to the shuttle driver."

To her it felt like the only option.

The building housing the climbing wall was a smallish metal deal, and Duke pulled the door open to let her pass through first. He smelled like...Duke. Duke after he'd worked up a sweat during sex. Duke and the faint spice of something different from his cologne. Probably something he used in the shower.

Inside, the space was dim with only two small windows for light. But the huge walls heavily dotted with colored plastic shapes were clearly visible, as were the pads on the floor six feet out from the walls.

She grinned. "It kind of reminds me of a playground. What are all those—"

He wrapped his arms around her from behind, pulled her

against him, and pressed his mouth to her neck. A wild, hot lust broke free inside her.

"Wanna climb?" he asked, lips moving down her neck, across her shoulder.

"You." How could she be breathless already? Her entire body thrummed with the need to feel him. To have him touch her and kiss her and turn this damn day around for her. "I want to climb you."

"I'm gonna get you dirty."

She wrapped one arm up and around his neck, arching against him to press her ass against his hips, and turned her head to look at him over her shoulder. "Dirtier the better."

He groaned and covered her mouth with his. His kiss was hot and wet and wild, his skin still held the heat of the sun, and his natural scent made her head light and her body ache.

He wrapped both arms around her and pulled her fully against him, his hands sliding down her belly, avoiding the piercing, over her hips. His hands slid from her waist to her ribs and pushed her top up, exposing her breasts, then covering them with greedy hands.

"I knew you weren't wearing anything under this." His weight pushed her forward, and she put out a hand to catch the wall. "Jesus, sometimes you make my heart stop."

He caught her mouth again, swept his tongue in to find hers, slid his thumbs over her nipples, making them pucker.

The sudden erotic onslaught thrilled her. She pushed her free hand into his hair, arched and rubbed her ass against a quickly hardening erection.

She felt like an entirely different person. Bold. Risky. So damn *alive*.

He broke the kiss and bit her neck. "I haven't been able to think about anything but this since the wedding."

One hand traveled down her body, between her legs, and she moaned. Then both his hands found their way under her skirt and grabbed handfuls of her ass. "I want my hands on you all the fucking time."

She pressed her other hand against the wall and used both to push back against him. He gripped her hips and gave her counterpressure. She'd never experienced this kind of lust or passion, and she was drunk. Euphoric.

Then her panties were sliding down her legs and his hands were everywhere. He lifted one ass cheek and slipped the other hand between her legs and stroked her. She couldn't classify the sound she made. Moan? A whimper? Both?

He stilled, his mouth on her shoulder, hot breath on her skin. "I love how wet you get for me."

Then, just his fingers moved, stroking through her heat and making her writhe. His other arm tightened around her hips, holding her still, while his other hand played between her legs, touching and stroking, exploring and teasing.

She arched her back, wanting to move, but he was so strong, she couldn't get what she needed.

"What do you want, sugar?"

"You. More of you."

His hot breath brushed her neck, his voice at her ear, low and rough and edged with excitement. "Tell me what you want, sugar. You know I love it when you talk to me."

"Inside me." The words rushed out with her breath. "Want you inside me."

One of his feet nudged one of hers sideways, opening her to more of his hand. He pushed one finger inside her. "Like that?"

She huffed. "Not even close."

He drew out and pushed back in with two fingers, and her pussy squeezed. "So tight. So wet."

He pulled out and thrust again, shooting pleasure through her pelvis. "Oh my God." She turned her head and whispered at his ear, "More. All of you. *Need it.*"

His breath rushed out on a groan. "Hearing you beg tears me apart."

He pulled his hand back, slid her wetness up between her ass cheeks, making her pucker. Then pushed right back in again.

"Duke."

He chuckled at her ear, and the sound was wickedly sexy. "Someone's impatient."

"You've got no one to blame for that but yourself."

He dropped his head to her shoulder and laughed. God, she loved the rich, joyful sound of it.

One hand disappeared, then it was back, holding his wallet. She took it out of reflex, but didn't want to search for the condom. Didn't want his hands off her for even a second.

"Do we need it? I'm on the pill." She turned her head and ran her free hand through his hair. "I don't want anything between us."

He made a sound against the skin of her shoulder. Longing, relief, excitement. "Fuck, sugar, you're killing me."

He groaned as he ran his hands over her body again, shoulders to hips. Used both hands to pull up her ass cheeks, then one to position himself. She braced for one of his signature thrusts, hard, deep, and long, but she didn't get that. All she got was the brush of his cock across her wetness and his groan in her ear.

"So wet." He bit her ear and kept rubbing the head of his cock through her folds. She fisted the hands braced against the wall, his wallet still in one.

"Stop being selfish. Share with me," she chided, hoping to get a rise out of him. "I want it all. You're being a tease."

He laughed again, and she closed her eyes and relished the sound. "That's something no one's ever called me."

She opened her mouth to poke at him some more, but he thrust, pushing himself halfway inside her.

"Ah." Caitlyn saw stars. Her vision hadn't cleared before he pulled out and did it again, making her whimper.

"Is that what you want?" he asked, his voice low, rough, a little dark. Before she could answer, he pulled out and thrust again. The strength of it almost buckled her arms. But still only halfway.

"You're a little slow on the uptake today, aren't you? I want *it all.*"

He stilled and burst out laughing. Laughing and laughing and laughing, head pressed to her shoulder.

His laugh made her laugh. Her arms collapsed, and her upper body angled toward the wall, her cheek against the cool metal.

The position change moved him deeper, and they both groaned at the stretch and slide.

They were still trying to catch their breath when he finally filled her with a stroke so complete and so forceful, her throat closed, cutting off any possibility of making a sound. And he didn't give her time to adjust. He just hit her with another mind-blowing thrust.

This time, Caitlyn did cry out, part whimper, part moan. "More, more, more."

This time, he gave her exactly what she asked for—more. More depth, more force, more passion. And all with a deep, hungry sound in his throat. It was utterly glorious.

"God, yes."

He gripped her hips and pulled her back against him to meet his thrust, and she choked out a whimper. "Don't stop. It's perfect. So perfect."

His thrusts were measured, but complete. No rush, no limits. Just his thick cock driving pleasure between her legs, filling her pelvis, weakening her knees.

"Perfect, perfect, perfect."

He raised her ass cheeks again and went deeper.

"Oh my God." The pleasure was indescribable. That extra half an inch hitting her at what felt like the very center of her body. Surging pleasure gathered, building outward.

His hot breath washed her shoulder, neck, back. Sweat slid from his forehead to her shoulder, between her back and his chest. Dripped from his chin and followed her spine. His hands slid effortlessly over her sweaty skin.

"Perfect," he agreed, breath coming quick and shallow, his voice gravel and lust. "Never...felt anything so...motherfucking perfect."

The pleasure was indescribable. Immobilizing. She'd never come anywhere close to experiencing this kind of sexual bliss. "Don't stop. God. Insane."

She'd been reduced to single words. Words that fell from her lips. Her mind had evaporated. All she could think about was the pleasure, the passion, the lust, the need. "Don't stop. Tell me...you won't stop."

His teeth slid along her shoulders. "I won't stop until you scream. I want to hear you scream. No whimpering. No moaning. You're going to *scream*."

Caitlyn was sure she could climax to his voice alone. It was like a catalyst, whipping everything else he did into a froth. She couldn't think anymore. She was singularly focused on the feel of him inside her, the way he held her, drove her, coached her.

The pleasure built and built and built until she ached with the fullness. "Duke..."

His name was a plea, a surrender.

"Patience, sugar pop." His voice dragged her back to their first night and all his sexy direction. *Tilt your hips, baby. Take me deeper. That's it. Ease into it.* "We're building. This is going to be...epic. Be patient. Enjoy...the rise."

Another rivulet of sweat slid between their bodies and teased the small of her back. Duke's arms wrapped around her. His hands cupped her breasts, stroked her nipples. Continued down her sides to her ass where he lifted her cheeks again, more aggressively, allowing him to go even deeper for three hard thrusts before he paused.

And yes, she absolutely whimpered. Whimpered and moaned and begged. "Please." She choked out the plea, not sure how much longer she could stand. "Duke..."

"I love hearing my name roll out of your sexy mouth." He pinched her nipples, shocking Caitlyn back from the stratosphere with a gasp. Then he stroked, soothing the pain, only to do it again. "You like that? You grip me so hard when I do it."

She did?

He did it again. The strike of momentary pain mixed with all the other luscious sensations tugged between her legs, as if there were a direct connection. And she did indeed squeeze around him.

He exploited the new find, stroking, pinching, and twisting while he thrust and she whimpered.

"Christ," he ground out. "You're going to fucking milk this orgasm out of me way too soon." He bit the flesh between her neck and shoulder. Hard. Hard enough to make her eyes fly open. Hard enough to sink deeper into her flesh.

"Fuck." He laughed the word. "Someone likes a little pain with their pleasure."

He bit her again, at her hairline on the back of her neck. The pain mixed and melted and layered. Her sex squeezed, released, squeezed.

"*Yes,*" he growled. "drag it out of me, sugar. Suck me off the way you do with that sexy Southern mouth."

She was dizzy. Unsure where the pleasure ended and the pain began.

Duke release one ass cheek and smacked her, open palmed. The shock of it made her gasp. The sting made her moan. She pressed her forehead to the wall.

He did it again, and the sound of flesh on flesh ricocheted

off all the metal. Her pussy squeezed him long and hard, until the sting subsided. He pulled out, thrust hard and deep, smacked her ass again.

"Fuck." She barely got the word out.

"I won't stop until you scream, sugar." He bit her neck again, his teeth sinking in as he thrust. The combination of squeeze and thrust, pain and pleasure was insane.

She needed relief. She pulled one hand off the wall and reached between her legs.

Duke caught her wrist, his grip hard. "No cheating. You're going to break from the inside out. I promise it will be worth the wait."

And he continued to torture her with the thrill of pain, the ache of pleasure, and the decadence of the two combined. His voice flowed over her skin like his sweat.

When her legs gave, Duke wrapped one arm tight around her waist, his hand on her breast, fingers on her nipple. He thrust quicker and combined the pinch of her nipple and the sting of his hand on her ass. The combination lifted her high and fast.

She felt the orgasm crest, somewhere deep inside her. "Yes." Thrust, bite, slap, pinch. "Ye-he-hes."

Everything intensified, harder, deeper, faster. And while the pain pushed her higher, quicker, it also distracted her body and held the orgasm just out of reach. Until she was begging. Open, shameless begging.

"Duke, please. Please, please, please."

The sound of his pleasure rang in her ears even as she broke. If he hadn't been holding her up, she would have hit the floor. The pleasure was so intense, it rushed through every damn cell, wrung out all thought. Her body locked her out, bucking, shivering, bucking again.

And she most definitely screamed.

21

Caitlyn stood on the sidelines, hugging her clipboard to her chest, trying to keep her mind on the approaching press conference.

Duke had showered and changed into fresh jeans and a T-shirt and now stood in the back, bullshitting with Troy, Keaton, and Wes. He'd wanted to take a shower with her, but by the time they'd returned to the hotel and he'd gotten the water temperature right, Caitlyn had passed out across the middle of her bed.

She'd told the guys they didn't have to come or stay for this press conference. They'd all had a full day of work, and Duke had also had mind-bending sex to tire him out. But they'd all insisted on being here, and after having Brett, her family, and her friends duck out of supporting her at every turn, the encouragement of these guys, guys she'd known for such a short amount of time, meant a lot to her.

All the invited journalists had a drink in their hand and chatted among one another. So far, it was a very relaxed atmosphere with like-minded people rubbing elbows.

The evening was a perfect seventy degrees, and she'd

arranged with catering to have food after the event. She'd borrowed two overstuffed high-backed chairs from the prop department and set up folding chairs for journalists in a semicircle facing them, all right smack in the middle of the movie set.

As far as press conferences went, this setup was curious. It would either bring journalists closer to Leo and Kendra, making them feel like insiders and acquaintances, or it would fail, creating a shitty way for Caitlyn to bomb her first event.

But something inside her thought it might just work by creating good will between the Woodses and the media. And she hoped that would pay off with positive stories in the tabloids, even though she rarely saw those. Only tonight, *People Magazine* journalists and photographers were here, so her chances of a positive spin grew.

A sting in her mouth made her realize she was biting the inside of her lip and pulled it from between her teeth.

"Hey."

Her stomach flipped at the sound of Duke's voice. She hadn't seen him come over.

"Hey." She smiled at him and bumped his shoulder. "You smell so damn good. I want to wash my sheets in your cologne."

That made him laugh long and deep, drawing attention. Female attention.

"How about I roll around on them instead?"

"What a thrilling idea." She glanced at him. "Could you at least appear tired? I can barely keep my eyes open."

"Oh no, sugar pop. You energize the fuck out of me." He bent his head toward hers. "You look amazing. Did I tell you that already?"

"Thank you." She glanced down at the stylish one-shouldered dress Andi had chosen because it was the color of her eyes. "Another roommate pick."

"Can't wait to meet this roommate."

She grinned and tried like hell not to think about where they'd been just hours before. Maybe her family and friends had something to worry about after all. What she'd done with Duke today had been impulsive and completely out of character. Yet she wouldn't change one single second.

Caitlyn shifted on her feet. She couldn't even stand near the man without wanting him. Would that eventually change, the way her relationship with Brett cooled off over the years?

No, she couldn't compare the two relationships. They were apples and oranges. Dogs and cats.

"This is an unusual setup for a press conference," Duke told her. "I love your out-of-the-box thinking."

"I'll love it too, if it works."

"You haven't done it this way in the past?"

"I've never done it, period."

"Kinda risky. How will you control them?"

"Every journalist signed an agreement to keep questions within the subject goalposts I specified. If they don't, I threatened to blackball them from all future Excel promotional events."

"Can you do that?"

She smiled at him. "No, but they don't know that. And you know those two photographers we had to pay for pics? They were turned away at the gate, so I think I've got enough street cred to make this fly. If I fail, I'll fail in a major way."

"Street cred." He chuckled. "You're a real go-big-or-go-home kind of girl, aren't you?"

"I didn't think I was, but..." She shrugged and smiled at him. "I guess I am, because there's you."

Duke was laughing when Keaton walked up and handed him a beer while speaking to Caitlyn. "This is more like a talk show than a press conference. Add in the liquor and the food and we've got a veritable party. I like the way you put a warm, welcoming spin on something that can be dry and often confrontational."

"Thanks." Caitlyn grinned. "Here's hoping it works."

"Who knows," Keaton said, "maybe you'll retool Hollywood with a softer edge. If anyone is going to do it, it would be someone from the LaCroix family tree."

She laughed. "Right? God, I wish Lexi were here."

"She'd be proud," Duke said. "Really, really proud."

A sweet sensation melted through her. She turned and wrapped her arms around him, cheek to his chest. "Thank you."

Her phone alarm chimed, and she stepped away from Duke. She pulled the cell from the discreet pocket on the dress skirt, silenced the alarm, and sent Leo a text. Then she smiled at Duke and Keaton. "Showtime, gentlemen. Wish me luck."

"You won't need it," Duke said, "but I'll give it to you anyway."

She reached for his hand and gave it a squeeze. Then Caitlyn walked toward the front of the group and stepped up on a small platform she'd borrowed from another location on-site.

"Welcome, everyone. Thank you for coming. I'm Caitlyn Winters with Excel PR." Caitlyn remained a little on the businesslike side. She didn't want to appear nervous or giddy. No one other than those closest to her needed to know this was her first press conference. Ever. "Go ahead and find a seat. After we talk with Kendra and Leo, catering promised us something worth waiting for."

Leo came out of the trailer holding Kendra's hand and led her to the stage, pausing to make sure she didn't trip on the step up. Then he settled her into a chair before sitting himself. The audience clapped in welcome, and Caitlyn realized Keaton was right. This setup was like a talk show.

Photographers stood in the back and camera shutters clicked like crazy, and the red light on the filming camera glowed. She'd done a lot of mock interviews in school. She had to focus on being as authentic as possible and hope it translated to the camera. If it didn't turn out, she'd just trash the tape.

Caitlyn sat in a chair opposite Kendra and Leo. She greeted them and thanked them for taking time to connect with their fans. Then she addressed the audience, keeping her gaze off Duke. She didn't want to lose her train of thought.

"Justin," she said, gesturing to the stagehand who'd offered to help out, "the tall, handsome man standing in the aisle, will be passing the microphone through the audience. Just raise your hand and we'll get to everyone who has a question at least once."

She turned to Leo and Kendra, welcoming them and congratulating them on all their recent successes, including the baby. Caitlyn set the scene for approved questions by asking basics about the pregnancy and Kendra's clothing line and said very little about *American Valor*.

Then Caitlyn invited the audience's questions, and time flew. Caitlyn was shocked at how well it went. The media was respectful of Caitlyn's rules and asked great questions, ones she wouldn't even have thought to ask.

On deeper subjects, topics that shone a glowing light on Leo and Kendra, Caitlyn teased more information out of them before moving on.

If Caitlyn didn't know how both Kendra and Leo had jumped at this as a promo op, she would have believed he and Kendra were head over heels for each other.

Hell, what did she know? Maybe they were. Maybe this was just a California-style marriage she didn't understand. Or maybe more likely a Hollywood marriage. Now, that made sense.

She learned a lot about the couple. Kendra was involved

with several charities, and her clothing line was a longtime dream come true. Caitlyn had instructed Leo to give Kendra time in the spotlight for a change, and he'd been a good boy. After all, it benefited him in the end.

A little over an hour later, Caitlyn thanked the audience again and invited guests to mingle over dessert and wine. Leo and Kendra could easily have gone on their way, but were willingly swept up with attendees and their questions. They played the perfect couple awaiting the birth of their son. They even seemed as if they enjoyed talking with journalists.

Duke appeared at Caitlyn's side with a Sprite and handed it to her. "I'd say this has been a smashing success."

She warmed up all over. "You think?"

"Oh, yeah."

She eased closer, lowered her free hand, and wrapped two fingers around his. "I think it's time to head back. I've got this incredibly sexy stuntman waiting for me."

"What a lucky guy."

"Oh, I don't know. I think I'm the lucky one."

She was just about to make the announcement that they were winding down when one of the security guards came forward.

"The gate guard says someone is here to see you," the middle-aged man told her.

She frowned. "Me? Are you sure?" She took out her phone and found no messages waiting. "I don't know anyone here."

The guard spoke into the radio. "What's the name?"

"A Brett..." He asked the man his last name, and Caitlyn heard Brett's voice. "Brett Mulligan."

All her blood drained from her face, leaving her dizzy. Her ears rang, drowning out others talking to her. She couldn't believe he'd found her. Caitlyn knew exactly how much work had gone into that. He had to have been on a plane all day.

And guilt pushed through her in one big swoosh.

22

Duke slid an arm around her waist as Caitlyn clawed her way out of the bizarre cocoon she'd retreated into.

She swallowed, pulled herself together, and told the security guard, "Tell him I'm coming." She looked at Duke. "No one knows I'm here. Not even my family. I have no idea how he found me."

"He probably went to LA first. Your roommate probably gave him the information. That's how I would have done it."

Caitlyn turned toward the attendees, surveying them with a nervous edge. "I'm not sure if I should break this up so I don't have to worry about something going wrong or treat them like adults and let them leave when they want."

Duke caught Wes's attention and waved him over. Keaton came along. "I'm taking Caitlyn to the main gate. Can you guys keep a check on the temperature here? Break it up if anything goes sour?"

"Sure," Keaton said.

"Is everything okay?" Wes asked.

"A family member showed up." Duke didn't want to get into

the messy ex-boyfriend thing right now. He gave Caitlyn's arm a squeeze. "I'll grab a golf cart. It will get us there faster."

She looked at him with confusion, as if she'd gone to sleep in Kentucky and woken up in LA.

"If you need anything," Keaton said, "just yell."

She thanked them as a security guard who had anticipated their need pulled a golf cart up beside them. Wes and Keaton returned to the event. Duke thanked the guard and was about to slide in when he saw Caitlyn staring off into space.

"We can get him a hotel room," Duke offered, "let him get some rest. He's got to be wrung out. You two can talk in the morning."

That would also give Duke one more night with her before she faced her ex-boyfriend of seven freaking years. When the guy was halfway across the country, Duke hadn't thought twice about him. But now he was here, which meant he'd put considerable effort into the journey.

The guy would either be groveling or pissed off. Duke didn't want to leave her with him in either of those moods. Okay, in truth, he didn't want to leave her with her ex at all.

"I don't know," she said. "I'll see how he is first."

They were silent on the drive to the gate, but the tension in the cart was palpable. By the time Duke turned the last corner to the main gate, tension strung his shoulders tight, and Caitlyn had picked off nail polish from two fingers.

The area was lit up with floodlights, and Brett paced in front of the gates. He was tall and slim, clean-cut from his conservative hairstyle to his black dress shoes, wearing slacks and a button-down.

"Can you stop here?" Caitlyn put a hand on Duke's arm.

Duke stopped the cart.

"Seeing me with you would hurt him. I've already hurt him enough."

A tear spilled over and slid down her cheek. Duke reached

over and cupped her face, wiping the tear from her skin. "Ending a relationship like you had with Brett is never easy. I've watched my sister go through all the roller-coaster waves. But you're doing it in the most thoughtful way possible."

"It's just...I broke it off nearly six months ago. I guess leaving for LA triggered something all my talking couldn't. Only..." She shrugged. "It's over. It's been over a lot longer than six months. It just took me a while to find my path out—of the relationship, of Kentucky. I know this is hard on him, but it's not all rainbows and glitter for me either. It hurts me to hurt him."

"How he's reacting to the breakup is his responsibility, not yours."

She blew out a breath, looked toward the gate, and rubbed tear streaks off her cheeks. "You can go back to the party. You've got to be hungry."

"I'm fine. I'll be waiting for you."

She met his gaze directly. "Thank you."

She looked like she wanted to say something else, but didn't.

Duke pulled her in and kissed her. Just a soft, simple kiss, but a kiss. He was sending her back to someone who'd shared her life intimately for seven years. He'd heard what she'd said about her relationship with Brett, but Duke also knew how emotions didn't always line up with logic. He'd seen it with Kristy when she'd had such a hard time agreeing to a protection order, even after Peter had left her with a split lip, a bloody nose, and a black eye. Duke could only hope Caitlyn had ended things with Brett in her heart and not only her mind.

She stood, took a deep breath, and walked the last couple of hundred yards, leaving Duke in the shadows.

When she approached the gate, the guard opened it for her. Duke wasn't ready for the passionate way Brett took Caitlyn in his arms, with a sort of familiarity that made Duke's whole body take a hit. His hand squeezed the steering wheel. His stomach clenched.

She wrapped her arms around his middle and let him rock her back and forth. Duke's heart sank a little. He'd never had a relationship like the one they'd had. The longest he'd ever dated anyone was a year. He had no idea how hard it would be to leave someone after so long, and he found himself jealous of all the history they must have. All the memories.

"I was beginning to think I'd never find you." Brett pulled back and held her at arm's length.

Her voice was softer. Duke couldn't hear what she said or even the tone of her voice.

"What are you doing out here in the middle of nowhere?" Brett asked.

Duke didn't hear her answer.

Brett's posture stiffened. "Look, you've tried it out, had your fun, now come home. You don't belong here. You should have figured that out by now."

The hurtful jabs sure didn't take long to come out. Duke expected Caitlyn to pop off the way she did with him when he crossed a line, or the way she had with Leo when he was being a shithead. But she didn't.

They continued to talk in circles. Based on his side of the conversation, Caitlyn told him she was staying, and Brett said she wasn't. This was the kind of conversation most women would rage against. This was not the age of telling a woman what to do. But she seemed to have endless patience and a consistent, kind manner, even as Brett grew angrier.

"Your brothers are a mess," he said. "Cody got suspended for fighting, Evan is sick all the time, missing a lot of school, and little Sam's grades have dropped. Your mother is barely keeping her shit together, and your dad's still depressed."

Jesus freaking Christ. Talk about a guilt trip.

"...not my responsibility..." she said, and "...they've all been leaning on me. They need to..."

Eventually, when Brett realized she wouldn't be changing her mind, hurt rose and joined the anger. Frustrated words followed by an angry, pained "I love you, dammit."

Brett's declaration tightened Duke's shoulders. He got up and paced in the darkness while Brett made promises to change, to bend the relationship to give Caitlyn what she needed, to back off the engagement if she wasn't ready.

Engagement? Duke hadn't known about that.

He thought of how shitty this job had turned out for Caitlyn. What a bitch of a boss she'd gotten and what an ass Leo had been. Maybe home didn't look so bad to Caitlyn right now. Sure, he and Caitlyn had amazing sex—like off-the-charts sex—but it was still just sex.

Despite what she'd said about her breakup, Duke feared that just the right words from Brett would take her away. Duke tried to tell himself that if that happened, it was the way it should be, but he didn't believe that.

Then Brett pulled out all the stops.

"Okay, look," Brett said, standing close with a begging posture. "I've thought a lot about this. If you really want to stay, I'll quit and move here. We can start over."

"Holy shit," Duke muttered. This was a potential game changer.

He leaned against the cart's front fender. He still couldn't hear what Caitlyn was saying, but she was still rubbing tears from her cheeks. And Brett was pacing, hands clasped on his head, gaze on the ground.

This was awful. Heartbreaking. After twenty minutes of talking and arguing, Brett sat on a curb, head in his hands, defeated. Duke experienced a complex feeling of both relief for himself and sympathy for Brett. If Duke was losing Caitlyn, he'd be just as inconsolable.

Because, shit, he loved her too.

She moved toward Brett, crouched in front of him, and rested her hands on his knees. God, she was so fucking sweet. So caring. So kind.

They stayed like that for what felt like a long time. Duke sat down, bounced his knee, chewed his fingernails, checked his watch.

Eventually, Brett stood, head hanging as he walked to his car. Before he got in, he hugged Caitlyn one more time, a long, hard hug that she returned. And when he drove away, she stood there until his car had disappeared down the road.

Duke stood, not sure what to do. Give her space? Go to her? Then Caitlyn started back toward him, head down, steps deliberate.

As she grew near, he heard her sniffles and offered a soft "Hey, are you—"

She walked right into his arms, face against his chest. He held her tight, stroked her hair, murmured reassuring things.

He had no idea what this meant, but she'd had ample opportunities to give Brett what he wanted and evidently hadn't.

Her quiet tears morphed into choppy breaths. "Can w-we go h-home?"

He knew she meant the hotel. "Yeah." Duke looked around and found one of the shuttle buses parked by the main gate. "The guys can close out the press conference."

She nodded against his chest. Her hands fisted in his shirt, her weight a solid force against him. A shaking solid force.

Duke called Wes, then wrapped his arm around Caitlyn's shoulders and walked her to the shuttle.

He sat and pulled Caitlyn across his lap sideways. She rested her head against his shoulder, her hand covering his. The first few minutes, they were silent. Her sniffles slowed, her breathing leveled, and her tension drained.

"I knew this wouldn't be easy," she said, voice soft and pained. "He was settled, comfortable. All of them were—Brett, my parents, my brothers. But I was tired of being taken for granted. I didn't leave to get them to see that. I left to find where I belonged."

"I heard something once," he said. "I can't remember where, but it was something to the effect of by the time a woman physically leaves a relationship, she's already been gone emotionally for a long time."

"That's true. At least for me. But it doesn't make hurting Brett any easier."

"You couldn't easily hurt anyone. I thought I heard him mention an engagement. Were you engaged?"

She closed her eyes. "Yes, but no. I was getting my words together to end the relationship when he dropped to one knee in the middle of a birthday party for my dad. I had to say yes. I couldn't embarrass him by saying no. I let it go for a few weeks before I returned the ring and told him I was leaving."

"How old are your brothers?"

She snuggled her head beneath Duke's chin. "Fourteen, eleven, and eight."

"Big gap."

"My mom was sick for a while. She had really high blood pressure, and they had to get that under control before she got pregnant again. Took a while, but as soon as her doctor gave her the green light, they started trying again."

"They made up for lost time."

She laughed. "Yeah, they did, though I don't think they planned Sam, the youngest."

"So, you were like a second mom to your brothers?"

"Yeah. My parents worked so much, they really needed me to watch over the boys. I miss them. They're the reason I stayed in Kentucky as long as I did."

"Maybe once you get settled, you can have them come out

and visit. I can tell you, nothing thrills a kid more than visiting a real movie set. I could even do some stunts with them."

She laughed softly. "Oh my God, they would love that. Have your nieces been on set?"

"They're a little young to see it as cool. Plus, their father is a producer, so Hollywood isn't as flashy to them as it is to others."

She moved her head to his shoulder and ran a finger along his jaw, her gaze following the motion, then she lifted her head to kiss him. It was soft and salty and made his hope soar.

She kept it light, and as badly as he wanted her right now, he didn't search for more.

"You're a really good person." The words didn't do the sentiment justice. "You were really kind with him."

"He's a good man. And he really does love me, just not the way I need to be loved. Watching him tonight, struggling to find a way to get me to come back..." She closed her eyes and a few more tears leaked out the sides. "It was awful."

"Was it like this when you left for LA?"

"He didn't think I was serious—about the breakup or leaving. He thought the whole idea was stupid, so he didn't even take me to the airport."

"He's got some seriously well-developed denial skills."

"I had to get an Uber because my parents wouldn't take me either. I guess Kentucky is the *state* of denial."

"Then you really do belong here. You're too amazing to be treated like that." He combed his hand through her hair. He loved the feel of it, thick and soft. "You've had a rough start. And that new boss of yours sure threw you into the fire."

"She did. I keep hoping it will get better."

"You're as resilient as they come."

She turned her face into his chest, and they went quiet for a few long moments.

It felt so good to be this comfortable with someone. No

chitchat required. No nerves. Just the two of them, fitting together like lost puzzle pieces.

Her hand skimmed through his hair, drawing his attention back to her heavy-lidded eyes and what had become a familiar expression of desire. She slid her hand around the back of his neck and pulled his head down. The kiss evolved into something he most definitely wanted to take to the bedroom.

One kiss, then another, a little longer, and another, tongues involved. Then they were in full free fall, and Duke fought to remember they were on a shuttle van. The driver might be the only other occupant, but he was still an occupant.

She was more passionate tonight. He wasn't sure what to make of it. He wanted to believe it was because they were gelling, because she was getting comfortable with him, that she was growing to trust him. But her ex of seven years had just left, and Duke was fully aware that this might just be her way of making herself feel better. A temporary escape from the pain. He didn't want to get his hopes up. She was in such a rough place.

She pulled back and looked him right in the eye when she said, "I want you," with the kind of conviction that shot excitement down to his toes. "How can I want you so soon?"

That certainly helped quell his concerns. "It's just that good. Can't get to the room too soon for me."

Before he could kiss her again, the van pulled into the hotel's roundabout. On the way out the door, Duke thanked and tipped the driver.

He and Caitlyn held hands on the way through the lobby and past the bar. Duke was sure there was more than one member of the crew in there and that by tomorrow, everyone would know he and Caitlyn were together. He liked that. Liked Wes's idea of showing a little ownership. He liked the idea of the other guys on the set knowing they didn't have a chance with her. At least not while Duke was around.

What he found so interesting was that she seemed clueless about how many other men would kill to get with her. He'd seen the way they looked at her. He'd watched them flirt with her. He'd heard what they said when they were talking to each other.

As soon as they stepped into the elevator and the doors closed, Duke pulled her close and kissed her deep. She swayed into him, and a geyser of happiness warmed his whole body. They kissed until the doors opened on her floor. They tried to kiss down the hall toward her room, but ended up tripping and laughing the rest of the way.

And when he closed the door of her room behind him, he turned and found her waiting. She slid her hands under his shirt and ran her nails over the skin of his back, making goose-flesh pop up as she pushed him up against the door, then leaned her body into his.

She kissed his neck and jaw, her hands moving to the front and traveling all up and down his stomach and chest. "I want you."

He couldn't stem the smile that seemed to reach all the way to his heart. He found the zipper of her dress and got his big fingers around what had to be the smallest tab on the planet.

But before he could slide it down, his phone rang. And it was Kristy's ring. He couldn't ignore it like he would so many other calls.

"Dammit." He slid his hands down her arms. "It's Kristy. I'm sorry."

"It's okay. I'm not going anywhere."

23

Caitlyn watched Duke hold the phone up so his family could see his face, and his smile was radiant.

"Hey, Cocoa Puff. You been eating toast? Don't go to bed like that. The jam will stain your sheets."

From the background, a girl yelled, "You forgot story time."

Duke's eyes went wide before they closed. "Oh, sh…oot."

He darted an apologetic look at Caitlyn, making her laugh. As soon as the sound came out of her, she covered her mouth.

"Who's there?" another girl asked. Sounded like the oldest one, closest to the phone.

"A friend." He took Caitlyn's hand and walked to the bed, where he dropped to his stomach. Caitlyn sat in the chair nearby to stay out of the frame.

"Can we meet her?" she asked, insistence in the question.

"Maybe. What chapter did we leave off at last night?"

"No." This came from a woman who could only be Kristy. "If you're busy, we can skip story time tonight."

A chorus of whines erupted, making Caitlyn laugh again.

He looked at her as if seeking permission.

"Go ahead," Caitlyn murmured.

"She's going to listen to story time too. Let me just find our place."

"No *Secit Garen*." The baby talk had to have come from Willow, the very terrible two.

"You love *The Secret Garden*," Duke said, fiddling with his phone. "I'm looking for it on the internet. I don't have the book with me."

Caitlyn did a quick search, found the book online, and held her phone up for him.

"Okay," he said. "Everyone have their blankets and bunnies?"

A chorus of Mmm-hmms and uh-huhs filtered over the line.

God, this was sweet.

"What's your friend's name?" the oldest wanted to know.

"Caitlyn."

"That's pretty."

"Catin read," the littlest said.

"Hey," he said. "You're going to hurt my feelings."

"Yeah," came from Kristy, amusement in her voice, "let Caitlyn read."

"Enough from the peanut gallery," he said. "Chapter sixteen, '"I won't!" said Mary.' Huh, sounds a little like Willow."

That made everyone laugh, and Duke started reading.

The girls went quiet, and Caitlyn soaked in this side of Duke, loving on his family. He could easily have ditched the nightly tradition. Kristy had given him the perfect out. And he was lying on the erection that had been pressed against her just moments ago. But he still stopped everything to be there for these girls.

It didn't take long for the girls to insist Caitlyn join in story time.

He looked at Caitlyn. "Suddenly, I'm chopped liver. Get your beautiful self over here. It's story time."

Caitlyn lay on the bed on her belly, next to Duke. "Hi."

She gave a finger wave, and all the girls smiled.

"Is Catin," Willow said around a pacifier, her excitement comical. "Oook, is Catin."

"She's pretty," the middle one said.

"Are you Uncle Duke's girlfriend?" the oldest asked.

"Enough with the questions." Kristy popped into the frame. "Sorry. Hi, I'm Kristy."

"Not a problem. They're beautiful."

"Thank you. Lord, you really do look a lot like Lexi."

Duke saw similar features, but he didn't see Lexi. He just saw Caitlyn.

"Sorry I'm not able to help out with them like I planned," she said. "This trip was completely unexpected."

"I appreciate the offer. I hope we get to see more of you when you get home."

"For sure."

"May we continue reading now?" Duke asked with an eye roll in his voice.

"Catin read," Willow insisted.

"She's a force," Caitlyn said, grinning.

"Oh, you have no idea," Kristy said.

"How about if we both read?" Duke asked. "Will that keep you from interrupting?"

That seemed amenable, and Duke and Caitlyn switched off reading paragraphs.

When Caitlyn's turn came, she put emphasis behind the story and used different voices for the characters.

When it was Duke's turn again, she found him smiling at her. "You're a hard act to follow."

"You'll do just fine."

They continued to trade off paragraphs until they'd finished the chapter and all three girls could barely keep their eyes open.

"Bedtime," Duke announced softly, to a chorus of sleepy complaints.

The oldest and middle daughters said good night to both Duke and Caitlyn and blew kisses. But that wasn't good enough for Willow. She had to climb over her sisters, dragging her blanket and her bunny and holding the pacifier in her mouth and got right up to the camera to kiss the screen. "Nigh-nigh."

The girls scuttled away, and Kristy took the phone. "Thank you. They just don't know what to do with themselves if you're not in their routine."

"They're going to have to figure it out," he told her.

"Don't tell them that." Kristy looked at Caitlyn. "Thank you for appeasing them. I'm sorry we cut into your time together."

"Not at all. I've been missing my youngest brother, so this quieted that for me. At least for now."

"How old is he?"

"Eight. I see a lot of his feistiness in Willow."

That made Kristy laugh.

"How are things going there?" Duke asked her.

"I'll let Cam talk to you while I put the girls to bed. Nice to meet you, Caitlyn."

"You too."

Cam took the phone and moved to the living room. When he looked at Duke, Cam's gaze caught on Caitlyn. "Oh, hey."

"Hey. I'm Caitlyn. I didn't get a chance to meet you at the wedding."

"That's because Duke monopolized you. I'm Cameron."

She grinned, looked at Duke, and bumped his shoulder.

"What's happening?" Duke asked.

"The Corolla's tires got slashed last night. No idea how that happened," he said with mock confusion, "but it hasn't gotten rid of him. He just showed up in a different car tonight and parked on the side street."

"Shit." Duke rubbed his eyes.

"I've still got a few tricks up my sleeve. Tomorrow morning, I'm going to follow him home, watch his house, see how he likes it."

"Jesus, don't go getting yourself in trouble. You've got to work, and I need you to be there for the girls."

"Stop worrying, dude. I've got them. That fucker will have to go through me to reach them. But speaking of work, I think we need to get someone to hang with them during the day until this is over."

Duke got an intense look on his face. "Did I hear you telling Jax you have a CCW permit?"

"Forever ago." Cam laughed and tapped his temple. "Look at you with a steel trap."

"What's a CCW?" Caitlyn looked at Duke then back to Cam.

"Concealed carry permit," Duke told her then asked Cameron, "Are you carrying?"

"Does it matter?" Cam asked.

Duke glanced at Caitlyn as if checking to see what she thought of this. "I guess not as long as you're keeping it on you and the girls can't get to it."

"Of course. Stop worrying, it's all legal and I've taken all the classes. And, in case you've forgotten, I was a marine not all that long ago."

"Aren't those hard to get?" Caitlyn asked. "The permits."

"In California," Cam said, "yes, but I did it fair and square. Took all the classes, proved my neighborhood was dangerous, been robbed at gunpoint a couple of times on my way home. No one needed to hear that I took care of the fuckers without any gun. And I might have had a word or two put in."

"Your ex?" Duke asked.

"Guess she did something good for me in the end."

"Your ex?" Caitlyn asked.

"A cop," Cam explained.

Duke put his head down and ran both hands through his

hair a couple of times, clearly uncomfortable with the thought of his nieces that close to a weapon.

"I grew up around guns," Caitlyn told him. "Respected, they're very safe. They can keep others safe. And there is no one who understands weapons better than a marine."

Duke gave her another one of those looks of disbelief. "You shoot?"

She laughed and shook her head. "Girls can handle guns too." To Cameron she said, "Let's hit the range when I get back."

"Definitely."

Duke blew out a breath and talked to Cam another minute. When he disconnected the call, his head swiveled toward her. "The range?"

Caitlyn laughed. "Your expression is priceless." She slid her hand under his T-shirt and scratched his back, drawing a pleasure-filled groan, her mind turning back to Duke's family. "This is Kristy's husband? Sending other people to watch her?"

"Yeah. Man, I can't wait for this to be over."

"I can see why. But I don't get why he's having her watched."

"Intimidation. He's pissed she's going through with the divorce. And if he can catch other men in the apartment, he can twist it to imply Kristy's having an affair, which could be a blow for custody." He smirked at Caitlyn. "This wasn't the way I saw tonight going."

"Let's fix that."

The interruption was just what Caitlyn had needed to reset and refocus. She didn't want to think about Brett or the breakup or her family. She wanted to move forward, continue creating Caitlyn 2.0.

She pushed at Duke until he rolled over, then moved on top of him. "Where were we?"

He slid both hands into her hair and over her shoulders to the zipper tab on her dress. "Somewhere about here."

The man made it so much easier to step outside her comfort zone.

The metal pressed against her skin, made her shiver. She loved the look on his face, deep and intimate. He was one hundred percent present, right here with her, with nothing else on his mind, nowhere else he'd rather be. Only now, with this level of focus and intimacy with Duke, did she realize how superficial her relationship with Brett had become over the years. Maybe it had always been that way.

And there she was comparing again.

On the surface, it all looked fine. Her relationship with Brett didn't look that much different from those of her friends. But all it took was the deep warmth Duke stirred inside her to get a glimpse of just what she'd been missing. He made her come alive.

With her zipper down, Caitlyn slipped off the bed and stood between Duke's spread thighs. He propped himself up on his elbows and watched Caitlyn slowly strip off her dress, revealing some pretty lace beneath. Duke's expression went from happy to hungry and sent a shiver down her spine.

Her gaze traveled over his wide chest, thick biceps, six-pack abs.

He pushed to a seated position and ran his hands all over her body. His gaze tilted down to hers, he asked, "What's going on inside that head of yours?"

"I was just thinking of how unbelievable you are. And not just this incredible body of yours, but just...everything. The way you gave me the space to deal with Brett. The way you supported me with the press conference and hung in the background. How incredible you are with your family."

She realized she was waiting for the other shoe to drop and cut off the thought. "I feel really lucky I met you when I did. Before all the women heard you were off the bench, so to speak."

She held his head in her hands and leaned down to kiss him, then fisted the back of his shirt and pulled it up and off, before settling back into the kiss.

They melted into a fierce heat. This wasn't like their first time together, when Duke made sure she was okay with every touch, every move. Or their second time, earlier that day, lust filled and begging. *Begging,* for God's sake.

This was sexier. Deeper. This was more than what she'd expected when she'd spent the night with him. But she would think about that later, because right now, her body and her brain were screaming for him.

24

Duke stood and watched her small hands unfasten his jeans in a rush, her fingers a little shaky, like she was a little out of control, and the idea made Duke's head light.

He found the clasp of her bra and flicked it open, then let his hands drift down her spine. He wrapped his arms around her and pulled her into a hug where every inch of her bare chest was against his. Duke swore he could feel the happy chemicals release from his brain and spread through his body.

He hyperfocused on the moment, the softness and warmth of her skin, the intoxicating scent of her. He slid both hands over her ass and pulled her against his erection with a moan. She rocked her hips, then pushed his jeans and boxer briefs down. Duke toed out of his cross-trainers and stepped out of his jeans before Caitlyn pushed up on her toes and offered her mouth. He obliged and kissed the hell out of her.

Caitlyn pushed him to a seat on the edge of the mattress and climbed on his lap, straddling him. He combed the hair off her face. "I want you naked, but those panties are so fucking sexy."

"I may or may not have been thinking about you when I bought these."

He grinned. "I may or may not love the fact that you may or may not have been thinking of me when you bought these."

She pressed her forehead to his and whispered like she was telling him a secret. "Then why don't you look at my panties while I suck you? Because I really want to suck you."

Electricity arced through him. "That may be the sexiest thing I've ever heard."

Especially coming from a woman who'd probably never said those words—at least not in that order—in her life. This was a different side of the woman he'd slept with last week. Even different from the one he'd had sex with earlier that day.

He liked to think she was able to express herself this way because he made her feel safe and confident, but that would be giving himself one hell of lot more credit than he deserved. Still, it was good to have dreams.

"I so badly want you to suck me." He kissed her slow and deep until he was out of breath.

"And you want to watch," she said with a hot little smile.

"Jesus." He closed his eyes and shook his head, trying to understand this complicated woman. "I *really* want to watch."

Caitlyn slid off his lap and knelt on the floor between his thighs. Her breasts were exposed, pale and bouncy, her gaze on his as she stroked his cock. The sight of her small pale hand on his big, reddened length was thrilling. As was the sight of her, between his legs, looking so sultry and hungry.

He stroked a hand through her hair. "You are one big surprise after—"

She spiraled her tongue around the head of his cock, then opened her mouth and took him deep.

"Ah, God." Lust rushed his bloodstream, burning in every cell in his pelvis, settling into a deep throb between his legs.

Then she sucked, and he lost his mind. He fisted the sheets at his hip with one hand and slid the other into her hair.

She dove into a series of full-length plunges that blinded Duke with ecstasy, sucking, sucking, sucking until the pleasure was so exquisite, he dropped his head back. "Fuck, you're so good at this."

"Only good?" she licked his length before pumping him with her hand. "Guess I'm not trying hard enough."

He huffed a laugh. She was beyond amazing. He still couldn't quite believe he'd gotten this lucky. He was just waiting for her to downshift into the friend zone.

"I love the way you watch me," she said. "Do you like this? Seeing yourself in my mouth, all wet and swollen."

He fisted both hands in the mattress. "You keep talking like that and I won't be wet or swollen for long."

"You like that? Guess I'll have to brush up on my dirty talk."

He was having a hard time processing the fact that she even *had* dirty talk in her vocabulary.

"I'd love to keep sucking you all night," she told him, "but I'm pretty obsessed with getting you inside me right now."

Who the fuck was this woman? From angry to lust driven, timid to confident, reserved to sexually open, all in a matter of days? He wasn't complaining, but he would pay to know what button to push to get her here again. He planned on using it —a lot.

"I'm completely onboard with that idea," he told her.

She smiled and stood, giving him a great view of the panties. He made a show of slowly hooking his fingers into the waistband and letting them drop to the floor. Then his hands were all over her warm, curvy ass.

She was perfect. From the top of her head to the soles of her feet, inside and out, this woman was as close to perfect as he'd ever met.

Caitlyn brought her knees to the mattress on either side of

his hips, gripped his cock, which was acting quite proud of itself, and positioned it before sinking down inch by amazing inch.

He moaned, gripped her ass, and sucked her breast. Then he dragged her ass cheeks up and pulled her into him, driving himself deeper. Caitlyn pulled in a sharp breath.

Once he was seated inside her, he wrapped one arm around her hips, used the other to brace himself on the bed, and kissed her while he rolled her to her back in the middle of the bed.

Caitlyn broke their kiss, laughing. "You really do have good moves, don't you?"

"I pulled them out and dusted them off just for you. Kinda surprised they still work." Duke got comfortable between her thighs, rested on his forearms, and brushed hair out of her eyes. "They come along with being a stuntman—a package deal. Like burgers and fries."

She laughed, a dark sexy sound, and she rocked her hips, moving Duke inside her and delivering a fresh jolt of lust. He gripped her ass and held her steady as he thrust. Her eyes closed, and a sound of utter pleasure rolled from her throat.

Duke lay back, then rolled with her again, putting them closer to the middle of the bed. He braced one knee on the mattress and locked his gaze on hers while, thrust by thrust, he pushed her higher, searching for control. After seeing how many orgasms she was capable of, he wanted to pull out every one possible. But even after having her earlier, he couldn't quite get himself under control.

He stilled. "Sugar," he said, breathless. "I'm not gonna make it much longer."

"You won't have to."

25

Duke pressed his face against Caitlyn's neck and breathed her in. She was warm and sweet. It was 3:00 a.m., and she'd fallen asleep only about thirty minutes ago. Now, they lay on their sides, the back of her body resting against the front of his. He had an arm over her waist and his fingers threaded with hers.

Her cell vibrated on the nightstand, and the screen lit up with the name Dad. It was 6:00 a.m. in Kentucky. Brett had texted her several times between the time he left her at the gates and now. Drunk texting, he guessed, based on the content of the messages, covering all they'd already talked about.

Hey, baby. Her father texted. *Sure miss you. Brett told us he talked to you. I'm sorry that wasn't enough to bring you back.*

Duke felt for them all. He knew what a diamond they'd lost. And, now, it seemed, they did too.

Another text pinged. *Your brothers are so unruly that life is a constant challenge. Your mother took them to JCPenney to get new school uniforms and the boys were all over the place. She came home crying. They obeyed you so much better.*

Anger struck. Why in the fuck didn't her parents act like

parents and take control of their boys? It was one thing to have Caitlyn help out with her brothers, it was another to expect her to raise them.

I understand why you left. I know that your job here with the city was boring. Maybe you could find something else closer to home. There are so many people who love and miss you.

According to Caitlyn, she didn't have as many people there to stay for as her father was alluding to.

Callie had her baby. They named him Tyler. He looks just like his dad. You've got to see it. And Dustin passed his test. He's a general contractor now.

Those messages exposed the intimate weave of Caitlyn's life before LA. She'd been embroiled in the daily lives of her family and the friends that she and Brett had shared. It gave a kind of texture to the little he knew about her and showed just how intricately her life in Kentucky had been woven.

He slipped his fingers from hers and slowly lifted his arm. When she stayed asleep, he rolled out of bed, stood, and looked down at her.

Her expression was relaxed, her lips full, blonde hair tangled on the pillow.

Duke pulled on boxer briefs, quietly took a bottle of water from the fridge and stood at the window, shoulder against the wall, looking at the lights shining in the darkness.

He thought of how angry she'd been earlier and smiled. She sparkled when she was mad. He loved her passion. He loved other things too. A lot of other things.

"Hey." Her sleepy voice drew his gaze. She rolled over and sat up, sheet around her naked body. "Everything okay?"

He smiled. "Better than okay."

"Couldn't sleep?" Her sexy smile glowed in the dark room. "You should have woken me up."

Duke chuckled. "At least one of us should be getting some sleep."

"Then it should be you. You're the one climbing mountains."

She stood from the bed and let the sheet fall away. Duke's bones melted a little. He set the water on the windowsill and faced her, thrilled when she walked into his arms.

He hugged her tight. "Oh my God, you're so warm."

She pulled away just enough to look up at him. "Are the girls okay?"

Her concern for his family warmed him. "Yeah, they're fine."

"Then what's got your mind spinning?"

He took a deep breath and plunged. "This. This thing between us."

Worry flitted through her eyes. "What do you mean?"

"I mean... What are we doing? Is this just you having fun and testing the waters after a long relationship? Or is it more? I've never felt the need to slap limits on relationships, but I guess I just want to know where to park this in my head."

And his heart.

"Oh. Yeah, okay."

Duke smiled. "You have no idea what I'm talking about, do you?"

She made a face, which only made her more adorable. "Sort of. I mean, I've heard friends talk about different types of relationships, but I was already in one, so I guess I never paid much attention."

"Last week, at brunch, you said you didn't want to get into anything serious. But that was when we were going to be apart for a month or more. Now we're here, and the fire between us clearly isn't going anywhere."

She let out a long breath, worry clear in her gaze.

"Let's set it aside for now," Duke said. "There's no rush to figure things out."

"No, you're right." She paused, thought about it, then said,

"I still don't even know the way around my own neighborhood, and this," she said, making a vague gesture to the landscape, "only makes everything more confusing. I feel like I've been dropped into an alternate reality, trying to find my way in the dark. What business do I have pulling someone's heart into something when I can't even handle the basic tasks of life?"

When Duke looked at it that way, he understood. Even admired her for thinking about how the consequences would affect him. LA had always been its own beast, but Hollywood was that beast on drugs. She was being cautious and smart. Duke was the one daring to go for it. But he guessed that was what made him a good stuntman, that willingness to go all in and figure things out on the fly.

"All that said," she kissed his chest, "I'm open to options, even though I don't know what those are."

The tension drained from his body. He hadn't realized until just this minute how desperately he'd hoped she'd say that.

"Anything is an option," he told her. "If you can think it, it becomes an option. Like casually dating, which means we keep the relationship superficial and open, and we can both sleep with other people."

She made a face, and he laughed.

"Or fuck buddies," he said, "which is just like it sounds. You only get together for sex."

She rubbed her forehead. "I never could understand that."

"Then there's friends with benefits. That's for people who are friends, but occasionally have sex—"

"Take the 'occasionally' out of that, and I vote yes. Do you like it?"

She made it sound like they were choosing a paint color, and Duke smiled. He couldn't help it. He pulled her into his arms, kissed her. "I like that one too, but while we're taking out 'occasionally,' can we add 'exclusively'?"

She gave him a why-would-you-say-that look. "I didn't realize that's something that had to be clarified."

"The crew is already vying for space in your bed."

"Pffft, that's ridiculous."

"You don't hear them talking when you're out of earshot. I do. I don't want to be with someone who wants someone else."

"I don't want to be with anyone else."

That sure sounded nice, but he knew these movie crews. The guys were just warming up, getting the lay of the land, looking at all their options. The only reason they weren't hitting on her already was because Duke was always close by, and he'd had words with a few of the cockier guys. Walking into the hotel hand in hand with her tonight would also help.

But he feared getting too far in with her only to have her wake up one day and realize he was just a breakup bridge to another life, one where she was free to date and sleep with whomever she wanted. One where she could play that field that had been overgrown for years.

In fact, that possibility really scared him.

But so did the thought of letting this opportunity pass.

"Okay, then," he said. "Friends with benefits—and exclusivity—it is."

She pushed up on her toes and kissed him. "This feels a little too contractual for me. Why don't we give it a personal touch?"

26

Caitlyn's eyelids fluttered open. For a millisecond, she stared at the ceiling, trying to get her mind to kick into gear. Her body felt heavy. In a good way.

Then Duke filled her mind, and she smiled. He'd woken her at 5:00 a.m. before he left. A kiss goodbye turned into another sultry session of sex.

A laugh of joy bubbled out of her. Their night had been amazing. A mix of wicked lust, affection, and humor.

She stretched and rolled to look at the clock, then sat up in shock. "*Ten?*"

Caitlyn thew the covers off and hurried through her morning routine. She braided her hair because straightening it would take too long. She threw on an outfit Andi had loved, because she was too freaked out to try to put something together herself. She used wipes on her face instead of her usual scrub, grabbed mascara and a blush-lipstick combo, and jumped in an elevator down to the lobby.

As soon as the doors closed, she dropped her head back. "Shit."

She tried not to think about what trouble Leo had gotten

himself into by now, which, of course, made her think about the trouble he had gotten himself into by now.

Caitlyn scanned her phone, but found no messages or alerts. "Why didn't someone call me?"

She grabbed a few tabloids from the gift shop and headed out front, where the doorman hailed her a taxi.

She texted Duke. *Hey, slept through my alarm. On my way to the set. How are things?*

He didn't always answer his phone, but he must have his feet on the ground because he texted back, *Could be better.*

When he didn't elaborate, she texted question marks.

A, you could be here, he texted, making her smile. *B, Leo could stop being an asshole.*

What's he doing?

Right now? Hanging upside down from his safety harness, swearing a blue streak. If I wasn't annoyed as hell, I'd think it was hilarious.

She laughed. *Having a hard time with the wall?*

He won't use the wall. Insists on going straight to rock.

Caitlyn groaned. *I'll get to you as soon as I can.*

I love the sound of that.

She smiled and sent him a happy emoji.

He sent her back a smiling devil emoji.

She looked out the window at another gorgeous British Columbia summer day, feeling on top of the world, despite the trouble of her present and the insecurity of her future.

She was crazy about Duke, but with so little experience, she kept second-guessing herself. Was it because he was so different from Brett? Was it because he did crazy-sexy things, in and out of bed? Was she one of those women who always had to be in a relationship? Had she jumped at the first attractive man who'd shown her interest? Or maybe it was the California effect? The way everything new felt exciting.

Caitlyn didn't have all the answers, but she knew he was a

really good man. And sure, he was shiny and different, but there was so much to love about him, especially the way he put his family first. But he was also dependable, capable, generous, funny, sweet, dedicated. Damn, she *really* cared about him.

Caitlyn opened the three newspaper-like magazines she'd pulled from the hotel gift shop. The cover of the *Star* showed Leo and Kendra sitting together in the overstuffed chairs, holding hands, smiling at each other. The title read *Could It Be Twins?*

"Jesus, Mary, and Joseph. Seriously?"

Instead of reading the article, she pulled out the second magazine. Another great picture of Leo and Kendra on the cover, caught in conversation with guests over wine—which Kendra did not have. This title read *Will a Baby Save Their Marriage?*

Her stomach dropped. "*Shit*. I should have known."

The final magazine showed a posed smiling pic of the two of them, holding the ultrasound image and a title which read *Baby News for the Woodses: Boy or Girl?*

Okay, all in all, not too bad. She'd have to read the articles later and hope those were favorable.

Her mind turned back to Duke. Last night, he'd told her Lexi would be proud. But she secretly hoped Duke was proud too. Childish, maybe, but she'd had far too little praise in her life.

She closed her eyes, relishing the feeling of caring this way about someone again. Looking back, she realized she hadn't been in love with Brett for a long time before she finally called it quits. Sounded like Duke was right about the difference between men and women based on when they left a relationship.

At the gate, one of the guards took her to the climbing base camp, where everyone was looking up at the cliff face. She followed the path to the base of the mountain, where she knew she'd find Duke.

He was easy to pick out from the small group, with his height and dark, dark hair. She also pegged Wes, Troy, and Keaton, as well as the three belays, one of them working Leo's line. Hadley and Kingsley were there too, looking at cameras and discussing angles and shots.

Arms crossed, hip cocked, Duke watched Leo, who hung in midair about fifty feet up the short cliff face for practice. He was reaching for, but not connecting with, the closest ridge.

"Use your body," Duke called to him. "Get some swing. There you go." Leo finally managed to get back to the top of a boulder. "Now take a break. Let your muscles—"

Leo reached for the ledge above him.

"Or not," Duke muttered with a sarcastic tone that made Caitlyn grin. "Match your hands. Don't reach for the—"

Caitlyn didn't know what matching was, but Leo raised his free hand to reach for a ledge a foot above him.

"Don't use your arms to pull. Use your legs to push."

Leo ignored Duke again, and fell again, swinging in the air, swearing.

Duke dropped his head, rubbing his eyes with a groan. "This is an uphill battle."

"Woods," Kingsley called. "Are you hearing impaired today? Listen to Duke, for God's sake. If your bullshit causes trouble, I'll be on the warpath. I may not be able to fire you, but I can make your life a living hell. Get your shit together."

Kingsley disappeared down the trail to the main rock-climbing set, and Caitlyn pressed her hand to Duke's back. "Hey."

Duke looked over his shoulder, smiling in a way that made her feel all gooey. "Hey." He dropped his arms and curled his hand around hers, then looked up at Leo again. "Do you know what's going on with him?"

"Out of sorts again?"

"Out of sorts doesn't begin to describe his mood. He's been a shit to everyone, demanded to climb 'for real.' Said he had all the training he needed. Wouldn't hear of using the climbing room."

They watched as Leo tried for a ledge too far out of reach, missed, and fell. Again.

"That belay needs a raise," Troy said, laughing.

"You know it," came from Milo, a member of Duke's climbing team, controlling the rope to keep Leo from hitting the ground every time he lost his hold on the rock.

Caitlyn clicked her phone to video and focused on getting film of Leo making a fool out of himself.

"Leo," Duke called to him. "Let's hit the climbing wall for a while."

"I'm doing just fine."

Duke sighed again and gave her hand a squeeze. "I wish I'd known he was going to be such an idiot. I would have stayed in bed with you longer."

Caitlyn laughed and pressed her hot face against his arm.

"Well, good luck with that," Keaton said, looking at the mountain. "I'm headed out to fight. Yes, I'm just that lucky." He pointed at Duke. "And no, don't even think about trying to switch jobs."

"He's just one problem after another," Caitlyn said. "Get him down. I'll talk to him."

Duke relayed the information to the belay.

"We're going to play with Cavill," Wes said, indicating himself and Troy. "He likes kids in his sandbox."

Duke smiled at Caitlyn. "That roommate of yours sure knows her styles."

She glanced down at herself. She wore skin-tight jeans, boots, a white top that showed a little more cleavage than she was used to, and a pink blazer over the top. "You wouldn't think so if you saw her. Very...punk."

"Caitlyn." Hadley's bark tightened her stomach. "He needs to understand the gravity of safety on the set, despite his shitty moods. I don't want him back here until he's mastered the wall and he can control himself."

"Of course." Though she didn't think she had any sway with Leo at this point.

Hadley followed Kingsley down the trail as Milo eased Leo to the ground.

"He's right," Duke told her. "If Leo fucks up, it will be my head on the chopping block."

"Yeah, okay. Let me see what I can do."

As soon as Leo touched down, he started yelling. "Where's Hadley? This is bullshit. I shouldn't have to learn to climb. If I could climb, I wouldn't need a stunt double."

"Eesh." She pressed her fingers against closed lids. "I could have stayed home if I wanted to babysit."

Once Leo was detached from the harness, he approached, attacking Duke first. "Answer me. Why do I need to learn to climb?"

"That is the stupidest question I've ever heard," Duke told him. "At least from a real actor. Anyone else would know exactly why."

Caitlyn approached Leo, pushing him back a few steps so they could talk in a semiprivate way.

Leo's angry gaze turned on Caitlyn. "I don't need to climb. They can just put me in for a few face shots."

"You've used up all your good will around here," Caitlyn told him, voice lowered, hoping Leo would follow suit. "They're paying you a lot of money to do this job. And this is part of your job. You'd have an easier time learning on the walls they set up for you. Just give it an hour."

Caitlyn was pretty sure after an hour of climbing, Leo's

temper would have settled. But nothing satisfied him today. He continued to rant, repeating a lot of what he'd already said.

"*Stop it.* My eight-year-old brother is more mature than you are right now. Why are you acting like this? Did something happen with Kendra?"

"She's always talking about that stupid clothing line, and when I want to talk about something else, she accuses me of not listening or not being interested in her life. It's asinine."

"Asinine? Or true?"

"You're a woman. I should have known you wouldn't understand. There's not one mention of me in any of the articles. It's all about her, the baby, the maternity line."

"Get used to it. A mama and baby will always steal the show."

When he popped off again, she put her foot down. "Leo, check yourself. There's very little I can do about videos uploaded to the internet from outside sources. And if you're portrayed in the media like you're acting right now, you'll look like a two-year-old having a tantrum. That's not going to win you any friends or get you any jobs."

"I'm done with this bullshit." He gestured angrily toward the boulders. "Let them figure out how to substitute my face where it needs to be for these climbing scenes. They'll just have to work around—"

"What makes you think you can act like an ass?" Her direct, stern voice cut into his tirade. She'd given up on keeping her voice down, and she was sick of babying this man. "You're nothing but another good-looking guy among thousands of good-looking guys in LA. The only difference is you got lucky."

That stunned Leo into momentary silence.

"You're as well known as you are because you got a break. You got lucky with *Outcast* when Simpleton got in that car accident. Yeah, I've looked into your background. And because of that job, you got another, then another. You're *lucky*. That's all you are, a good-looking guy who was at the right place at the right time. If you want to keep that lucky streak going, you're going to get your ass into that climbing room. And you're going to appreciate Duke teaching you what you need to know."

"You can't tell me how or what to do—" Leo took a step forward. In her peripheral vision, she saw Duke do the same, placing himself within reach to grab if Leo decided to get too close. "Who the fuck do you think you are?"

"I think I'm your direct lifeline to the media," she said with a clear you-dumb-shit tone. "I thought I demonstrated that last night. I think I'm your assistant with the power to make and break appointments and appearances. Think twice before you speak to me that way again."

"The hell you—"

"Don't make me call Porsha."

Leo stopped on a dime. Then offered a tentative "Porsha doesn't care—"

"You're her client. Your life is an extension of her skills and professionalism. She cares about everything that happens with you. If Porsha finds out how much trouble you're giving me, she'll fire me, and then she'll show up to be your PR rep instead. Is that what you want? Porsha looking down her nose at you all day, every day for the duration of this film?"

Leo's mouth twisted with anger.

"If that's fine with you," Caitlyn pulled her phone out, "I'll just call her now, because to be honest, I've had about enough of your bullshit and hers."

"Don't." Leo shifted on his feet. "It's fine. Whatever. I'll practice on the wall."

Pouting, Leo disappeared down the trail leading to the climbing walls.

When Caitlyn looked at Duke, she didn't find the amused expression she'd expected. He looked... She couldn't even define the emotions playing over his face, but she knew she didn't like them.

"Take lunch," one of the site managers called to the crew. "I'll call the truck to come over."

Everyone started down the trail leading to the main rock-climbing set.

"I'm sorry he's such an asshole," she told Duke. "I'll work on getting some leverage over him to keep him from—"

"Who is Porsha?"

The question was more of a demand. "My boss, why?"

"What's her last name?"

"VanDyke."

Duke's expression went dark. So dark, Caitlyn was suddenly cold.

"You work for Porsha VanDyke."

"Yes." Caitlyn was growing frustrated. "*Why?*"

His jaw muscles jumped, and his entire expression had gone rigid. "Because she's the reason Kristy and I have been living in hell the last two years."

"I don't understand."

"She's the fixer Kristy's husband hired to get dirt on Kristy. She's the reason there's always someone stalking our family. She's the reason we live in fear of Peter taking the girls away."

Caitlyn's temperature dropped a few degrees, and a pit formed in her stomach. "Are you sure? You said you didn't know anything about Excel PR."

"She must have broken away from the other company and started her own. There's only one Porsha VanDyke working PR in LA. Everything that's been happening with you and this job makes sense now. How bitchy she's been to you, how demanding, threatening even."

Her jaw dropped, and a sudden rush of guilt chilled her. But logically, she knew she had nothing to feel guilty about.

And something about this exchange was bringing back unhappy memories from her too-recent past.

She had to curb her desire to apologize. It was a knee-jerk reaction to anything that upset anyone. The last crew member started down the path. In the distance, the lunch truck's horn sounded.

"I agree she's miserable to deal with," Caitlyn told him, "and I'm sorry for what you've all been through, but what happened with Peter doesn't have anything to do with me."

"You can't work for her."

Caitlyn hit an emotional wall. "Excuse me?"

"She's unethical. She uses illegal tactics. She's a shitty human being. You can't keep working for her."

She really didn't like the ugly feelings bubbling up. "You're not making any sense. How does one relate to the other?"

"Didn't you hear me?" The force of his tone pushed her back a step. "She is the reason our lives have been a living hell. She's the reason we moved away, the reason I have Cam staying at the apartment, the reason my nieces can't have friends, the reason Kristy doesn't sleep, the reason I'm broke. She's the reason all our lives have been on hold for two fucking years."

"Again, what does that have to do with me? I'm not doing those things."

"You're working for the woman who did."

"So, what? I'm guilty by association?"

"This isn't just about a shitty job anymore. You're on the wrong side of this, and she's insidious. How long will it be before you're doing those things?"

Caitlyn's jaw dropped, and a slicing pain cut through her stomach. "*What* did you just say?"

"You have to quit."

Caitlyn's temper pushed heat into her chest, her neck, her face. She crossed her arms, putting counterpressure to the pain welling inside her. She couldn't believe this was the same guy she'd spent the night with.

"What I have to do is hold a job to pay my rent. What I have to do is grow my career so I'm not living on rice and beans the rest of my life. What I have to do is live up to my obligations. You're not my keeper, and you don't make decisions for *my* life."

She started to turn, to walk away from the conversation, but a revelation made her turn back to him.

"Everyone in Kentucky may have doubted my abilities, but even they didn't question my character. As far as I'm concerned, you can figure out how to deal with Leo from here on out. I'm done with both of you."

27

Duke finished his third beer, wishing he could keep drinking until he passed out. But there was no room for error on the cliff face waiting for him in the morning, so he pushed the glass away and declined a refill from the waitress, then pushed his food around the plate some more.

Troy, Keaton, and Wes were volleying crew gossip. In between, they talked about what they all needed in the upcoming stunts.

Duke had been fighting himself to stay away from Caitlyn since their argument this morning. He was a triple-threat loser—he felt guilty for attacking her, angry she wasn't as appalled at her situation as he was, and really, *really* fucking wanted her.

Now he had one more thing to hold against that bitch Porsha. How could one woman cause so much misery?

"Reid."

Duke came out of his fog and looked at Troy. "What?"

"I asked how Leo did on the climbing wall."

"Shitty, but possibly just well enough to hold a position so they can get the footage they need to swap us out."

"Stop pouting," Troy said. "Just bite the bullet and apologize."

"Can't apologize to someone who won't talk to me." She'd ignored his messages and sent his calls to voicemail. "Besides, I don't know if I want to apologize."

When he looked up from shredding the beer bottle's label, all the guys were giving him that what-the-fuck look. "The only thing I'm sorry for is hurting her feelings. I still think she should quit. I still think she's in dangerous territory working for Porsha. And I hate knowing that by handling Leo, Caitlyn is helping that bitch."

"That's some twisted logic," Troy said.

"You know," Wes said, "if that's how you really feel, leave her the hell alone. She deserves better."

"She's in a tough spot," Keaton said. "She's been thrown into a cesspool. She's just trying to escape the alligators and snakes until she can find solid footing."

"She needs this job," Wes said, "and she hates her boss almost as much as you do. Now, she's in conflict with her man over the whole thing."

"Your life, on the other hand," Troy said, "is looking up. You're working, you've got a network of people you can trust to help with the family, the custody hearing is coming up, and by all accounts, favor is bending toward Kristy."

"And you had a really great girl—" Keaton said.

"For about a minute," Wes added.

Duke sighed and sat back. "I'll go by her room on my way up." His phone rang, and he saw Kristy's name on the display. "Gotta get this. See you guys tomorrow."

He stood and wandered from the hotel restaurant into the lobby, where he answered Kristy's call. "Hey, how's it going?"

"I'm calling to ask you the same thing."

"What do you mean?"

"I talked to Rubi earlier today, then got a concerned call

from Brook an hour ago. I anticipate calls from Ellie and Zahara before I go to sleep. And, I swear to God, if Lexi calls me from her honeymoon, your name will be Royal Shit."

He closed his eyes and swore. He'd forgotten how everyone in this self-made family was always in each other's business.

"What's going on with you?" she wanted to know. "You hit the jackpot with Caitlyn right out of the fucking gates and then screw it up?"

"You never let me talk like that at home."

"The girls are asleep."

"Is Cam there?"

"Yes. Stop avoiding my question. What's going on?"

Duke groaned, sat on a planter ledge in the lobby, and explained the issue. The line went silent for a long moment before Kristy exhaled heavily. "That sucks. It really does. But she's an innocent bystander in this thing with Peter and Porsha. We've both developed a knee-jerk reaction to anything involving either of them. I'm sure she'd understand if you explained it to her."

Duke opened his mouth to tell Kristy he *had* explained it to her, but a woman in cut-off shorts with killer legs drew his attention and spiked his heart rate. Caitlyn wandered into the hotel store, her hair in a high ponytail, and strolled around aimlessly. The sight of her pulled his heart into his throat and ramped up the heat he'd been trying to bank. He was so fucked.

"God, I can't wait to be rid of Peter, Porsha, and this whole mess," Kristy was saying, but Duke had lost track of the conversation.

A group of crew members left the restaurant and headed toward the elevators. As they passed the store, a few glanced in and stopped walking. Guys working the sets. They parted ways with the others and roamed into the store—Sully, Dax, and Warren. Duke had worked with all three at some point in his career, and all three were dogs with women.

Within minutes, Warren and Dax were chatting up Caitlyn. Sully stood nearby, leaning on a display, giving Caitlyn his I-so-want-to-fuck-you smile, and a steel strap cinched around Duke's chest.

"You can't blame what's happening on Caitlyn," Kristy said. "It's not like she had anything to do with Porsha taking Peter as a client. She's not connected to Peter at all."

Wes's earlier words mixed with Kristy's. *If that's how you really feel, leave her the hell alone.* Maybe he should. Let her find someone without as many demons.

The guys drew out their conversation with Caitlyn and got her talking. Duke had to unlock his jaw to say, "Hey, I've got to go. I'll check in tomorrow."

He said goodbye and disconnected, pushed to his feet, and slid his phone into his back pocket. He wandered toward the store and heard the guys laughing. They were young and cocky, using tired lines, but if Caitlyn noticed, she didn't show it. And while they did pull a laugh out of her, Duke could tell she was subdued.

Inside the store, Duke put himself at Caitlyn's back and leaned his shoulder against a shelf, in the direct line of sight of the men facing her. Warren saw him immediately. His smile fell, and he elbowed Sully. Sully followed Warren's line of sight and saw Duke.

All Duke had to do was lift his chin in their direction to have Warren and Sully begging off. Dax frowned at his friends, then saw Duke. While he didn't jet out like Warren and Sully, Dax left Caitlyn with an open invitation for a hookup. He was lucky he didn't use those exact words. Duke would have given the man a reason to max out his dental plan.

Once the guys were gone, Caitlyn seemed to exhale in relief and the tension in her shoulders melted.

"Hey."

Caitlyn turned, surprised. And judging by the complex

expression and fleeting emotions, he was pretty sure she shared the conflict dogging him.

She took a step back. "Hey."

"I was going to swing by your room on my way up to see if you'd talk to me."

"Guess I saved you a trip, but I don't want to talk."

He glanced at the Snickers bar in her hand. "Dessert?"

She looked at the candy bar like she'd forgotten she had it. "Breakfast, lunch, dinner, and dessert."

"You haven't eaten all day?"

"Someone let me sleep late, so I didn't get breakfast. Then that same someone pissed me off to the point of a stomachache." She looked at the candy bar again and turned it over. "Figured a little protein wouldn't hurt."

He grinned. "Protein."

She lifted a shoulder and made a silly face. "It's got peanuts, right?"

He laughed. If anyone told him five minutes ago, he would be laughing with her, he would have told them they were crazy.

"I don't have the energy to deal with much else," she said.

"Room service?"

She sighed as if she thought that was too much to contemplate. "I'd have to read the menu, make decisions, deal with people."

He looked past her to a refrigerator case. "Let me make you something better than a candy bar."

"Do you have a pop-up kitchen in your pocket?"

"No, but I've done this job long enough to know how to get my body what it needs when there are limited supplies."

She looked down at her candy bar. A strand of hair fell from her ponytail and swung into her face. He reached in and tucked it behind her ear.

Her eyes fluttered closed, and the look of longing on her face sent flash fire through his body.

"Long hours, hard work, stress," he told her, letting his touch slide along the softness of her cheek, the angle of her jaw, her bottom lip. "You've got to take care of yourself, or you'll get sick."

She pulled away from his touch and took another step backward. "The stress seems to be my biggest problem."

"I have two really big problems."

"Oh, yeah?" she said with a healthy dash of sarcasm.

"Yeah. Those fucking *hot* cut-off shorts of yours..."—that got a smile out of her—"and my piss-poor ability to apologize."

Her gaze softened, but she looked away and shook her head. "It's just... I'm not... You can't..."

She shook her head. "I googled Peter and the divorce. Got information on Porsha repping him through Merissa. He's a shitty human being. I feel for her. And you. And the girls. You've all been through the wringer. That said, it doesn't give you the right to treat me like the enemy."

"I shouldn't have."

"You also shouldn't have underestimated me or questioned my character."

"I shouldn't have. It was wrong, not only ethically, but factually." When she didn't respond, he asked, "Can I make you something real to eat?"

She shrugged.

Duke took that as a yes, grabbed a Stouffer's French bread pizza from the freezer, a handful of mozzarella sticks from the refrigerator, and grabbed a couple of beers. He put them on his room tab, along with the Snickers so she wouldn't have to part with it, and she reluctantly wandered toward the elevators with him.

28

She felt listless. And pained. She was in a battle between her head and her heart. Being with Duke just made it worse.

The elevator doors opened, and they stepped on.

When the doors closed, she said, "Leo said the climbing went well in the gym."

"I don't know if it went well, but it went. He may have just enough skill to hold still in one place so they can get the photos they need. Then Keaton had to deal with him for a few fighting scenes. Keaton escorted him back to his room and told him to stay there."

She nodded. "I got a call from reception when he returned. He's having dinner with a producer at the hotel restaurant, and they said they'd call if they saw him leave again."

"How'd you manage that?"

"Money. A hundred bucks for any tip-off."

"Do you know which producer?"

"Thomason? Shandon? Something like that?"

"Shandon," he agreed. "He's here working on a Netflix series."

"Leo said the guy saw the interview on *ET*. It put him in a good light."

He shook his head and stared at the elevator doors. "You're amazing."

"I sure don't feel amazing."

"I shouldn't have done that today," he said, voice sincere. "I reacted without thinking. I'm really sorry."

Tears swelled in her throat. She cleared the block and blinked hard.

"I have no excuse. I should have handled it differently."

She had to fight against the need to tell him it was okay, because it wasn't.

"Apology accepted," she said instead and lifted her chin to look him in the eye. "But it won't happen again."

"No, ma'am, it won't."

A little weight lifted from her heart, and his "ma'am" made her smile. "Be careful, next thing you know, you'll have a lilt in your voice and be saying things like 'who licked the red off your candy?'"

His brow fell. "Who licked what off what?"

She laughed. And, God, it felt as warm as a summer rain.

She couldn't keep herself from easing toward him, more of a shoulder roll against the wall to face him than an overt approach. Then she leaned into him and looked up to find the most affectionate expression she'd seen in a long time, including Brett's visit.

"Since I was a kid, I've been programed to let others off the hook. My family taught me that obeying or being good or liked was more important than standing up for myself. But I'm not a kid anymore, and that fawning behavior has caused me more than my share of heartache. It's also built some really lousy self-esteem. I'm not accepting anything less than what I deserve anymore."

Damn, that was hard to say, especially to a man she really,

really wanted. She might know logically that if he walked away because of her limits, he wasn't the guy for her, but her heart was holding on to him hard.

"I don't want to give you mixed messages," she told him, "so let me be clear: telling me what to do is not okay. Neither is judging me for my choices."

He tucked a knuckle under her chin and lifted her gaze to his. "Understood."

Then he kissed her, and the world fell away. The pain she'd been living with all day evaporated. He did all those things that made her melt—the soft kisses before he went deep, the way he could kiss forever without pushing for more, the way he held her, one arm tight at her waist, the other in her hair.

She didn't hear the elevator ding on her floor. Only realized they'd stopped when Duke broke the kiss to put his arm in the way of the closing door. Caitlyn's head was light as Duke took her hand and guided her to her room, where she fumbled with her phone to pull up the QR code that opened her door.

Before they were even through the door, Duke had one strong arm around her middle, his mouth on her neck. He put the food on the counter, and Caitlyn ignored the little voice in the back of her head telling her there were deeper conflicts between them. That this wasn't the answer. But it wasn't near loud enough to kill her desire for Duke.

He let the door close behind them, and in seconds, Caitlyn was in his arms, her legs around his hips, her hands in his hair.

A couple of weeks ago, she didn't even know this kind of passion existed. Now she couldn't get enough. She tilted her head and stroked her tongue against his until he moaned. The sound shivered through Caitlin's blood, flowing through her body, slowly filling every cell.

She fisted the back of his T-shirt and pulled out of the kiss to drag it over his head. The look on his face told her everything she needed to know right now—he cared about her, and he wanted her. She could worry about all the other stuff later.

He put her down to pull off her tank top and his gaze scoured her body as if he'd never seen it before, touching her like he wanted all of it, all at the same time.

"Skin, sugar." His rough, low voice tugged deep inside her. "I need more skin."

She lowered her legs to the floor and scraped her teeth over his collarbone while her hands worked at his jeans, then slid inside to feel his length. His hands tightened on her arms, and his head fell forward on a curse.

He picked her up again, then lowered her to the bed on her back. He usually stopped here, when she was under him, when they were face-to-face. He stopped just to catch his breath and look into her eyes, making her feel like nothing existed outside this room.

But not tonight. Tonight, he opened her bra as easily as he pushed down the zipper of her shorts, then slid off the bed to pull them off, along with her panties. His gaze stayed riveted to hers as he got rid of his jeans and boxers. Excitement streaked through her stomach. His expression was one of pinpoint focus. Wicked desire. Deliberate intent.

Instead of joining her on the bed, he dropped to his knees. The move made her stomach clench and her heart soften. He gripped her thighs and pulled her to the edge of the mattress with a force that made her gasp.

Then his mouth was on her, and she gasped for an entirely different reason. His tongue was warm and insanely soft against her. Working in concert with his lips, he had her doing things she'd never imagined she would do—lifting her hips to get more, fisting the sheets, thrilling over the sight of his dark head and wide shoulders between her legs.

He seemed to know exactly how to slowly push her to a

peak, until she'd fallen into the no-return zone, then kept her there until she couldn't stand it. Until she pushed a hand into his hair and begged.

Still, he took her over the edge in his own time, in his own calculated way that shot three deep orgasms through her before he kissed his way up her body. She felt heavy in the aftermath. Bubbles of pleasure stung her veins and lightened her head.

He slid an arm between her back and the mattress and moved her to the middle of the bed. Then he eased his hips between her legs and propped himself up on his forearms.

Caitlyn was still trying to recover as he kissed her—lips, cheek, temple, jaw, neck, throat. Again, no hurry to find his own release. His restraint made her feel like he didn't want to be anywhere else. Like he would spend all night like this if she asked. Like she was important.

It was an alternate reality for her. Not just the incredible sex, but the way he treated her during that incredible sex.

Duke reached between them, placed himself and rocked his hips. He thrust just enough to get as deep as he could go, and she and Duke groaned together. Then he stilled and pressed his forehead to hers. His eyelashes fluttered, and his expression spoke of pure joy.

Nothing had to be said for butterflies to fill her belly. He made her throat tight, made tears sting her eyes. Even as she identified all the feelings of being in love, she couldn't admit it to herself. Love created far too many risks. She'd taken her share of risks for a lifetime, and she knew there were still lots in her future.

Duke pulled her upright and maneuvered them face-to-face so smoothly, she had no idea how he'd done it. She lost herself in him, and the way they moved together. Slid her fingertips along the grooves of his sweaty muscles, tasted his salty skin, wrapped her arms around his neck, and pushed her hands into his hair, holding tight as the first of what she knew would be a slew of climaxes ravaged her.

29

Duke was so pumped, he felt like he could scale Everest.

He pushed into a double knee bar, wedging both knees in a triangular gap between granite slabs. Resting his quads, hammies, and glutes, he leaned back, hanging upside down and letting his arms hang free twenty-five hundred feet above base camp.

They didn't have to film this far up to make it look like he was climbing, but Kingsley was always looking for drama. It was a gorgeous day. The sun was out, the sky was bright blue, the air crisp, and Duke was in his happy place, on the face of a mountain.

Scratch that, he had a new happy place, and it was with Caitlyn.

Just the thought of her made him smile. Laugh even. He loved being with her, fighting with her, talking to her, scheming with her, hanging with her, sleeping with her.

Especially sleeping with her. There was no slow burn between them. They lit up in bed. Every time. In fact, it just kept getting hotter. She let go of the inhibitions she'd been living with, game to try all kinds of things. And she was incredible at everything she tried.

Hands down, the best sex of his life. And that was because of more than the physical. Sure, they hadn't known each other long, but he loved everything he knew about her. Though her intense independence was a problem. But that was Duke's issue, not hers.

He'd been protecting four precious females for two years from someone who clearly meant them harm. His instinct to control Caitlyn's exposure to danger wouldn't just evaporate. And the closer he got to Caitlyn, the more protective he felt. He just had to keep a handle on it.

"All your blood's going to go to your head," Troy said. "You're gonna make it fatter than it already is."

Duke had almost forgotten Troy was there.

He pulled himself semiupright as the chopper carrying Hadley, Kingsley, and several senior cameramen, took another slow pass. The chopper blades created a wind that picked up small rocks and tossed them around.

"Ouch," Troy said, a mild, sarcastic response to what was, in perspective, a very small issue.

Duke lifted his hand to his earbud, about to press the mic and tell the chopper to back off a bit, when a drone popped up beside Duke, creating a river of fear.

"What the...?" He pressed the mic. "Who the fuck is flying the drone while the chopper is in the air? Get it down. *Now.* And whoever got it up here has relinquished the privilege of flying it. Forever, as far as I'm concerned. Get someone else to take over."

The drone immediately dropped, and Duke breathed easier. "Jesus Christ. That's all we need."

The chopper was low, scouting for camera angles. They were going to do the same with the drone, but the two shouldn't have been in the air at the same time. Best case scenario, the drone was killed instantly. Worst case, it got caught up in the chopper's blades and caused the chopper to crash.

He refocused on the rock. Troy climbed beside Duke, looking for places for extreme shots. They'd already discussed the ledge Duke, Troy, and Wes had found, and they'd filmed that from every angle. Now they were getting close to the top, where the camera angles would widen to exploit the incredible view.

Above, below, and on the other side of him, cameramen filmed different angles. There were more cameras at the summit, attached to arms that stretched out over the edge of the granite for yet another angle.

Tonight, after dinner, everyone would gather for the dailies, where they would check out all the film from the stunts—Wes's driving, Troy's rigging, and Keaton's fighting, which was where Keaton was now, managing fight scenes between Cavill and Woods. Duke absently wondered if Woods would act like a normal human being with another star around.

Once they'd done the work, nailed down the angles, and blocked out the stunts, filming would begin, and they'd be working their asses off. Lots of long days for retakes, specialty shots, and close-ups to allow the editors to splice it together and make it look like one badass climb.

Duke couldn't lie. Knowing Caitlyn would be here while he filmed set his heart on fire.

"You should try that overhang," Troy said. "You know, climb on the underside, then wing yourself up and over the edge at the tip. That would be amazing."

Duke studied the rock jutting out from the mountainside. He hadn't plotted his path for that, but Troy was right. And that was really what this climb was about, to look at the rock from a camera's perspective. The idea also gave Duke a thrill. He hadn't been challenging himself much over the last two years.

"I'll give it a shot."

Duke pushed one hand into his chalk bag, scanning the ledges and crags available for his hands and feet. He chalked his hands. He'd be essentially climbing horizontally, keeping tension on three hold points at a time to keep him on the underside of the outcropping, while still moving.

"I'm going to have to move relatively fast once I start." Energy in climbing was precious, and once Duke started moving, he wanted to move quickly and efficiently.

Troy got on the radio and explained what they were doing so the chopper could swing back around and film. As soon as Duke heard the whap of the blades, he set off.

He reached to his right, put one finger in a round gap, and used it as leverage to pull his feet up. He worked his toes into inch-wide divots, used one hand to grip a small crag, and reached for the next.

Then he was climbing, horizontally, body up against the underside of the rock, held in place by the tension he created with his limbs.

"You're like fucking Spider-Man," Troy yelled, making Duke laugh.

He worked from muscle memory and experience, basically winging it. Left hand on a crag, right foot against the face, right hand into a crack on the roof. He found another hold for his other hand, but not for his feet, so he took a minute to set an anchor, then clipped his rope into it.

The next place he'd be able to secure his feet was eight feet to his right. So he tightened his handholds and let his feet drop. Now, he was taking the rock like a jungle gym, his hands all that kept gravity from dropping him to his last anchor.

"Jesus," Hadley said. "That's amazing."

Troy laughed and told Duke, "I forgot how damn good you are."

Duke continued across the rock until he reached the end of the horizontal surface. At the very tip, he found a nice round rock the perfect size for his hand, grabbed hold, and let his other arm fall free so he was holding the tip of the outcropping with one hand.

"Mother of God." That was Kingsley's voice in Duke's ear. "I knew we picked the right team for this."

"That's nothing," Troy said into his mic, which meant everyone heard. "Do that other one, that cross thing."

He was talking about the reverse iron cross. An advanced climbing skill rarely used in actual climbing. As far as Duke was concerned, that move was all about showing off. In all his years of climbing, he'd never needed it, though he'd practiced it, but only to enhance his other skills.

"Are you fucking kidding me right now?" Duke yelled at Troy, off the air. "Dude."

"You've got this," he yelled back.

"Payback."

"It'll be worth it. Wait until you see it on film."

"Jesus Christ," Duke muttered.

If Troy had brought that up just between them, he would have told him no. Duke found this move one of the hardest, but he was in the perfect location to do it, and he really didn't want to say no to the producer and the director. He absolutely would if it would risk his safety, but the way Duke had his path anchored, the risk was low. At least relatively low considering what the hell he was doing.

The chopper took another swing around the summit, and Duke switched arms, resting the other. He prepped his mind, took a few deep breaths, and chalked both hands.

When the chopper came back around, Duke looked left and found his target. He blew out his breath and swung his free arm out and around, turning away from the mountain. He caught another ledge with his other hand, arms extended, legs dangling, creating a human cross.

One one thousand, two one thousand, three one thousand...

It was taking everything Duke had not to drop, so he didn't hear the accolades until he'd released the pose after five one thousands, once again dangling from one arm. His hearing returned to cheers and praise that Duke was too exhausted to appreciate.

He used his abdominal muscles to pull his feet up and monkeyed over the edge of the horizontal plane, leading back to vertical surfaces.

Duke was working his way toward the perfect gap in the rocks for a double knee bar where he could rest, when the outcropping on a rock snapped off in his hand. He immediately slid down the slant, grabbing at anything that would help him stop. While the rock was rough, it didn't give Duke a handhold. His belly and chest took a beating, and his feet were already over the edge, so he couldn't get any help there.

"Fuck, fuck, fuck," he muttered even as he went over the side. At the last second, he grabbed for that rock he'd been hanging off just minutes ago and was shocked to realize he'd caught it just in time.

With his heart beating like a freight train, he looked up at Troy, whose eyes were wide, flashing with a little terror.

"Jesus," he breathed. "Stop fucking around. You almost gave me a heart attack."

They both knew Duke wasn't fucking around. They both knew just how close Duke had come to falling. Sure, he was anchored in, but that didn't calm any nerves during free fall. And there was always the off chance the anchors wouldn't hold for some unforeseen reason.

His grip started to slide. Duke quickly chalked his free hand and switched off.

"Seriously," Troy said. "Fun and games are over. Get your ass back up here."

A whistle sounded in their headphones.

"Hot damn," Hadley said. "I can't fucking wait to see that on film."

"You're welcome," he said, pressing the mic when his hand passed his head to reach for more rock. He worked his way back to the main chunk of granite that was the mountain face, and when Duke finally slid into a double knee bar to rest, his muscles were on fire.

He drank some water, chalked his hands, and took a minute to look around. A lake sparkled to his right. Tall trees dotted more of the mountain. And now that he was safe, he felt a familiar rush of gratitude mixed with adrenaline.

"How are things with Caitlyn?" Troy asked from his own comfortable perch. Probably trying to get his mind off Duke almost falling.

Duke sighed, released himself from the rock, and started to climb again. Right hand on a rounded boulder, matching that hand with his other. Finding footholds, stretching, pushing, reaching, as he made his way toward the summit.

Troy followed suit.

"It's a little more volatile than I like," he told Troy before he took hold of a crag and pulled both legs up and stabilized them.

"Makes for some killer sex," Troy said.

Duke laughed. And laughed some more. His night with Caitlyn was still bubbling through his blood. He could swear this was the best he'd climbed in years, despite his almost fall.

He reached for an anchor, placed it, and gave the metal a couple more taps with the hammer, then he pulled like hell to make sure it was secure and snapped his safety line into the clip.

"She's skittish of relationships," Duke told him, "but I got her to agree to friends with benefits."

"Based on how your eyes turn green every time you see a guy even look at her, I don't see that kind of arrangement working very well. You're too much of an Alpha. We all are."

"We agreed to not sleeping with other people."

"Friends, sex, and exclusivity? That sounds like a relationship to me."

Duke took hold of ledges above his head and leaned back, letting his arms go straight to rest for ten seconds.

He laughed. "I know. Just don't tell her that."

30

Caitlyn stood beside Kingsley, who had just arrived from the climbing set, now watching the fight playing out in front of them on green mats and green walls. All the green, she'd learned, would disappear in postprocessing, and be replaced by whatever setting was required for the film.

Keaton coached Cavill and Leo through fight scenes against each other, and Caitlyn might not know a damn thing about fighting, but she could clearly see Keaton was a master. He was also a great teacher, and Cavill was a great student. Their fight scenes often left her breathless.

"How was the climbing shoot?" she asked Kingsley.

"Incredible." He shook his head without looking at Caitlyn, his gaze on Keaton showing Leo how to take fake blows. "Really incredible. They're going to be the highlight of the film. Duke is amazing. I'm so glad we got him for this shoot. They're packing up and heading down to camp. Should be here soon."

She was disappointed she'd missed it, but she had limits on how much danger she could witness before coming unglued.

Cavill threw a very believable right punch at Keaton's face. Keaton's head whipped the opposite direction, and he stumbled. It looked so real, Caitlyn tensed and grimaced, only for both Cavill and Keaton to drop back into their normal postures and talk about the hits.

"Can I take a few minutes to talk to you about promotion?" she asked Kingsley.

He didn't answer, his attention on the crew attaching wires to the back and top of Cavill's harness. This was all for just one little part of one little fight scene in the grand scheme. And they filmed things over and over and over. It seemed so tedious to Caitlyn.

She decided to jump in and ask for forgiveness because she hadn't gotten permission.

"I've been working on some possibilities that leverage Paramount's, *American Valor*'s, and Leo's popularity online. Keeping Leo's promotion within the scope of this movie, I would arrange a promote-one, promote-all plan. Leo's got four million Twitter followers and close to as many Instagram followers. That's almost triple the other two.

Caitlyn had spent all day embroiled in this full-fledged marketing plan with input from both Andi and Merissa. She was so freaking excited about the possibilities, she wanted to jump out of her skin. Not for Leo; Leo was an ass. But for herself. For her to knock Porsha's socks off, as Merissa put it.

Kingsley didn't offer more than a distracted "Uh-huh."

On the green mats, against green walls, Keaton faced Cavill and counted, "One, two, three."

Cavill made an aggressive move toward Keaton in slow motion. Keaton, just as slow, leaned back and kicked toward Cavill's face. Even though Keaton hadn't made contact, Cavill arched backward just as Keaton took another shot at Cavill's middle, making him fold forward while the wires pulled Cavill back on the mats as if Keaton's kick had sent him flying.

"Got it?" Keaton asked Leo, who assured him he did.

It took a few seconds for Caitlyn to process what she'd seen and how they made it look so damn realistic.

She refocused on Kingsley. "I'm looking at some exciting ideas. On the larger side, I thought we could build mini sets from *American Valor* in a few big cities, maybe here, Boston, and Atlanta or DC, where the public could participate. A rock-climbing set designed to mimic some part of the wall Duke is climbing where participants can follow a path to the top. Or a shooting set that looks like one in the movie where participants use paintball guns. It would be like living part of *American Valor*."

Kingsley cut a look at her, then turned his attention back to the monitors, showing more work by Keaton, Cavill, and Leo. "That's a creative idea."

Actually, it wasn't. She'd stolen it from a similar setup for *Game of Thrones*, but who was she to say so?

"Social media and other digital avenues can be a low-cost, high-reward way to go, like recreating *American Valor*'s atmosphere in a video game. And that could not only garner interest in the film but be another revenue stream."

That deepened his attention. "I'm listening."

Caitlyn silently blessed her brothers for playing those damn games she was forever bitching at them to stop playing so they could do homework or chores.

"On a smaller but still impactful scale, there could be a mystery hunt, where participants find clues in movie posters, websites, and/or social media channels to win prizes. Video content could be posted on social media and used to create online games, which, again, could be monetized if they became popular."

She took a breath and pushed on, all the ideas spilling out of her head. "Releasing behind-the-scenes snippets has been shown to create major buzz among die-hard fans. And there could be a chat room where fans can talk about the film and characters, where there can be games and prizes."

The high-pitched sing of wires preceded a hit to the pad against the wall, breaking into her overly zealous ideas.

When Kingsley returned his gaze to hers, she said, "I could go on, but I know how busy you are, and I tried to get an appointment with you, but you're full up."

Kingsley didn't say anything for a long moment, during which Caitlyn's palms started to sweat.

"Your ideas have merit, and I admire your out-of-the-box thinking," Kingsley said. "Unfortunately, the movie's marketing budget is always spread thin, and the money is taken almost before it's budgeted. There's no money left for what you're talking about, but, if you do go with ideas that promo the film, let the marketing department know. We can at least get the information out through our regular channels. And they may be able to implement some of your ideas that cost little or nothing."

Caitlyn nodded despite her disappointment. She wasn't sure how many of her ideas would make it to any type of screen, but she wasn't through trying to take them live. She could use some of these ideas without anyone's help. "Of course, I understand."

His gaze moved back to the fighters, and Caitlyn prepared to move on.

"Saw your impromptu press conference the other night," Kingsley said.

She tilted her head. "You were there? I'm sorry I missed you."

"You didn't. I wasn't there. Caught it on *ET*."

Her heart skipped. "*ET*? As in *Entertainment Tonight*?"

"There's only one *ET*," he said, grinning as he watched the fight on camera where the background was in, turning everything green to a desertlike setting. "You made Leo look like fucking husband and father of the year. I don't doubt you could do exactly what you're proposing for marketing. You're just throwing your hat in the ring a little late."

Caitlyn's heart was still pounding at the idea her interview had been on television. Why hadn't anyone called her? She'd distributed the video file to Excel's media partners, but didn't really think the segment would get picked up. Merissa hadn't mentioned it when Caitlyn had talked to her earlier, but then she did work for Porsha, which would distract anyone from anything. But then Porsha should have told her. Then again, that would require praise. Porsha didn't seem big on praise.

"Right, okay. Well, thanks for indulging me."

Caitlyn moved to the side for a good view of the mats, clicked her phone over to video, and filmed the end of that fighting session. She'd send it to her brothers and post it on social media.

"Seriously, they're all hot as hell," a woman said somewhere behind her, "but Duke, there's something insanely sexy about the way he conquers those mountains. I get wet just watching him."

Caitlyn's ears perked, but she didn't turn around. A strange annoyance tripped down her spine. She didn't like the idea of Duke making another woman wet, but she couldn't exactly blame the other women either. Nor could she do anything about it. And it wasn't like he was doing it on purpose.

"I've never seen a body like his."

"And he's so sweet," the other woman said, a sound of pleasure-pain filling her words. "I met him a couple of years ago, but he had to leave the set before I got any time with him."

"I heard he's hooking up with the woman working with Leo."

"Carmen told me the same thing."

Sounded like small towns weren't the only places running rampant with gossip.

"Have you seen her?"

"Fucking gorgeous." Then she added a playful "Bitch." Making them both laugh. Almost making Caitlyn laugh. She wasn't anywhere close to fucking gorgeous, but, hey, she'd take it.

"Hard to compete with LaCroix family genetics."

"I didn't know they were related."

"Cousins, I heard."

She sighed. "Oh, well… That explains a lot."

"He'll be here for a while, and all the guys are eye-fucking her. Maybe they'll both move on to new pastures. Give it time."

The women's voices faded as they walked away, and Caitlyn glanced over her shoulder to see them wandering to join another group of people. They were about her age, one with long dark hair, the other woman a sandy blonde, both pretty.

While Caitlyn was considering what they'd said, and how she felt about it, someone came up to her, and she refocused on Duke.

He stood beside her to watch the guys fight. "Tired of watching me already?"

"Hardly." She glanced around before saying, "You look insanely hot right now."

He was unshaven, sun-kissed, and sweaty. He had cuts and abrasions on his arms and body, but didn't seem to even know they were there. And his smile made everything inside her fizz.

"But when you started doing those crazy-ass things," she said, "like hanging off a rock with one hand, I decided this was a safer alternative. My heart won't blow up over here."

He chuckled. "I'll give you a pass. How was your day?"

"Judging by that smile, not as good as yours."

"I may be able to help you out with that."

"Oh, yeah?"

"I'll give it my very best shot."

"That sounds promising."

She wanted to lean into him and lift her mouth to his for a kiss. After hearing what the other women had said, she found herself wanting to put her mark on him. She'd never had to deal with jealousy before, on either side. This was new, and she didn't like it. At all.

Her gaze dropped to the scratches on his chest, deeper than she'd first thought. "But I want to treat those scratches first."

"Letting you get your hands on me? Don't have to ask me twice."

After a moment, he tilted his head, frowning down at her. "What's up?"

She laughed softly. No one back home ever noticed when she was upset or unsettled, not even when she *told* them. But Duke could tell with one look. "Not entirely sure."

He took her chin between his fingers, tilting it back so she was looking directly into his eyes. Eyes that were now more worried than happy. "What happened?"

"Nothing, nothing." She took his hand and squeezed it.

Before he could dig deeper, Kingsley came up and slapped Duke on the shoulder. "You're an amazing climber. You gave us some killer options for these scenes. Let's head to the hotel and see how the dailies look."

He released Duke's shoulder and looked at Caitlyn. "You two are a good match. I can see you ten years out as a behind-the-scenes power couple in this jungle."

Kingsley found his way off set, and when he was out of earshot, Duke looked at Caitlyn for answers. "What was that about?"

"I just pitched some promo ideas to him earlier, telling him how I could use Leo's popularity to help the film and for the film to help Leo."

"Cross-promotion."

"He said the ideas are great, but that the marketing budget for the film is pretty much spent before they even get it."

He tucked a strand of hair behind her ear. "Yeah. The money in these movies can be turbulent. Budgets are a big deal."

With everyone headed toward the gate, she leaned in and kissed him. "Kingsley's right. You're incredible. I've been thinking about you all day. I'd really like to get through these dailies, grab some dinner and spend our time in bed in ways other than talking. Not necessarily in that order."

31

Duke ran his gelled hands through his hair to get it under control, then hit the door and boarded the elevator to Caitlyn's floor.

He'd been away from her for barely thirty minutes, just long enough to catch a shower and change, but his nerves still tingled. There was something going on with her. He could only pray she hadn't changed her mind about their relationship status. And he realized that this nervous feeling was only a glimpse of what Brett must have felt—at least when he pulled his head out of his ass long enough to realize he'd lost her.

Duke stepped off the elevator and turned the corner toward Caitlyn's room. When she opened the door, she took his breath away. Literally. Her hair was down and wavy, framing her angelic face. She was wearing the same jeans as earlier, but she'd changed her blouse, and the way she looked in the one she was wearing made his head light.

"Okay," she said, almost before the door was open, "you have to—" She stopped, took him in and slowly smiled.

"I have to what?"

She curled her hand into his T-shirt and pulled him into the room. "You have to get in here and kiss me."

His smile melted into heat. He wrapped her in his arms, pulled her close, lifted one hand to brush her hair over her shoulder. Then slowly, slowly, slowly lowered his mouth to hers.

Her moan sent shivers through his body. Her tongue sought his out, and Duke almost buckled at the knees.

A few kisses later, his hands were under her pretty top, sliding across soft, warm skin. She pulled from the kiss, and he rested his forehead against hers.

"We can't miss these dailies, can we?" she asked.

"You can, but I can't. They're shots of the climb from all angles. If I let Kingsley and Hadley have free rein, I'll be performing double back flips all the way up the rock."

She pulled back. "Really?"

"Really what?"

"They're going to show the pictures from the plane and the drone?"

"That's what the dailies are—time to go over the day's filming and decide if they're keeping, refilming, or editing the footage."

"Oh no. We're not missing that." She deliberately stepped away from him and smoothed her hand down the front of her top, a pretty smoky-purple thing with spaghetti straps and lace—some of that lace backed by nothing but Caitlyn's skin. "I was going to say, you have to be honest. Is this too casual? Too...I don't know...revealing?"

He had no idea how a thin piece of fabric could make him want to touch her so badly. When Duke didn't answer, she dropped her head back and turned. "I knew it. I'll change really qui—"

Duke wrapped his arms around her from behind and

pulled her against him. He dropped kisses on her shoulder. "I didn't answer because you take my breath away. You're perfect. Don't change."

He meant that in so many ways.

She turned her head to look at him. "Really?"

"Really." He kissed her.

When he pulled back, she was smiling again. "Okay."

She turned and wrapped her arms around his neck, pressing her body against his and fiddling with his still-uncooperative hair. God, she felt perfect against him. Fucking perfect.

"Maybe we can switch up the order of our plans," she said. "I need you more than I need dinner."

His nerves settled. "I'm good with that."

She grabbed her notepad and phone, and Duke held her hand for the walk to the elevator. "I may need to get my hands on you as soon as those elevator doors—"

As if on cue, the elevator stopped and the doors opened. Troy, Wes, and Keaton stared back at them. So much for Duke getting his hands on her.

Caitlyn laughed, clearly thinking the same thing. "Hey, y'all."

Duke wondered if he'd ever get tired of hearing that Southern drawl. He couldn't imagine it.

They stepped on and faced the doors.

"It's so unfair for you to have your girl here when we don't have ours," Wes complained.

Duke scoffed. "You've all had your girls for years."

"Fair point," Troy said.

"I'm dying to see these dailies," Keaton said. "Troy told us how you nearly fell off the rock. That would have been priceless."

Duke winced just as Caitlyn said, "You almost *fell off*?"

"Not for real," Troy backpedaled. "I mean, he wouldn't have gone far, not with all the safety anchors."

"Kingsley's got the best eye," Wes said, trying to defuse the situation. "I bet today's test shots are sick."

Then they were at the top floor walking toward one of the conference rooms, talking about the schedule for the rest of the shoot.

Duke reached the doors and pulled one open, standing aside for Caitlyn to enter.

As she passed, she paused and looked him in the eye. "You almost *fell off*? We need to have a talk."

Duke shot Keaton a glare before ushering Caitlyn in and following her with a quiet, but stern "What happened to not telling the girls?"

"She was gonna find out when she saw the dailies anyway," Keaton said as he fell in behind Duke, followed by Troy.

"*Surprise!*"

The rowdy greeting startled all of them. Ellie was the first to come forward, her gold hair down and bouncy, her gorgeous face open and excited. Troy wrapped his arms around her and pulled her off her feet. "Hey, beautiful. This is an amazing surprise."

With her legs wrapped around Troy's hips, Ellie framed his face and said, "Happy birthday, baby."

Troy was beaming. "Best gift ever."

The room erupted in excitement, the cast and crew cheered Troy's birthday—only, Troy's birthday was in December, and it was August. Wes cut a look at Duke, confirming he was thinking the same thing.

Wes found Rubi and Keaton found Brook and their boy.

And from the back of the room, Scarlett yelled, "Uncle Duke! Surprise!"

Caitlyn released his hand right as Scarlett and Paisley hit him, Scarlett grinning up at him, Paisley clinging to one leg.

"Wow, surprises all around." He reached down and pulled Paisley to sit on his forearm and ruffled Scarlett's hair with the other hand.

"It's Uncle Troy's birthday," Scarlett told him.

"I heard," he said as if it were really exciting. When Duke searched the room for Kristy, he also found Cameron, and the looks on their faces only deepened Duke's concern.

"Uh-oook," Willow called her abbreviated version of Uncle Duke. "Yuk, Mama, is uh-oook."

"Sure is, baby," Kristy said, managing a smile.

He barely heard Willow's greeting. He went straight to them, searching Kristy's and Cam's faces for the answer to the unasked question, even while giving Paisley to Wes and taking Willow from Kristy, settling her into his arms. Paisley would catch on to what they were saying; Willow wouldn't. At least not yet. Wes took Paisley toward the others.

"What happened?" he asked, keeping his voice down.

"If you'll save the rest of your greetings until after the dailies," Hadley said, "we'll get this started."

The room dimmed, and clips of the day's film filled the screen. Luckily, they began with footage from fight scenes with Keaton.

He glanced around for Caitlyn and found her sitting beside Rubi and Ellie, then refocused on Cameron.

"What happened?" he asked again.

Cam moved to the other side of Kristy, beside Duke. "Maybe Scarlett can sit with the others, closer to the screen so they can see the movie."

Kristy took Scarlett up to a row with the others and settled in. Duke repositioned Willow to his other side and stroked her hair to get her to put her head on his shoulder. Worked like a charm.

"The forensic accountant's report came in today," Cam said.

"He found a shit ton of money Peter was hiding. Someone broke into the apartment and trashed the place while Kristy was at the park with the girls. Tore up the kids' room, ruined everything. Even cut up their stuffed animals."

Peter's attorney most likely got a copy of the reports and told Peter. This was retribution for finding the money. They all knew it. And the best way to hurt Kristy was to hurt the girls.

"That mother*fucker*."

"No good word," Willow said, her voice sleepy.

"I know, baby. Close your ears and go to sleep."

"We're getting the locks changed and adding more security measures," Cam said. "I got a service to clean everything up before we get back."

The others were laughing at something on the screen. Keaton's fights were usually entertaining. He had a way of fitting his sense of humor into the way he fought. Sometimes those antics made it to the final; sometimes they ended up on the cutting room floor.

"Did you call the police?" Duke asked.

"Yeah. They took a report. I showed them the security footage, but the guy wore a hoodie, gloves, and face mask. Couldn't even tell if he was Black, Caucasian, or Hispanic. Or male or female, for that matter."

Shit.

Duke felt torn again. He needed this work. But he needed to know his family was safe too.

"Maybe they should stay here," Duke told Cam. "There are two beds in my room, and I can stay with Caitlyn."

Cam's brows shot up, and he grinned. "Is that right?"

Duke laughed. "Yeah."

Cam held out a fist, and Duke met it with a smirk. "Nice catch, dude. Really nice catch."

Duke glanced toward Caitlyn, where her head was bent to

listen to Kristy. He loved the way Caitlyn slid into the family seamlessly. "Yeah, she is."

"I've got a guy," Cam said.

"You've got a guy?"

"He owes me a favor. He's going to stay with them during the day, while I'm on the set."

"Yeah?"

Cam nodded. "Ex-cop. He's working as a PI. Most of his work happens at night anyway. I'd trust him to watch my kids, I mean, if I had any."

"Okay. Yeah. We can try it. The girls have had so many changes, it would be better for them to stay in LA, but not at the expense of anyone's safety. The second any of you feel like things are going sideways, pack them up and bring them back."

"You got it."

"Thanks, Cam. I owe you."

"No sweat."

Duke exhaled long and deep, feeling fucking helpless. "No one told Jax, right? I don't want to bother him. He and Lexi work their asses off. They deserve this time."

"We all agreed," Cam said. "No one is calling Jax or Lexi."

Duke's jaw pulsed. He'd spent the last two years fighting a feeling of powerlessness when it came to Kristy's divorce. He was so over it. They all were.

"The final hearing isn't too far away," Cam said. "Things may calm down after a judge puts Peter in line."

"Only if it's a judge who *will* put Peter in line and not someone whose pockets have been lined with Peter's money."

"Shit," Cam said. "I didn't think of that."

"I can't wait to be done with this motherfucker."

"Kinda weird coming to Canada to escape him when he's here."

"He'd never do his own dirty work, which means he can be

anywhere and cause trouble. Anything else happens while I'm here, I'm going to hunt that fucker down."

"I don't see confrontation doing anything good when it comes to this guy."

"Maybe not, but losing a few teeth might make him think twice."

32

Caitlyn really wanted to focus on the incredible footage of Duke climbing, but she was distracted by the knot in her gut.

The crew was one hundred percent into the film, cheering and gasping at the appropriate moments, while Caitlyn drifted into the muck of guilt.

She knew it wasn't her fault, that she had nothing to do with Peter or the divorce, but somehow, working for Porsha, knowing her boss was causing all this hell for these amazing people, made her sick. It also made her hate her boss even more than she already did.

Caitlyn would rather be working for Kristy, using her skills to put this mother of three in a good light and exposing Peter for the narcissistic sociopathic criminal he was.

Of course, that wouldn't pay the bills.

She refocused on the screen. On Duke moving up a giant cliff face by his fingers and toes. Close-ups showed how every muscle bulged any time he used them, which was every second. Caitlyn tried to lose herself in his raw, God-given beauty, then, without warning, a piece of rock broke off in Duke's hand.

Caitlyn gasped, and her whole body went tight. Then he started sliding, creating a dust cloud that did nothing to hide his attempt to find something to grip, only grabbing something after he'd fallen off the slope.

While the crew cheered like crazy, Caitlyn covered her face with both hands and tried not to throw up.

A hand closed on her shoulder. It was Duke, standing at the end of the row. "Looks more dramatic than it was."

The lights came up, and Hadley and Kingsley waved Duke over. He gave her shoulder another squeeze before heading that direction.

Everyone was talking and laughing, refilling drinks, eating snacks. She watched Duke talk with Kingsley and Hadley before Leo joined them. Then Hadley walked away, clearly fed up with Leo. Caitlyn couldn't blame him.

With Willow still asleep on his shoulder, Duke used his other hand to plot something on a whiteboard, explaining whatever it was to the other two. Whatever they were discussing pissed Leo off. But, then, everything seemed to piss Leo off.

The sight of that little toddler all safe and secure in Duke's big, strong arms made Caitlyn ache on a deep level. She'd wanted kids all her life, had dreamed of being a mom from the moment she got her first doll as a kid. But she'd never imagined having a man who was as equally competent with children as herself.

Her dream started to fade when she'd returned home from college and realized just how much she and Brett had grown apart. He wanted to wait for kids. He worked long hours, trying to advance his career, while expecting Caitlyn to be satisfied with a boring, unchallenging job and putting their family on hold. They never went out or took trips. He had no hobbies for her to share. And he'd been adamantly opposed to the idea of couples counseling.

She'd fallen out of love with him one day at a time.

Now she was looking at an incredible guy who'd sacrificed his job—really, his entire life—to keep his family safe, to make sure they had what they needed. A completely different kind of man from Brett, and Caitlyn couldn't be happier about that.

"Are you okay?"

Caitlyn popped back to the present and tried to smile at Kristy. "Yeah. I just... That footage about knocked me off my feet. And I feel so bad about what Peter and Porsha are doing to you."

Kristy gave her forearm a squeeze. "None of this has anything to do with you. Peter is Peter. He would have found a way to stab me in the back, Porsha just made it easier for him."

Caitlyn released a long, troubled sigh as fatigue set in. She glanced at Duke again and smiled. "He's a natural, isn't he?"

Kristy laughed. Then laughed harder. "Sorry," she said, wiping tears from her eyes and catching her breath. "That man isn't a natural at anything but scaling cliffs. I spent our first six months living together waiting for him to bail out. We were all one big hot mess for a while, but he stuck it out. He still amazes me."

"I guess that would have been tough. Three baby girls, no experience with kids, all that stress."

"Yes. But once we all settled in, he turned out to be incredible with them. He's been more of a father than Peter ever was. He's the father figure and the fun uncle all in one. Duke is the reason the girls are so resilient. He's always teaching them how to get up, dust themselves off, wipe the tears, and keep going. I guess in a way, he's done that with me too. We've all grown so strong, it's hard to imagine anything we couldn't bounce back from now. I don't know how we would have gotten by without him, but it's time for him to get his life back."

Scarlett and Paisley were busy at the snack table, where

other members of the Renegades family helped them fill plates and get drinks.

Kristy stood. "I need to head downstairs and book a room."

"Oh no. Really?" Caitlyn stood as well. She knew their finances were tight. "Why don't you and the girls take Duke's room? He has two queens. Duke can stay with me."

Duke strolled up, grinning. "I like the direction of this conversation."

"If you're sure," Kristy said.

"She's sure," Duke answered, making Caitlyn laugh.

Her gaze drifted past Duke to where Leo stood arguing with Kingsley. "I'm beginning to think that man doesn't have a happy bone in his body. All that happiness at the press conference was bullshit, wasn't it?"

"Yep."

She shook her head, sick of all the fakeness, the lies. "What is he pissed about now?"

"He doesn't like the way Hadley wants to film his part of the climb. Even though all he'd be doing is getting into position and holding still, he's battling it." Duke glanced toward Leo, serious. "I'm starting to think he's afraid of heights."

"Oh, man." Her eyes went wide. "That would explain a lot."

Troy, Ellie, Keaton, Brook, Wes, and Rubi joined them.

"Dinner?" Troy said. "Downstairs?"

Everyone agreed and headed that direction. Duke passed up the first elevator car for an empty one all their own. With Willow still asleep on his shoulder, he used his free arm to wrap her waist and pull her up against him.

"Look at you, multitasking like a pro."

He smiled and kissed her. Then kissed her again.

"You realize the sight of you with that baby on your shoulder made every woman in that room wet, right? Maybe even a few of the guys."

That made him laugh. He slid his hand under her hair,

cupped her jaw. "You're the only woman I want wet for me. Speaking of… Let's make short work of dinner. I want to get you into bed."

Excitement percolated inside her. This thing between them seemed to have jumped the tracks, speeding into unknown territory, and she felt like she had no control over it, which was both terrifying and thrilling.

She looked at Willow's face all scrunched up against Duke's shoulder. "She's precious."

"She's precious when she's sleeping. Awake, she is another thing entirely."

"You're going to make a great dad." Her gaze skipped to his, unsure whether or not she should have brought that up.

But he smiled and stroked a lock of hair off Willow's forehead. "I've certainly had enough practice. At least at the young stages. The thought of these three as teenagers seriously scares the living shit out of me."

"Do you want kids?"

His gaze settled on hers again, and he didn't answer right away.

"It's okay," she said. "You don't have to—"

"I don't know. I mean, kids aren't something most men think about. Not the way women do."

The elevator doors opened, and he wrapped his hand around hers. "I'm not sure I've ever seen myself as having kids, really. With my job, I'd be lucky if I found a woman who'd stay long enough to even contemplate kids. But after living with these little terrors, I can't imagine the rest of my life without kids of my own. I think it would be the biggest adventure of my life."

"That's saying something based on what you do for a living."

He grinned. "I guess so."

A slow smile crossed her face until her cheeks hurt.

"What?" he asked.

She shook her head. "You're just...I don't know...different from any man I've ever met."

He stroked his thumb across her cheekbone. "I'll take that as a compliment."

In the restaurant, the Renegades' table was already the loudest in the place, and they hadn't even put in drink orders yet.

"I swear I threw that damn rifle to him *twenty* times," Keaton said, sharing funnies from the set.

This used to be Duke's favorite time of day, sitting around bullshitting with the guys after a great day of filming. He'd missed this.

"It started out legit," Keaton said. "He was going to catch it and reposition, prepared to shoot. But he couldn't catch it, or I couldn't throw it. Then we started laughing, and catching it was even harder. In the end, we got sloppy and just threw it at each other for fun. After about a dozen tries, Jeb knew every take would be blown, so he started putting his tongue in the clapper." Keaton's laughter faded with a sigh. "Good times."

"My favorite," Wes said, "was when Cahill was filming that intense scene where he's down on his stomach, hiding in brush, waiting for the enemy—"

"And the gun kept getting leaves stuck in the hammer," Keaton finished, laughing and shaking his head. "I love my job."

Kristy sat between the two older girls helping them with the games on the child's paper place mat. When Duke slid into the booth with Willow, the baby didn't move. Didn't even lift her head to see what all the noise was about.

"Man, she's out," Caitlyn said.

"Probably travel and stress," Kristy said. "She loves to be in everybody's business, but she forgets she's two, not twenty."

"Troy forgets he's two every damn day." Wes's comment

brought another round of laughter. Caitlyn loved being around these vibrant, happy people. She knew exactly why Lexi was so damned happy with her life. Caitlyn was excited to be stepping into an incredible life of her own.

Willow's cheeks looked overly pink, and Caitlyn pressed the back of her hand to Willow's neck. "She feels a little on the hot side, but then she is chest to chest with a wall of muscle that kicks off heat like a furnace."

"True."

They managed to get the drink order in before crew and cast started coming to the table to say hello. A lot of hand-shaking and shade tossing ensued. When she glanced at Duke, she found him watching her with a soft look in his eyes. One that made joy break open inside her.

"You want me to take her for a while?" she asked Duke.

"No, I'm okay, but I may take you up on that offer if I can't find something I can eat with one hand."

They were thigh to thigh in the booth, and Duke slid his free hand along her leg while he looked at the menu. Caitlyn wished they could have gone with their original plan—sex, then dinner.

She didn't know how she could be so crazy about anyone this fast, but there was no doubt she was head over heels for this man. She covered his hand and threaded their fingers together, giving his hand a squeeze.

"You could do a burrito," she told Duke. "Or something you could cut with the side of your fork." She smiled and met his gaze. "Or I could cut your food for you like I did with my brothers."

"Funny."

Someone walked through Caitlyn's direct line of sight in the lobby. Leo, on a mission.

"For the love of God."

Duke looked up and saw Leo. "Let him go. He needs to feel some of the consequences of being a prick and an idiot."

"You have no idea how much I'd love to do that, but I can't." She gave his thigh a squeeze. "I'm sorry. Can I get out?"

He heaved a sigh, but stood. "Want me to come?"

"No. You've got your hands full." She apologized to the others and pushed to her toes to kiss Duke.

"Call me when you get back?" he asked.

"Most definitely."

She was beyond annoyed when she caught up with Leo, out front waiting for a taxi. "What happened to a quiet night in?"

"I got another invitation to dinner. All that publicity from the press conference put a bug in another producer's ear. He wants to talk jobs, and you're not coming."

"You're welcome."

"This is business. You have no reason to come."

The taxi pulled up, and Caitlyn stepped into the open doorway before Leo could close it the way he'd done the first night they were there. "I go where you go."

He rolled his eyes as Caitlyn sat next to him. "I'm going to fire Porsha."

"Great. I want to get rid of you just as much as you want to get rid of me. And I'd love to use at least some of the footage of you acting like a prick."

When his head jerked toward her, she lifted her cell phone and wiggled it. "I'm sure *Star* would pay more than my yearly salary for what I've got."

"Where to?" the driver asked.

Leo was throwing daggers at Caitlyn, but he said, "Five Sails."

Caitlyn looked up the restaurant and cringed. It was a five-star restaurant on the water. She googled their dress code and found that they'd done away with it and now accepted everything down to a T-shirt and jeans. The article said if that was the guest's choice of dress, be prepared to feel out of place and field disapproving looks.

She breathed easier. She'd spent her life fielding disapproval, and she didn't give a flying fuck how others looked at her.

"You're not sitting at our table," Leo said, looking out the side window.

"Fine with me."

"And you're not cutting our night short because you want to leave."

She thought of Duke waiting on her, and her heart sank. "Whatever. But my dinner is on your tab."

"No, it's not. Expense it."

"You didn't give me any notice, so I don't have my wallet," she lied. She had a credit card and cash tucked into her cell phone's case.

She texted Duke. *Looks like it's going to be a long night for me. Sorry. Rain check?*

Well, you were right about Willow. She's burning up and just puked all over me, so it looks like it's going to be a long night for me too.

I'm not sure which of us got the worse end of the deal.

He texted back an upside-down smiling emoji and: *Double rain check.*

Caitlyn glanced out the window at the countryside slowly turning into city. "What kind of role?"

"Leading, what else?"

"That's not what I meant. You do know being a prick is optional, right? You can change that any time you want."

That was the end of their conversation, and Caitlyn enjoyed the silence for the rest of the ride.

The restaurant was in the middle of downtown Vancouver, a relatively modern business district. She followed Leo into the foyer and was greeted by a host who did indeed look down his nose at her.

"Mr. Woods." The man offered Leo a stiff smile. "It's good to see you again. I didn't see your name on the reservations list, but you're always welcome, of course. Will it be just the two of you?"

"No. The reservation is under a different name. Fontaine."

The name hit Caitlyn like ice water, and a chill snaked around in her stomach.

"Oh yes, I see it now," the host said. "But the reservation is for two..."

"It is," Leo said, "just Peter and me. You can put my assistant anywhere you have an extra seat."

Holy mother of God. Peter Fontaine. The man was lucky Duke wasn't there.

"As long as I can see him," Caitlyn added quickly. "He's good at disappearing acts."

The host gave her a nod, and she and Leo followed him through the restaurant.

Maybe Caitlyn did care what others thought, at least a little, because other diners most definitely, purposely looked at her. She distracted herself with the ornate chandeliers, gilded posts and tables dressed in, not one, but two linen tablecloths with elaborate place settings.

She felt like she did when she flew first class. Strange. Tense. Uncomfortable.

She was relieved when the host gestured to a table at the windows offering an amazing view of the water, the boats, the city skyline. All just before sunset.

"Mr. Woods." The host gestured to the table, and Leo took his seat, then claimed the menu the host offered.

The host gestured to another table, away from the windows across the walkway. A tiny table snuggled up against one of those rotund pillars. The table couldn't have been any closer to the kitchen. In fact, she was pretty sure that every time someone came out of that kitchen, she'd get the jolt of the door against the back of her chair. "Miss."

He pulled out her chair, then offered her a menu.

Caitlyn looked around the other tables to take in the view. This was surreal. Truly. The day before she'd left for LA, she'd had dinner with her family at Chuck's Ribs, on an old picnic table, outside, under a torn awning while her brothers fought.

She settled in, and a man dressed in a black vest, black pants, and a crisp white shirt immediately stopped at her table to pour her ice water.

"Good evening, ma'am."

"Hey."

"Your server will be right over."

"You're not the waiter? This place sure has some fancy busboys."

He laughed. "Can I get you anything to drink?"

"Do y'all have Mississippi Punch?"

His smile deepened, but not in a condescending way. "A woman who knows how to drink."

She grinned. Mississippi Punch included three liquors—bourbon, cognac, and rum.

"If the bartender doesn't know how to make it, I'll tell him," the busboy offered.

"You don't sound Southern."

"I'm not, but I have friends who are, and your accent tells me you're a ways from home."

"Oh, you have no idea."

He laughed.

"Can you have them add a little peach liqueur to the punch?"

"Absolutely."

"Thank you."

"Of course."

He headed toward the bar, and Caitlyn looked at Leo. He was leaning forward, elbows on the table, hands clasped as he appreciated the view. Her mama would have knocked her arms out from under her if Caitlyn put her elbows on the table like that.

Her stomach growled, and she looked at the menu. Thankfully, it was in English. Mostly. She scanned the very short list of offerings and deflated. Froufrou food. And judging by the plates she'd seen on the way in, a very limited amount of froufrou food.

The server stopped by the table. He wore a half apron and carried a linen over his arm. "Hello, I'm Christopher. I'll be your server tonight. How are you?"

"I'm hanging in there."

He smiled. He was in his midthirties, light hair, balding on the crown. "Do you have any questions about the menu?"

"Yes. Are there any rules about eating dessert first?"

He laughed. "No."

"That's great news. It's not exactly dessert, but it's on the dessert menu. I'll start with the cheese plate." Various cheeses, candied pecans, toasted fruit and nut bread sounded like the best way to start.

"One of my favorites," he said.

"And I'll be ordering real dessert at some point. I'm here with my boss." She gestured to his table. "So the longer he talks, the more I'll eat."

Christopher seemed to enjoy her sense of humor. "Very good."

Not two minutes after Christopher left, the busboy returned and set her drink down. "Complete with peach liqueur."

"Fantastic. Thank you."

He nodded, and Caitlyn was alone again. There were two empty bar glasses on Leo's table. She hoped he didn't get stupid drunk. She really didn't want to deal with that.

Another man, who could only be Peter, swept in and shook Leo's hand before sitting, facing Caitlyn. He had a deep voice, one that carried, which was perfect for her.

He gave the space a casual glance, as if looking for others he might know. His gaze rolled past Caitlyn, then bounced back and held. He smiled at her. She smiled back. He was handsome. And well dressed. And, judging by the way he was smiling, both charming and sleazy.

Caitlyn saw a lot of Scarlett in him—the chin dimple, the forehead. Paisley looked like Duke, and, though it was a little early to tell, she thought Willow looked like Kristy.

When Peter began talking with Leo, she tapped into her phone and scrolled through Instagram and Facebook. She'd planned to brainstorm promotion options, but Peter's presence really set her on edge.

She had the crazy urge to call Duke, but nothing good could come of that.

Caitlyn couldn't understand how Peter could be so damn vengeful. Kristy was the mother of his children. And a good one. That alone was enough reason to treat her with respect. Instead, he'd cut her off from all her resources and launched a smear campaign. How vile did someone have to be to do those things? Especially given he was hurting the kids.

As they jawed on about the industry Caitlyn tried to focus on her job, but she couldn't keep her mind off Peter and Kristy and the girls and Duke. She wanted to do something. Intervene in some way. Slay the fucking dragon.

Five drinks later—for the men, not Caitlyn—midway through dinner, trash talk edged into their conversation. They mentioned names Caitlyn didn't know, talked about situations and events she had no frame of reference for. But she knew trash talk when she heard it. She couldn't imagine their conversation was worth holding on to, didn't even know if she could capture it, but she tapped into an app on her phone and turned on the recorder anyway.

Three more drinks and the trash talk got dirty. This guy handled that movie wrong. That guy was fucking so-and-so's wife. Another guy got pushed out of that coveted role. Yet another guy's sidepiece was pregnant.

These men were mean, miserable people, looking for any outlet they could find to belittle others so they could feel big.

Caitlyn was starting to realize everyone had been right—LA was a swamp dressed up to look like an oasis. As soon as you dipped your toe in the water, a crocodile came up to bite your foot off.

A heavy feeling made her restless. She felt helpless. Hopeless. How did anyone beat someone with the kind of power and money Peter had?

Caitlyn covered her mouth to conceal a yawn. All she wanted to do was slide into bed beside Duke and let him take her far, far away from all her troubles.

It was long past dinner, and the chill feeling from her two Mississippi Punches had worn off. Mostly. The men enjoyed yet another night cap. Their livers had to be dead by now.

Out of the corner of her eye, she caught a strange movement at their table. She did her best to look side-eyed, so she didn't stifle whatever was going on there.

Peter slid his hand across the table toward Leo. Leo met his hand halfway and they transferred something beneath their fingers. There was no way she could see—

Then Leo lifted it off the table, and Caitlyn got a split-second look at a clear baggie hardly big enough for a peanut, holding a white powder. The exact same kind of baggie Duke had pulled out of the business card Leo had given her at the club not all that long ago.

The brazenness of the drug deal stunned Caitlyn. She'd

always imagined drug deals in dark alleys, not in a packed five-star restaurant.

That had to be bad for court, right? A judge wouldn't give custody of three little girls to a guy who traded coke in a crowded restaurant, would they?

Unfortunately, all she had was a recording of them trash talking. No video. No proof. Leo certainly wouldn't turn the coke over to Caitlyn.

Get it yourself.

It was barely a thought. More like a whisper in the back of her mind. Going over and asking for some, that would be bold and risky. And that was who she was now, a woman who picked up and left everything behind to take her chances in Hollywood.

All she had to do was think of those three adorable girls or the way Duke loved them to commit to the idea.

Caitlyn scanned her mind for all she'd learned about drugs during her internet searches after she'd been told Leo was an addict.

She took a deep breath, stood, and pulled her chair to their table, then dropped down, looked at each shocked face, smiled, and said, "Hey, y'all."

"We talked about this." Leo turned hostile immediately. "We had an agreement. Get back to your own table or leave."

"I'll go away," she said, turning her attention and her best smile on Peter. She lowered her voice. "But I could really use some of what you just gave him."

"You've got to be fucking kidding me," Leo said. "You wouldn't know what the hell to do with it."

"Sugar, what do you think we kids do with all our free time out in the country?"

"Introduce us, Leo," Peter said.

"She's just my assistant—"

"I'm his fixer. I know how to get anyone out of anything.

Confidentially. Just imagine what I've been dealing with, repping Leo. I could use a little high."

Peter laughed, loud and deep. "I like you."

She glanced left and right, then pulled her phone from her back pocket. "I don't have much on me," she said, voice low. "About forty bucks. I know prices here are probably higher than I'm used to—"

"You told me you didn't bring your wallet," Leo said.

"I didn't. This is my emergency fund."

"Coke is on your emergency list?"

"Shh," she chastised Leo, then smiled at Peter again and rolled her eyes, like Leo was such an idiot, making Peter laugh.

"I have to confess," she said, "I've seen your name on some of my favorite films." *Please don't ask which ones.* "And when Leo told me you were going to meet, I couldn't pass up a chance to meet *the* Peter Fontaine. Big fan."

"Thank you, sweetheart." He crossed his arms on the table and leaned toward her.

"I don't need much. A quarter, an eighth. Whatever you've got on hand."

"I think I can drum up a little candy for you."

"It's clean, right? I assume a man of your caliber wouldn't accept anything but quality, but I've got to ask. Good to be safe, right? I mean, with the fentanyl scares out there nowadays..."

"Beautiful and smart. My candy is always pure, but probably not quite as pure as you."

Somehow that statement made her stomach roll.

"Tell you what." Peter reached inside his blazer and brought out a bag just like the one he'd given Leo, thumb and forefinger pressed securely to the plastic. "I'll trade you, this for your phone number."

She grinned. "Hand me your phone, and I'll add myself."

He unlocked his cell and handed it to her. Caitlyn navigated to his contact list, added herself with her real first name, but a random number with a Whitley County, Kentucky prefix.

She handed it back to Peter, took the baggy by the very top, and let it rest ever so softly in her palm, praying she didn't mess up any fingerprints she hoped he'd left on the bag.

"I will leave you gentlemen to talk. There are no paparazzi in sight, so I'm going to head back to the hotel. You, be good," she said to Leo, then turned her smile on Peter. "And you, call me."

The walk back to the entry seemed to take forever. Her stomach jumped and twisted, her heart beat too fast, and as she grabbed the door handle, she was sure two big burly men were going to jump out and haul her off to jail.

But then she stepped outside and found the night cool and quiet.

After a thug-free moment, Caitlyn exhaled hard. She had to hold on to the banister to stay upright.

Once the fear eased, she was able to take in more air and get her mind working again.

She'd just traded her phone number—albeit fake—for coke. She was holding *cocaine* in her hand.

Sure, it was for the right reason, but she still had fucking cocaine in her hand.

She was shaking as she turned off the recorder and ordered an Uber.

She didn't know what to do with the coke. Her pocket? Her bra? She didn't want to risk losing the fingerprints, so she just left it lying lightly in her palm and acted like she was carrying nitroglycerin.

Once she was in the car, headed away from the restaurant, she could finally pull in a deep breath. She opened her palm to see the bag tilted just enough to keep the flat sides mostly off her skin. She had no idea what she was doing. She'd watched one too many true crime shows and now thought she was a goddammed private investigator or something.

Her mind opened from its pinpoint focus, and when she looked at things on a grander scale, she realized that in a single week here, she'd slept with a guy the same night she'd met him, taken a job she was elbowed into, lied to save face, done a drug deal, and now carried cocaine.

Still, she couldn't help but feel like she'd done something good for a change.

Now, she just had to find the best path to expose Peter.

33

Duke paced the floor of the hotel hallway, with Willow on his shoulder so Kristy and the other girls could get some sleep.

Willow had stopped puking about an hour ago. Tylenol had brought her temperature down, and she was finally asleep.

Without the immediate worry of Willow's flu, his mind strayed to Caitlyn. It wasn't exactly late, but later than he expected, and he wanted her back. He hated having her doting on Leo, cleaning up his messes, crossing lines she didn't even know were dangerous.

He hated Porsha for trapping Caitlyn into this job. For giving Caitlyn such a prick to manage for her first time. He didn't know who Leo was meeting, and there were a lot of amazingly awesome people in Hollywood, but Leo didn't fall into that category. So whoever he was meeting was probably not in that category either, and Duke didn't want any of them near Caitlyn.

He was so fucking possessive of her. He shouldn't be. But he was.

His cell buzzed with a message from Caitlyn. *I'm back. How's Willow?*

A deep sense of relief filled him, and he sighed and let his eyes fall closed for a second. *Finally asleep. Over the puking. Fever's coming down.*

That's great.

When I put her down, do you want me to come over?

An immediate answer didn't come. He waited. And waited. Tried to convince himself that she hadn't answered because she hadn't seen the message, not because she didn't want him to come over.

When had he turned into a damn chick?

I'd love that, but only if they don't need you.

He would have preferred something more enthusiastic like *I haven't been able to think about anything but you* or *Get your fine ass over here and fuck me.*

He texted back, *Be there in five.*

He settled Willow on the bed with Scarlett and put pillows between Willow and the edge of the bed. She was sleeping in a toddler bed at home, but he didn't want to take any chances.

"She okay?"

Duke turned toward Kristy, cuddled up with Paisley in the other bed. "Yeah. Asleep. Fever's down."

She sighed and rubbed her eyes. "Thank you. You're climbing tomorrow. You need to get some sleep."

"Caitlyn is back. I'm going to her room."

"I really like her."

"Me too. Call if you need me."

"I'll make sure not to need you. Enjoy Caitlyn."

In the elevator, Duke tried to curb his expectations. She was probably tired. Possibly annoyed as hell. It didn't matter. He just wanted to be with her.

At her door, he knocked softly with one knuckle.

Caitlyn opened the door as if she'd been standing right there and stepped aside as he entered.

"Hey," he said as he passed and turned toward her. "How was—"

His words evaporated. She was in nothing but a towel. And a second later, she was in absolutely nothing at all.

"Holy..." He didn't have the words. "God damn." He tried to take all of her in, all at once. "You're so fucking gorgeous."

She was small framed, delicate, yet curvy. He slid his hands down her arms around her waist, over her ass, and moaned. "You have no idea how badly I needed you."

Her hands found their way under his T-shirt, pushing it up, tugging it off. "Oh, I think I might."

Her hands were warm, and her touch made him lightheaded. He cupped her head and kissed her. She opened and stroked her tongue into his mouth, making him moan. Caitlyn worked his pants open, pushed them down, then pulled everything off.

Naked, he wrapped her tight and lifted her off her feet. She giggled. "You smell like baby."

"Not baby puke, I hope. I showered and changed."

"No, just sweet baby scent. It's surprisingly...hot. The way it's panty melting to see you with a sleeping baby on your shoulder."

"That's all well and good, but let's work on getting me smelling like you. Because you smell amazing."

Caitlyn wrapped her thighs around his hips, her arms around his neck, and sank into the kiss. Every time they slept together, she became a little less timid, a lot more exploratory. He loved every second of it.

"What happened with Leo?" he asked.

"Same stupid stuff, different day."

He laughed.

"Can we not talk about Leo? I really just want to get lost in you."

"I'm onboard with that." He turned and sat on the edge of the bed.

She pressed her knees to the mattress and shimmied a little, then kissed him again, like she was starved for him. This sure as hell beat her simply telling him she wanted him.

He broke the kiss for air and trailed his mouth down her neck and across her shoulder. As he stroked his hands up her back, Caitlyn palmed his cock until he moaned, then rocked her hips and took him halfway.

"Fuck." He rested his forehead on her shoulder and gritted his teeth as she rocked him deeper and deeper. "You feel so good."

She cupped his face and lifted his gaze to meet hers. "Couldn't stop thinking about this all night. How incredible you feel inside me."

Duke felt himself falling. Day by day, he just kept finding things to love about her, and in moments like this, he was just about ready to admit—at least to himself—he might be more than crazy about her.

He wrapped his arm around her hips and moved back on the bed. He lay back, and Caitlyn followed, chest to chest, her hands in his hair, her mouth exploring his neck, jaw, ear.

He wanted to let go, but he also wanted to hold on. They'd gone from zero to sixty in seconds. Duke wanted to savor her, but his control seemed to evaporate when he touched her.

She straightened, sinking deeper onto his cock, making them both moan. With her hands pressed to his chest, she rode him, slowly at first. Her hips undulating, hair falling over one shoulder, her gaze never leaving Duke's. He'd never seen anything so fucking beautiful in his life.

The wetter she got, the deeper she sank. The deeper she sank, the faster she moved. Watching her find pleasure was one thing. Watching her exploit it on her climb to the peak was one goddamned incredible thrill.

When she reached behind herself and braced her hands on his thighs, she was glowing with sweat and lost in euphoria. Still riding him, Caitlyn offered him a front-row seat at the most erotic show, maybe, in his life. Her piercing sparkled at him every time she rocked her hips.

She was all his, and he made sure he touched her everywhere. He gripped her hips, her waist, her breasts.

"God, you're beautiful." She was also soft and warm and gorgeous. He pressed his palm low on her belly and one at her hip, feeling the movements as he watched them, intensifying everything. He rested his thumb over her clit with the slightest pressure. She moaned and rode him faster.

"More, more, more." Her eyes were barely open, her head barely upright, lips parted and pulling in quick shallow breaths.

"Fuck." She brought one hand around and covered Duke's, adding the pressure she needed to climax. And what a fucking climax. Back arched, one hand gripping his thigh, the other squeezing his hand, head dropped back, a cry of pleasure joining the moans and whimpers. Duke continued to rock his fingers across her, drawing out mini climaxes until she melted against him, limp, panting.

"Jesus. That's insane," she said. "If I'd known this was what I was missing, I'd have broken up with Brett a lot sooner."

Duke rolled Caitlyn to her back, where he kissed her neck, her shoulder, her biceps, and thanked the gods she'd left Brett.

"I mean, it's crazy, right?" she said, voice soft, hands sliding over his sweaty skin. "Or is this, like, normal sex I just never figured out?"

He chuckled. "No, sugar. This is several levels above normal."

She tilted her head and laid her cheek on his biceps, her smile lazy, her eyes dreamy.

And damn... Yeah, he loved her. Like, *really* loved her. He felt the pull of it deep inside him. It hadn't exactly come out of nowhere, but it still seemed a little intense for such a short time knowing her. Though that didn't seem all that far out of bounds when he climbed mountains for a living.

He lay back. Caitlyn pressed her chest to his, touching him, kissing him. He let his fingers travel up and down her arm, let his lips touch whatever skin he could reach.

When she looked in his eyes again, she stopped and searched his. "What's going on? What aren't you saying?"

He let out a slow breath and tried to figure out how to tiptoe around this. He knew telling her how he felt right now was out of the question. Neither of them was ready for that.

Caitlyn shifted, rocked her hips, and stoked the heat. "Never mind." She kissed him. "Just fuck me."

He groaned a laugh. "God. That is so damn sexy coming out of that sweet Southern mouth of yours."

She leaned in and nipped his jaw. "This sweet Southern mouth wants to do more than talk."

"Bring it on down here, Sugar Pop."

She broke out laughing. Laughing and laughing and laughing. She was still catching her breath when he wrapped a hand behind her neck and pulled her down.

She'd become one hell of a kisser over the last week. Her mouth was loose and warm, and the way she used it made him ache.

He rolled and sank his hips deep between her legs. She sucked a breath. One hand fisted in the sheets, the other gripped his ass cheek. Duke pressed one hand to the headboard and wrapped the other behind her knee. He pulled her thigh wide, pressed it back, and gave in to his banked need.

She moaned, whimpered, cried out. Her sounds rang in his

ears, amped his need. He was having a hell of a time holding off. They just got hotter and hotter, and right now, he felt like liquid fire filled his veins.

"Come for me, sugar," he said, his voice low and rough.

"Oh my God."

"That's it. Talk to me." Sweat dripped off his chin and slid down her chest, between her breasts. "This is so fucking good."

"God..."

"Ready for you. Come on, bring it."

He swore she came on command. A fist-clenching orgasm that would leave nail marks on his neck and nearly tore the sheets.

Only when every last shiver had passed through her body, only when she sank into the mattress, only then did he let go.

Duke buried his face against her neck and breathed her in. She moved her hand from the sheet to his ass cheek, and the bite of her nails pushed him off the cliff.

Ecstasy ripped through his body in a white-hot wave, singeing the edges of his brain, drenching his closed eyelids with stars.

He floated for what felt like a long time, right there, tangled up with her. He couldn't believe how fucking amazing he felt. Couldn't begin to think of the last time he'd felt this good.

He wrapped her tight and rolled them to their sides, then dropped kisses all along her neck and back around to her mouth.

They stayed like that a long time. He stroked her arm, kissed her neck. Rubbed his thigh against hers.

His mind turned to normal life, and curiosity sparked. "So, who did you two meet tonight?"

She let out a deep sigh. "I try to ignore most of what Leo does. He wouldn't let me sit at their table. I was at a tiny table next to the kitchen. But have no fear, I still got some ridiculously overpriced food—on Leo. A couple of drinks too." She barely let a beat pass before she changed the subject. "Do you think Willow just has the flu? Poor little thing."

If that wasn't talking around a question, he didn't know what was. That only made him want to know more. But in the end, it really didn't matter. She was safe. She was happy. She was in bed with him.

"She had a really rough night," he said, thinking back to Willow's crying and puking. "But I think she's on the downhill slide. I bet she's bubbling again by morning. That kid is a fighter."

"You're so amazing." The affection in her words warmed him. She let her index finger trace the length of his nose and along his jaw. "You've got to climb tomorrow. And you're filming. Big day on the rocks. You should sleep."

Duke rolled to his back and Caitlyn repositioned herself so her head was on his chest, her body halfway on top of his. In three minutes, she was out, arm across his body, hand over his, fingers threaded.

They might be as close as they could get physically, but emotionally, there was something about her not elaborating on her night that left a little sliver of unease. One he did his damnedest to ignore, because it probably didn't amount to anything.

34

Caitlyn rose from sleep, heavy and confused. It was still dark. Duke still lay beside her.

Her phone vibrated on the nightstand. A call at this hour of the night was never good. She looked at the display, saw Leo's number, and groaned, imagining what trouble he'd gotten himself into now.

"Who's that?" Duke curled his fingers around hers, and tugged her close again.

"Leo."

"What would he possibly call about at this hour?"

"I wish I could say I don't care." She rolled away from Duke again, sat up on the edge of the bed, and answered. "Leo, this is way too late to—"

"You need to come. Now." His words were slurred.

"Why?"

"I don't know... They're not... Please come."

"You're not making sense."

"Get. Up. Here." Those words came out clear. "A big mess. Such a mess."

Caitlyn disconnected and stood.

"You're not going." It was less demand, more shock.

"It won't take long." She stepped into her jeans and slid into her bra and top.

"Caitlyn."

She leaned down to kiss him before she left, and he held on to her. "Don't go."

"I have to."

"No, you don't."

She exhaled and straightened. "I know it's stupid. I know I shouldn't go and should just let him get himself into trouble, but I really need a paycheck, and one call from Leo to Porsha would make me roadkill."

She grabbed her phone and headed toward the door. "Get some sleep."

Caitlyn stepped into the hallway and quietly closed the door behind her. She felt heavy and disappointed. She wanted this bullshit with Leo to be over.

In the elevator, she decided to wake Duke in a very sexy way when she got back. She was smiling as she knocked on Leo's door.

It swung open to Leo, stark naked and unhinged. "Come in, come in."

The sight of him hit her like a brick wall. "Holy hell—"

"Come in, come in, *come in*." He grabbed her wrist and jerked her inside.

She pulled away and was about to smack his face when the state of the suite hit her.

Bottles of alcohol—most empty—littered the kitchen counter, dining room table, living room floor. Assorted prescription bottles lay scattered on the coffee table, right beside a mirror dressed up in a mound of white powder, five lines, and a dollar bill.

She pressed her hands to both sides of her face, trying to understand what she was seeing. "What in God's name happened here?"

Leo weaved and swayed as he paced, hands in his hair, voice cracking with panic. "I don't know. I passed out and woke up to this."

"Go get some clothes on," she ordered.

He ignored her and gestured toward a sofa. Caitlyn got a seriously bad vibe. She sidestepped for a better view and found another completely naked man lying on the sofa, passed out. He was young. Really young. Too young.

Her stomach dropped like lead. "Who is this?" she asked as she moved toward him. "What happened?"

"We met them at the bar. Peter went back to his hotel, but these guys came here for drinks. Things got...a little wild."

"A little?" Then something else he said registered. "*They?* Is there someone else here?"

"Near the bedroom, by the table." Pacing and panicked, Leo rambled. "You told me I couldn't sleep with other women, so..."

"You twisted prick. Don't you dare put this on me." She lifted her phone, but only got the 9 pressed before Leo took it from her in a sloppy grab and nearly fell over after the fact.

"No, you can't call anyone."

She immediately lunged, trying to get her phone back. "Yes, I can."

When it was clear she'd have to get physical with this naked asshole to get her phone back, she let it go and moved to the sofa.

"This can't get out," Leo insisted. "*Can't* get out. I'll be fucked. Royally fucked."

The man's chest didn't look like it was moving. She swallowed hard and hovered her hand over his nose and mouth. The slightest flutter of air against her palm released the band of fear constricting her chest.

"I'm not gay," Leo insisted. "But this would make me look gay. I'd never be able to come back from this. Never."

"Give me the phone. I have to call for paramedics."

"You can't."

"Leo—"

"You can't. They'll tell. It will be splashed all over the front page of every sleazy tabloid by morning."

God, he was right. What a damn mess.

"It will be worse if this guy dies," she said. "Then you're looking at prison for the rest of your life."

"If they haven't died already, they won't. A coke high only lasts fifteen or twenty minutes."

"When did you become a doctor?" she yelled at him as she moved to the man near the bedroom. He too was also young, naked and unconscious but breathing.

Relief brought her to her butt. She leaned her back against the wall and glared at Leo while keeping her gaze off his very unappealing dangling privates. She was sick enough as it was.

"Give me my phone so I can google how to help them, or so help me, God, I'll be screaming this from the rooftops."

He handed it to her and continued to pace, muttering like Chicken Little. Not the vibe she needed at the moment.

"What did they take?" she asked. "What all do you have here?"

"Coke, vodka, Vicodin, Molly," he yelled at her as if this was her fault. "I don't know what else. I wasn't exactly taking notes."

"Get some fucking clothes on," she yelled back.

She tuned him out and googled how to sober up after snorting cocaine. Several articles suggested the same solutions: sleep and replenishing liquid for serotonin and dopamine production. There were apparently a few foods that would help that happen as well.

That seemed glaringly inadequate. She put her hand against her head and continued to search for a more reasonable solution, like make them drink coffee or put them in a cold shower or something. Her brain spun with crazy thoughts.

She pushed to her feet, grabbed the phone in the kitchen, and called room service. "Hi, can you send up..." She glanced at the article on her cell. "Bananas, nuts, and orange juice please? A lot. Like, really, a lot. Everything you have. Just leave it outside the door. Thanks."

"I am fucked," Leo continued to rail. "I am fuuuuuuucked."

Caitlyn was beginning to realize *she* was the one who was fucked.

She slammed the phone on the kitchen counter, turned, and slapped Leo's cheek, hard. Startled, he went quiet, eyes round and glazed. That seemed to have ended his downward spiral. For now.

But the sting burned through her hand, and she looked at her palm as if it belonged to someone else. She'd never hit anyone in her life. Tears stung her eyes, and her insides trembled. This was all a nightmare. She'd wake up, and none of this would be real.

Only, in real life, the man near the bedroom coughed and moaned.

She slid back into her shell—one she didn't even realize she was wearing—grabbed pillows and blankets from the closet, and got both unconscious men at least a little more comfortable, whether they could appreciate it or not. She was wickedly relieved when they both attempted some semblance of speech and curled up under the blankets.

Caitlyn turned on Leo, who'd dropped to a seat in a dining room chair. "For God's sake, man, *get some clothes on*, or I'll go Lorena Bobbitt on you. Then get back out here so you can eat something. Google, the all-knowing god, says it will help. Then you can sleep." When he didn't move, she said, "*Now.*"

Leo obediently went into the bedroom without a word, leaving Caitlyn to wonder how in the living hell she'd gotten here. And more importantly, how the hell she'd get out.

In the kitchen, she put a pod into the Keurig and made coffee. It might not help Leo, but it would definitely help her. And she had to stay up to keep watch on all three of them. At the first sign of distress, she would be calling the ambulance, fuck the consequences.

She dropped her elbows to the counter and rested her head in her hands, ticking off a mental list of to-dos. She needed to clean up the room so housekeeping didn't start buzzing. She had to find and clear both men's phones of any texts or photos that referenced Leo or anything about the hotel, the room, or what they planned to do tonight. She should create a sort of severance package for both of the men to ensure they didn't talk, even though that hadn't worked very well with the photographer. She didn't have many choices at the moment.

She lifted her head and scanned the eerily quiet apartment. Tears slid down her cheeks, and she rubbed them away with her palm. This was beyond surreal. Beyond nightmarish. Far worse.

This was reality.

It had only taken her a week to become an LA cliché. Everything Duke feared had come true. She had gotten trapped into compromising her values. Not only had she succumbed to the dirty underbelly of Hollywood, but she'd also crossed lines she couldn't uncross. Seen things she couldn't unsee. Learned things she couldn't unlearn. Done things she couldn't undo.

She'd changed, and not for the better. She didn't know exactly how, but she knew she'd never be the same. It was no wonder she didn't recognize herself in the mirror.

How in hell was she going to explain this to Duke? He'd told her this would happen. He'd even tried to cut her off at the pass. But, no, she'd gone full steam ahead, thinking she'd be different, and look where that had gotten her.

Now she was in a dirty city that had chewed her up and spit her out, and she wouldn't go back home even if she could. She didn't belong there anymore either. She didn't belong anywhere.

35

Duke exaggerated his movements for the cameras and climbed much more slowly than he normally would. He was supposed to be a member of the military in dire straits, trying to scale a mountain to reach help, not a rock climber doing his thing.

He didn't have to try to make it look hard. This climb was fucking intense. And he hated—absolutely hated—the camo pants he had to wear for the part. They didn't give him the range of movement he needed to climb this cliff efficiently. At least he hadn't had to wear a shirt.

As he made his way up the face of this monster, he let his fingers slip here and there. Lost his footing now and then. Those were always dramatic on film. And it wasn't hard given the bizarre shoes they'd given him, some sick combination of a climbing shoe and a military boot.

Spread-eagle against the cliff wall, he bent one knee and pushed with the other leg. He grabbed a ledge with his left hand and sank his fingers of the right into a hole. But his balance was off. His head wasn't in the right place. And his mind veered to Caitlyn, her side of the bed empty when he'd woken up.

He lost his footing and allowed the fallout to happen naturally—feet slipping, attached to the cliff with only his hands, his body swinging loose.

They'll like that, he said to himself. But he really had to keep his mind right here, right now.

With no other foot stability within reach, Duke had to use his arms to pull himself up until he could catch his heel on an edge. Then he went back to pushing with his legs.

Right hand, ledge, left toe, depression. Left hand, hole, right heel, cleft.

His fingers were beat up. His hands weren't used to this length of exposure to rough surfaces.

Climbing was usually incredibly peaceful—just one of the many things he loved about it. But now, he could barely hear himself think. The chopper was in full swing, getting dramatic footage showing how small he was in comparison to the landscape. Three camera operators hung in slings and filmed Duke from the top and both sides. One camera operator climbed alongside Duke, with handholds painted to match the rock screwed into the granite and a safety line from the top supporting him so that he barely had to climb.

Duke found the perfect spot for a double knee bar and slid into position, locking his legs into the rock, allowing him to let go and shake out his arms. It also allowed him to think about Caitlyn and how she hadn't come back to the room last night. She didn't answer his texts or calls this morning either. He was still pissed that he'd overslept and didn't have time to bang on Leo's door to find her. But that really didn't matter, because if she slept with Leo, she wasn't the woman he thought she was.

What a stupid thought. She'd never sleep with Leo.

Still, the knot in his stomach tightened a little. She didn't normally get up as early as he did. She could have responded to his texts and explained everything while he'd been climbing.

They'd dubbed the man beside him as the camera climber. His name was Bart, and he was in his forties.

He scanned the images he'd taken on the last leg of the climb, smiled, and nodded. "Nice. Really nice."

Duke turned his head to look at Bart. He wasn't even trying to hang on, both hands on the camera, that sweet harness holding him like a swing.

"Aren't you comfortable?" Duke said. "Can I get you a beer?"

Bart didn't even look up, but he was still grinning. "No, but if you find the remote, you might get lucky tonight."

Duke huffed a laugh. If he were in a better head space, he would have really laughed and bantered a little more. But he wasn't.

He eased out of the resting position and reached for more rock. In his ear, Duke listened to Hadley toss out orders to cameramen. The blades of the chopper created a windstorm and whipped Duke's hair into his face, making it hard to see.

Ledge by divot by cleft, Duke made his way to the summit, doing a push-up to get himself over the top. He was greeted by cheering from the crew who'd been dropped on the top of the mountain before Duke started his climb. They weren't his belays, but they'd all climbed, and now they would all rappel down the mountain together.

He bent at the waist and pressed his hands to his thighs to rest and catch his breath. The chopper took another dip and swung back out of the tight space.

One of the crew members brought Duke water, another handed him a sport towel, and they all started gathering equipment to head down.

"Another incredible job," Kingsley told him through the earbud.

"Really beautiful work," Hadley agreed. "Let's wrap for lunch."

Duke dropped to his butt, his feet hanging over the edge, and reached into one of the many pockets on the cargo pants. He drew out his phone and tapped the face. Two new messages. He already knew one would be from Kristy, letting him know she and the girls got home safe. If the other wasn't from Caitlyn...

He cut off his thoughts. He'd already decided to have the hotel staff do a welfare check on Leo's room.

Don't get ahead of yourself.

He unlocked the phone and tapped the messages icon. As expected, Kristy's message was waiting. And so was a text from Caitlyn.

His breath released on a whoosh. At least he knew she was okay. Then he read the text.

I'm sorry about going AWOL on you. Leo had a "guest" who needed attention. I didn't want to call and tell you because I knew you needed the sleep.

Relief flooded him. He dropped his head back and laughed, still catching his breath. "Thank God."

I'm headed down, he texted her. *Are you at base camp?*

Not yet. Pushing Leo today is like swimming in quicksand.

Leo was such an unprofessional prick. He hadn't hit stardom all that long ago, and he was looking at a very short stay if this kept up.

Now that he'd talked to Caitlyn, Duke's world had righted again. His mind cleared, his lungs expanded, and his shoulders released. Dammit. He was so crazy about her. He could only hope they could find a way to make it last long-term.

Duke methodically checked everyone's gear before they rappelled down together, then trekked to base camp.

A lunch truck was there, feeding the crew. Duke grabbed water and a protein bar from the snack table, one of the crew members handed him a hamburger, and he sat on a nearby rock to eat. A couple of guys came over and sat with him and talked about rock climbing.

Duke could talk about this topic all day, but he kept his eyes on the trail that led from the parking area to base camp.

It was another twenty minutes before Leo appeared, complete with scowl and tense shoulders. Duke should probably keep his distance until he had to work with Leo to keep the friction down. He was still waiting for Caitlyn to arrive when Hadley came into the eating area.

"Attention, please." Hadley waited until the buzz died down.

Caitlyn appeared on the trail and stayed on the edge of the area while Hadley spoke. She wore khaki-colored pants, drawstrings at the ankles, sandals, and another one of those cropped blouses that showed off her middle. She had her hair up, and damn, she looked tired. It was in the slant of her shoulders and the fatigue in her expression. He'd bet she'd been up all night taking care of this "guest."

"We've got a little summer thunderstorm coming in," Hadley said. "We've got about three hours left of dry weather, and we'd like to use the stormy skies as a backdrop. The bad news is we need to cut the lunch break short. The good news is you'll all get off work early."

The camp buzzed as everyone collected their things and returned to their jobs.

Duke started toward both Leo and Caitlyn, but Leo walked right past him.

Caitlyn stopped a few feet away. "It's been *a day*," she said, "and it's barely noon."

He slid his hand around the back of her neck and gave it a squeeze. "Give me a few hours to torture him on the rocks, and we can chill tonight, talk about everything."

She exhaled slowly and tried to smile. “Yeah. That sounds amazing.”

He gave her a kiss.

“Be safe,” she told him.

“Always.”

36

Caitlyn watched Duke grab gear and head down the path leading to the cliffs.

Today, she followed. She wanted an up close look at Duke doing his thing. She also wanted to be close to him. Probably because she knew their relationship had the potential to implode soon.

The guys all suited up in harnesses and their belays rigged ropes. Duke kept his distance from Leo and assigned him the most experienced belay. Beau, the set medic, hung off to the side, watching. He was quiet, but intense.

Caitlyn's mind went back over last night and this morning, minute by minute. All three men had gotten through the early morning hours fine. She sent the other two stumbling partiers home with a wad of cash in exchange for their signatures on the nondisclosure form. The cash covered the cell phones she'd confiscated, hoping to keep from repeating the same mistake she'd made at the club.

She found a spot well away from others and dialed Merissa, asking if she could have Porsha call her. It was urgent.

Urgent must not have translated, because Caitlyn waited for what felt like forever for Porsha to call back.

Duke was suited up in minutes, but Leo was causing problems for his belay, Ike, bitching at him, complaining about this whole thing. He'd been acting weird from the moment Caitlyn had woken him to get ready so they could head out. Dragging his ass, muttering stupid things, weaving as he walked. She'd never had a hangover, but plenty of people she knew had.

He'd shaped up on the ride there, and she was glad to be rid of him for a while, though she hated that Duke had to deal with him too. The plan was to get Leo to the right location with a harness lowered from the top of the mountain, much like the ones used by the cameramen, so Leo would have to climb as little as possible. He wasn't climbing far. He only needed to get into position and let the cameras roll, and they were sticking to the shorter mountainside for this.

Just as Duke, Leo, and the cameraman Joe were almost ready to go, Porsha called.

Caitlyn took a deep breath and answered. "Hi, Porsha."

"This better be good. Normally, I never take calls from crisis managers. But since this is your first assignment... Make it quick."

She wasn't sure she could make it quick, but she did her best as she described, not the nightmare in the early morning hours with Leo, but the dinner before and everything she'd learned about Peter's treatment of Duke's family.

Leo's belay, Ike, walked away to grab some gear. Leo didn't like that. He drew Milo's attention from the belay rigging for Joe, one of the cameramen. "This isn't right. Fix it."

"He'll be right back," Milo said, staying focused on the cameraman's harness.

But Leo wouldn't be ignored. He hit Milo's shoulder with the back of his hand. "You need to fix this. It's bugging the shit out of me."

Caitlyn described the situation to Porsha, what Caitlyn knew and what she'd seen. "I have evidence. I have a recording and the coke he handed me."

Duke started toward Leo, but Duke's belay, Deon, spoke up. "I've got it." To Leo, he said, "What's your problem?"

"This," he said, oblivious to everyone's annoyance. "It's digging into my hip."

Deon pulled out the knot and reknotted it in a way that kept it off Leo's skin. Ike returned to Leo, and Deon returned to Duke.

"Why are you telling me this?" Porsha asked, her voice ice cold.

"Don't you represent him?" Caitlyn said.

"Yes."

"Well, you must know that he's in the midst of a tough divorce."

"Get to the point."

She took a deep breath. "He's using coke, dealing coke, and he has three little girls who he is fighting for custody of. He shouldn't be allowed custody of kids while he's doing dope."

"Joe, you ready?" Duke asked the cameraman.

"Born ready."

"You start up to get ahead of us."

The cameraman swung his cameras to his back and moved up the cliff relatively easily. He was using the handholds Duke had screwed into the rock to make it easier for less experienced climbers.

"That is an opinion," Porsha said, drawing Caitlyn back to the conversation.

"That's not an opinion. I saw him trade cocaine. That is a fact."

"Your facts don't matter." She sounded like she was going to get off the phone.

"Wait," Caitlyn said. "This is really important."

"Get rid of the tape and the coke. That's what we're paid to do. Do your job, or I'll do it for you, and you'll never work in public relations in California again. I will blackball you from San Diego to Sacramento."

And she disconnected.

Caitlyn's heart dropped. Her stomach twisted. "Fuck."

She exhaled and stared at her phone without any idea how she would handle this. She'd just have to tell Duke and let the chips fall where they may. Which, of course, terrified her.

She refocused on Duke and the cliff wall.

The cameraman, Joe, was about forty feet up before Duke looked at Leo. "Our turn."

Leo, sitting on a rock, looking miserable, stood up. He swayed, and his first steps were awkward, making him fall hard against Milo, the cameraman's belay. The next thing Caitlyn knew, Joe dropped straight to the ground, hitting with a sickening thud and a grunt, and the rope that should be taut wasn't just loose, it flailed free, falling out of the stopping device altogether.

A scream pierced the air and sent a shiver down Caitlyn's spine. Then a flurry of movement erupted as the crew rushed in that direction.

It happened in seconds that seemed to last for minutes. Cold coated Caitlyn's skin. Her mind stalled. She couldn't move. Part of her didn't believe what she'd just seen.

Duke pushed his way to the front of the crowd from one direction and Beau from the other, backboard and C-collar in hand. They dropped to the ground and worked together to get Joe wrapped up for transport, and Jarrod sent a member of the crew to bring over one of their trucks with a camper shell.

This was awful. Shocking. Terrifying. A dark freeze sank deep into Caitlyn's body.

Joe was moaning. She decided that was good. It meant he was alive.

Milo was on his knees at Joe's feet. "Oh my God, I'm so sorry. Dude, fuck, I don't know... Fuck, I'm so sorry."

"Stay out of the way." Beau was firm, but compassionate. "There will be plenty of time for that later."

Duke gave Milo's shoulder a squeeze, then spoke to Joe. "Dude, you're such a problem child."

That got a laugh out of the guy, then he grimaced and moaned.

"Hold still," Beau told him, securing the last strap. "We'll get you to the hospital and fixed up in no time. I'll get you pain meds on the way."

"How bad is it?" Joe asked. "Do we need to call Wendy?"

Caitlyn assumed Wendy was his girlfriend or wife.

"Not right now," Beau told him. "We'll call her from the hospital."

The truck backed into the space and the crew member rounded the back to open the tailgate.

"Can I get two more guys to carry?" Beau asked of no one in particular.

Two crew members stepped forward, and the four of them loaded Joe into the back. Beau and one of the crew stayed with Joe.

"I'll head over in a few," Duke told Joe and Beau. To Joe, he said, "Take the rest of the day off, buddy," making Joe laugh again. Then he secured the tailgate and smacked it twice. "Good to go."

Now that the situation was under control, Caitlyn's mind cleared a little. She immediately replayed the sight of Leo falling into Milo, and another wave of ice prickled her skin.

She glanced around and found Leo hanging on the very edge of the space, right next to the path out, like he was going to bolt.

"Jeff," Duke called across the clearing. "Woods doesn't leave."

"You got it."

Jeff made his way to Leo and stood with his arms crossed. He was a big guy, three inches taller and thirty pounds heavier than Leo.

Her intuition told her things were about to go ballistic.

"Everyone who saw what happened, raise your hand," Duke said.

About ten men and women raised their hands.

"All of you head into the admin trailer with Jessica and recount what you saw," Duke said. "The rest of you can go."

The crew dissipated with rumbling undertones of concern.

"Milo." Duke tilted his head in a come-here gesture.

As soon as he stood beside Duke, words just fell out of his mouth. "I don't know what happened. I mean, Leo knocked me over, but Joe should only have dropped to the top anchor, but the rope kept going, right through the ATC. I had an end knot in, but it didn't hold."

"That's probably because Leo bitched at you to fix his equipment while you were tying your knots. You forgot to tighten it."

"Fuck." Milo dropped his face into his hands, looking as sick as Caitlyn felt.

Duke clasped Milo's shoulder in a reassuring gesture, then closed the distance between him and Leo. "What's wrong with you? Are you drunk?"

"No. It was just an accident."

Duke reached out and took Leo's chin firmly in hand, looking into Leo's eyes. "Or are you high?" Duke's blatant anger made Caitlyn nervous as hell. "Your pupils are blown, dude. Don't lie."

"Haven't touched anything today," Leo said, faking bravado in the face of Duke's anger.

"He hasn't," Caitlyn said, her heart beating out of her chest.

His gaze jumped to Caitlyn, and the look there turned her

body to ice. Then to Leo, he said, "But you were on a bender yesterday."

Caitlyn's mind skipped ahead, fearful that not only was Duke going to put this on her, but he might also be right. This might be her fault. Her legs felt weak, and she sat on a nearby rock.

"That was yesterday," Leo said.

Duke's angry gaze turned on Caitlyn again. "Is this why you were gone all night?"

"It's not that simple." That was a longer conversation, and she wasn't doing it here. She turned on Leo. "Are you high? Did you do coke when I wasn't looking?"

"Fuck you. I don't need this." He tried to turn, but Jeff kept him in place, which pissed Leo off.

"You're not going anywhere," Duke told him. "Jeff, drug test this fucker."

"Fuck off," Leo said.

"It's mandatory. Lined out in every contract. You don't get a choice."

Jeff took Leo's arm. "Let's go."

Leo tried to pull away but didn't get anywhere and was still bitching when Jeff took him across the lot to another trailer.

Caitlyn watched Duke pace, head down, one hand at his hip, the other in his hair. She didn't know what to say, but the silence was just too suffocating.

"He's not drunk," she said. "He hasn't had anything since last night."

He huffed what sounded like a laugh and shook his head. "You're so… You have no idea…"

Her hackles rose, but her guilt tamped them down. "He couldn't have had any coke unless he had some hidden, because I threw away what he had last night."

Duke dropped his hand and looked directly at her for the first time since all this happened. "He was drunk and high last night—which in reality was early this morning—and you thought it was okay for him to show up and do something as dangerous as rock climbing the next day?"

"He has a hangover." Tears clogged her throat and stung her eyes. "People all over the world go to work with hangovers. I don't understand what you're trying to get at."

"That is exactly the problem. You don't understand. I knew you weren't equipped to handle him."

That hit her like a punch, and her air whooshed out.

"Duke." He looked toward Jeff. "Point sixteen."

"Fucking bastard."

"What does that mean?" she asked as Jeff disappeared inside again.

"That's his blood alcohol level." His voice had a little too much of a condescending tone for her taste. "If he'd been driving, he'd have a DUI."

She shook her head. "How is that—"

"*He's drunk.* He's currently, right this minute, so drunk, he couldn't legally drive, let alone handle something as dangerous as rock climbing."

She shook her head. She still didn't understand.

"Alcohol metabolizes at different rates," he told her. "And the more someone drinks, the longer it takes to sober up. If you had the experience you need for this job, you would never have brought him to the set."

And Joe wouldn't be in the hospital.

The words didn't need to be spelled out. They hurt the same as if he'd said them out loud.

"And that's not even considering how this accident will affect me and my job. Me and Kristy and the girls." He rubbed his face. "I can't do this now. I have to get to the hospital."

He turned toward the admin trailer. "Jeff."

Jeff reappeared.

"Call the cops. Have them charge him with anything and

everything applicable. Reckless endangerment, battery. Hell, I'd settle for being drunk in public. But something."

He walked away and disappeared down the path without looking back.

It took a minute for all this to sink in. She'd instinctively had some barriers up, and now when they fell, all Duke's anger sank in like teeth.

Emotions whirled inside her. Her thoughts tangled with them.

His words, *That is exactly the problem: you don't understand. I knew you weren't equipped to handle him,* played against the sight of Duke putting a comforting hand on Milo's shoulder and speaking to him reassuringly.

She just wasn't good enough.

For anyone.

Ever.

37

Duke paced to the window in the hospital room, then back to the other wall, phone to his ear.

"It's not an automatic bounce," Wes was saying on the other end of the phone. "You get knocked back to zero and put on six-month probation only if you were negligent. I looked at the witness statements. You weren't negligent. If anyone is at fault here, it's Leo."

Duke thanked Wes and disconnected. He crossed his arms and stared out the window at the night. His conflict with Caitlyn sat in his chest like a rock. Duke pressed his fingers to closed lids. He shouldn't have said those things to her. And he shouldn't have said them the way he said them either. What he'd said was still true, but he'd handled it all wrong. She was doing her best, and she'd been able to keep Leo reined in for the most part. What he'd said had been unfair.

He didn't know how he was going to fix this fuckup. Maybe he couldn't. Maybe he shouldn't. But, God, he wanted her. Even though he didn't deserve her right now.

"She's great."

Duke turned at the sound of Joe's voice. "Hey. How are you feeling?"

"Drugged. I love it."

Duke breathed easier. "We've got Wendy on a flight. She'll be here in about an hour."

"Thanks. I was talking about Caitlyn. She's great."

"Yeah," he said on an exhale. "She is. And I seriously, royally created a clusterfuck with her."

"Give it time. She'll come around."

His cell rang with Kristy's name on the display. He wandered into the hall to take the call. "Hey, how's it—"

"They moved up the court date," she said, her voice filled with terror. "And he's going for f-f-full custo…"

"Custody" was lost in choking sobs.

Panic and fear rushed in. "He won't get it."

"Can they just do that? Move the hearing?"

"I don't know. Have you called Celeste?"

"I left her a message, but the hearing is Monday. I don't know if she can c-come on such sh-short notice."

"I'm sure that's what he counted on. God, he's such a bastard."

"I can't lose them." The agony in her voice felt like a flaming rod in Duke's heart. "I can't lose them. Half custody would be bad enough. I'd have to move to New York so they wouldn't have to be shuttled across the country or raised by a nanny. But full custody? I can't live without them. They're my whole w-world."

Her words faded into sobs, and Duke's heart broke open. He felt like he was losing his own kids. His life had turned into a flaming meteor.

"We won't lose them. I'll call Zach and Tessa." Tessa was an experienced attorney. "I don't think they've left for home yet. Zach said they were going to hang around awhile. Take Sophia to Disney and Universal. Tessa can slide in until Celeste is free. I'll grab the next flight home. You won't be alone."

He disconnected, looked up cheap flights, and grabbed one. He returned to the hospital room.

"That didn't sound good," Joe said.

"It wasn't. I've got to go, but the guys will pick up Wendy at the airport."

"Go," Joe said.

Duke pocketed his phone. "I'll check in."

"Get out of here."

Duke took a deep breath. "Yeah, okay, thanks."

He left the hospital room with terror clawing at his chest. In the elevator, he texted the other guys. *I need a ride to the airport.*

38

The phone woke Caitlyn.

She pried her eyes open. Eyes that were swollen from crying. Her brain wouldn't kick in. She didn't even know what time it was, but the darkened window told her she'd slept far longer than she'd meant to. When she picked up her phone, the question of time fled her mind. It was Porsha.

Her boss's name struck a match in Caitlyn's tired brain and reality poured in. She hadn't seen or spoken with Duke since he'd walked off the set after Joe's fall, thirty-six hours ago. Wes told Caitlyn that Duke had gone home for the rest of the weekend, but nothing more, which was fine. She didn't want to know any more.

She'd spent the last day and a half doing her best to pull her head out of her ass and fulfill her job responsibilities—keep Leo out of trouble. Something she'd believed would be impossible just ten days ago, now felt easy.

When she took away the complications of her relationship with Duke, she had far more room to focus on Leo and all his issues. A good chastising from the film's producer and director seemed to take a little fire out of Leo's arrogance. But the biggest change in his attitude had taken root after several hours with the police and the threat of reckless endangerment charges.

She groaned before answering. “This is Caitlyn.”

“I got an earful from Leo.”

Caitlyn rubbed her forehead. “I’m sure you did.”

“I got his side. What’s your side?”

She explained the situation.

“Leo said it was your lack of attention to the situation because you’re seeing one of the stuntmen.”

“That’s bullshit.”

“I believe you.”

Caitlyn was stunned silent.

“But in our business, the client is always right. Besides, it’s not professional to be sleeping with someone involved in your work. End it.”

Caitlyn’s jaw dropped. “Excuse me?”

“You heard me. End it.”

“No.” Caitlyn hadn’t known that was going to pop out of her mouth, but once it was there, she doubled down. Despite the issues they’d had, Caitlyn couldn’t just close the door on Duke. Nor would she because someone told her to. She didn’t work that way.

“Did you just say ‘no’ to me?”

“I’m not going to let you decide who I can and can’t see on a personal level. That’s an absurd overreach.”

She sighed heavily. “I knew this was coming. You’re fired.”

“I knew this was coming,” Caitlyn repeated. “You can’t fire me, I quit.”

She disconnected. Her stomach seized, then released. It was better this way. She’d just have to figure out what to do next.

She dug the cocaine out of the drawer where she’d put it inside another plastic bag, hoping to preserve any fingerprints. This was a big deal. She was going to expose one of the biggest producers in Hollywood. But it wasn't about the coke. She knew that was nothing more than a party favor around here. It was about custody of those innocent girls. And Caitlyn had already seen and heard about the lengths Peter would go to for vengeance when it came to his family.

If Porsha didn't level her career, surely Peter would. But she seemed to be doing a great job of that all on her own.

Besides, it was the right thing to do.

She sat on the edge of the bed and looked at the coke. "Good deeds never go unpunished."

Sometimes it was so much easier to be an asshole than a good person. Like Merissa said, no one cared about values here. They wanted power, money, and stardom.

"How did this happen?" She'd *just* gotten here. It had been mere weeks, and look where she was. "He was right—this place changed me."

With a heavy sigh, she slid the coke into the pocket of her shorts. She looked at herself in the bathroom mirror and groaned. Puffy, red eyes, blotchy coloring. She could do only so much with this mess of a face, so she used cold water in hopes of calm.

She picked up her phone and considered texting Duke, but she didn't want the whole back-and-forth. She just wanted to get this off her plate and hopefully help Kristy.

She made her way to his room and stood there for a minute, trying to get her emotions under control. Then she cleared her throat, knocked, and waited. Knocked again and waited again.

"Duke," she called through the door.

Still no answer.

"Dammit." She dropped her head back and closed her eyes. He was probably downstairs having dinner. Now, she'd have to go out into more public spaces looking like shit.

No, actually she didn't. She wanted to help, but she wasn't required to. He'd been mean to her the day of the accident, and she was still reeling from all of it—Duke, Porsha, Brett, her family, her job. She didn't have to do anything for anyone but herself. A truly novel idea after years of having expectations thrust upon her.

Exhausted, she returned to her room and ordered room service, that platter of potato skins she'd been wanting, and berry cobbler with ice cream for dessert. Then she slid under the covers, turned on the TV, and scanned for a good movie to take her mind off the mess that was her life.

39

Duke returned to Vancouver, hurting more than he'd ever hurt before.

He still couldn't believe that fucker had gotten custody of the girls. Tessa had done all she could in Celeste's absence and assured Kristy that this was temporary, that the ruling wouldn't stand, but that it would take time to straighten things out.

Going forward was going to be hell on earth for him and Kristy. He should have seen it coming. Peter had everyone who had any kind of power in his pocket, but Duke had hoped—and therein lay the problem.

The only way he'd been able to return to work was having the better halves of the Renegades team there to support Kristy.

Duke needed this job more than anything now. All those attorney's fees wouldn't be going away anytime soon.

Troy picked him up at the airport. "Dude, I'm really sorry about the girls."

Duke nodded and stared out the side window at the greenery, the mountains, the bright blue sky—all things that used to thrill him and now felt flat. Even the idea of climbing today left him numb, and that was a first. "Me too."

"What happens now?"

Duke shook his head. "Kristy only has a couple of days to get the girls ready to go. Then she has to find somewhere to live in New York so she can be close to the girls and take all the visitation she can get."

"The girls will be in New York even when Peter is out here working?"

"He'll just have a nanny raise the girls, which in the end is probably the lesser of two evils."

He thought of Willow and all her funny sayings as she learned to talk. Paisley and how she'd melted down when Duke left. Scarlett confused and scared and trying to understand something that couldn't be understood.

His heart was broken. Tears burned his eyes, and Duke pressed his fingers to closed lids.

"And unless the alimony gets straightened out soon," he said, "I have no idea how we're going to swing that, even with me working. She can get a job, but..."

He exhaled heavily, the weight of the world on his shoulders. "God. This is a nightmare."

And it was ripping his heart out.

"Why don't you stay in Malibu awhile, just till you're on solid ground again? That way, your rent money can go to a place in New York for Kristy."

Mention of Malibu made him think of Caitlyn. Regret swamped him, followed closely by sadness. He really was a prick. He didn't deserve her, but she was the only thing he wanted here. More than climbing, more than stunts, more than hanging with the guys, he wanted to be with Caitlyn.

"Maybe," he said. "Have you talked to Caitlyn?"

"No. Have you?"

"No."

"I hate to pile on when you've been dealing with so much bullshit, but that's what friends do. You don't deserve her."

"I don't."

"You've been acting like an asshole."

"I have."

"She's amazing, and you didn't just let her walk out of your life, you pushed her out."

"She is, and I did."

"Well, this is no fucking fun," Troy muttered.

Duke managed a laugh, but every time he thought of the girls, the scab on his heart tore off.

"How's Joe?"

"On the mend. Everything looks good."

At least that released a little extra air from his lungs. "What are we working on today? What's happening with Leo?"

"They want to fill in a few dead spots with more of your climbing, and Leo says he's ready to do his part."

"Heard that before." Duke was hoping he'd see Caitlyn on the set.

"Heard through the grapevine that Caitlyn set up scheduled drug testing for Leo three times a day, so you shouldn't get caught in that residual-hangover mess again."

"That's smart."

"I also heard she hired a twenty-four-seven security detail for him, so there's no doubt it's really his pee and not someone he paid to give theirs."

"Really smart."

They passed through the main gates, and Duke forced himself to focus. He'd find Caitlyn as soon as he was done filming today.

40

Duke had been climbing on rote all day. They'd resorted to lowering Leo from the top since he couldn't climb to save his life, and he was, as it turned out, afraid of heights. It had been beyond tedious to coax him into a pose so video could be taken. Leo didn't even have to act. He was utterly terrified.

Caitlyn didn't show up to the set all day. Duke figured she'd given Leo an ultimatum, because aside from being a pansy pain in the ass, he was doing his best.

Duke rappelled down the cliff with the others and spent an hour cleaning up and checking equipment, all while thinking about Caitlyn. If she broke it off, she'd be justified, but what little piece of his heart that still existed would be crushed.

If she stayed in LA, he could work on making it up to her, show her he had his shit together. If she didn't... He was so royally fucked. He didn't want to be without her.

As soon as they entered the hotel, Duke scanned the lobby and restaurant for her, then headed up to her room. He was a dirty, stinky mess, but he could shower later, after he'd apologized and begged her to give them another try.

At her door, he closed his eyes. He couldn't contemplate the negative outcome, only the positive.

He knocked, and the door opened, but the woman standing there was definitely not Caitlyn.

"Well," she said, all snotty-LA like, "at least she has good taste."

His gaze darted to the number on the door, then the other doors in the hallway. He had the right room. Which could only mean one thing, and his mood turned on a dime.

"You must be Porsha," he said. "You're the bitch who made us lose custody of our girls. You're the fucker protecting Peter."

"That would be me. Though, for the record, I had nothing to do with him getting custody of the girls. Even I have a heart, and children belong with their mother, especially in this case."

He glanced past her. "Where is Caitlyn?"

"I don't know," she said. "Probably still on the plane."

"Plane?" His gaze jumped back to Porsha. "Where did she go?"

"LA, I imagine."

"Why?"

"I fired her. She'll tell you she quit, but I fired her first, so she didn't have a job to quit."

All the air left Duke's lungs, and he pressed a palm to the wall. "But I heard she set up drug testing for Leo."

"She did, before she left."

"Why did you fire her? She's damn good at what she does."

"But she doesn't follow directions very well. As for why she quit, that tosses the ball back into your court. When I told her to end things with you, she said no. Nobody says no to me and keeps their job. Too bad, really. She had potential."

"What the hell are you doing in her room?"

"Cast and crew have the hotel booked solid. Only room available."

He narrowed his eyes on her. “You told her to end it with me?”

“Sleeping with a member of cast or crew is bad for optics, and she does—or did—represent me and the company.” She looked him up and down. “But I can see why she chose you over the job.”

41

Caitlyn stared blankly through the apartment's front window. She wanted to sleep. She wanted to slide into oblivion and forget all that had happened and all the worry over what would happen next, but every time she closed her eyes, all her mistakes rushed back, along with the betrayed look on Duke's face before he left the climbing set.

She knew he'd learn about the steps she'd taken to ensure safety on the set again, but she didn't expect that to erase the problems or excuse her mistakes. Joe was still in the hospital.

The front door opened, and Andi looked at Caitlyn on the couch. "Have you moved since I left?"

"I went to the bathroom."

"You've been in that same spot for two days." She tossed her purse and keys on the coffee table and sat on the edge of a chair.

"You're exaggerating." Only, she wasn't and they both knew it.

"I don't have time to give you a full-fledged verbal beating at the moment, but if you haven't moved your ass from the sofa by the time I get home from Bougie tonight, I'm taking you out and getting you shit-faced drunk." Andi pushed to her feet and wagged a comical finger at Caitlyn. "You've been warned."

"I think I'll head to Lexi's this weekend, spend a few days job hunting from the beach."

Andi shook her head. "Do it while you can, girl."

Her roommate disappeared into her bedroom and emerged ten minutes later to grab her keys and phone, shoot Caitlyn another I-mean-business look, and slam the door on her way out.

That would be Caitlyn soon, juggling two or more jobs to stay afloat. But to do that, she'd have to job search. Merissa swore up and down she'd intercept Porsha's blackball order and give her a glowing recommendation, so Caitlyn couldn't sulk anymore. She had to get up and get moving.

But first things first. She picked up the phone and dialed Kristy. As soon as she picked up, Caitlyn knew she'd been crying.

"Hey," Caitlyn said, "it's Caitlyn."

"Hi. Is Duke okay?"

"He's fine. I'm home. Long story." She hesitated, then asked, "Are you okay?"

"Ah, no. The judge gave custody of the girls to Peter, and I only have a couple of days to—" Her voice broke. "To get them ready to move to New York."

"Christ." No wonder she sounded like a mess. "I don't want to bother you, but I have something that may or may not help you. It's kind of hard to explain without the whole story. Can I come by, and we can talk about it?"

"Uh. To be honest, I'm a wreck. Can you call my attorney, Celeste? She's a new partner at Wells, Barkley, and Fine."

"Of course, I'll call her. Can I help you with anything?"

"Maybe, but I'll have to call you back."

She disconnected with Kristy, stunned and sickened, and immediately searched her phone for Celeste's law firm. When the secretary tried to push her off, Caitlyn hardened her tone. "I'm calling about Kristy Reid-Fontaine's case, and this is urgent and time sensitive."

"Hold a moment, please."

Caitlyn let out a breath of relief and prayed this could help.

"This is Celeste."

"Hi, hi. My name is Caitlyn, and I'm a friend of Duke's, Kristy's brother. I've been in Canada on a film set and I met Peter Fontaine while I was there. I may have some information that could help Kristy."

"I'm all ears."

42

The drive from Hollywood to Malibu gave Caitlyn time to decompress. So much had happened, and she'd been in a pressure cooker so long, stress plagued every part of her body.

Celeste had taken the audio file and cocaine, but couldn't tell Caitlyn anything about the case, so she had no idea whether it was helpful or a waste. Kristy hadn't called Caitlyn back for help with the girls, so she gave her space.

Now, all she could do was hope and job hunt.

She used the spare key to enter the house and wasted some time watering Lexi's plants, then popped a bottle of beer and wandered out onto the beach, where she dropped her butt on the sand, wrapped her arms around her knees, and looked out at the ocean.

She could see why so many people wanted to live on the coast. She'd never understood until she sat here on the warm sand, under a crisp blue sky, the waves rhythmic and relaxing.

Unfortunately, it didn't help with heartbreak.

She might not be able to figure out how she felt about the whole tense situation with Duke, but she felt really good about what she'd done for Kristy. She hoped it made a difference. Peter would ruin those girls.

She closed her eyes and rested her chin on her knees. She was so lucky to have this kind of setting to enjoy the silence and think about everything that had happened over the last two weeks.

Two weeks. She laughed and shook her head. She'd left home just two weeks ago, and her entire world had changed. She'd spent most of her life in Kentucky, and it had remained the same for years.

She already missed Duke. Missed the guys. Missed Lexi and Jax.

"You're a hard woman to find."

Duke's voice made her heart skip. She looked up and found him standing in front of her, his body blocking the sun.

"How did you find me, then?"

"Your roommate. Quite a character, that one. Threatened great bodily harm if I hurt you any more than I already have."

Caitlyn repositioned herself on the sand so she could see him better. He seemed rough around the edges. His hair had grown out of the stunt-double haircut, and it looked like he hadn't shaved in three days. He also looked exhausted. "Are you okay?"

"I am now." He sat next to her and looked out at the ocean. At an angle, with the sunlight in his eyes, they were a clear, beautiful deep brown. "Thanks to you."

She sucked in a breath of hope and rolled to her knees to face him with both hands pressed to her heart. "Did Kristy hear from the court?"

"This morning." He studied her for a long moment, the look in his eyes serious, but sweet. He reached out and brushed her hair off her cheek. "The court awarded Kristy full custody."

She gasped loudly. Tears stung her eyes. "Oh my God. Are you serious?"

He finally smiled, and it was a breathtaking sight. It might only have been a few days, but she'd missed the hell out of him.

"I'm serious."

She threw her arms around his shoulders and hugged him tight. "I'm *so* happy for you. All of you."

He wrapped his arms around her and pulled her into his lap and leaned away, tucking her hair, blowing in the breeze, behind her ear. "Kristy got an emergency hearing because the case involved the well-being of children. And after reading your affidavit for the audio and the report from the crime lab confirming Peter's fingerprints were on the bag of cocaine, the judge awarded Kristy generous alimony and child support. He only gave Peter the bare minimum visitation, and always supervised."

Her breath rushed out. "Oh my *God*. That's amazing."

"*You're* amazing. I can't even tell you how grateful we are. You made the difference between an upended, nomadic life and stability for all of us."

They slid into silence for an extended moment, and Caitlyn's heart mended a little. "I've missed you. How are things on the set?"

"Lonely. I miss you too. On the upside, the threat of reckless endangerment charges has made Leo easier to work with. A couple more weeks and I'll be done with him."

"A rough assignment all around," she said.

"Definitely." Duke paused then said, "Why didn't you tell me about meeting Peter or what you'd heard and done?"

"If I remember correctly, you were yelling at me."

He winced and closed his eyes. "Guess I was. I've been such a prick."

"Won't argue with you there."

"It shouldn't have happened, and I'm *really* sorry it did. I'm angry with myself and ashamed of how I acted. If you knew how much daily shit I catch from the guys, not to mention Kristy, you'd be happy."

She smiled and stroked his jaw with the backs of her fingers. "I feel like I haven't seen you in weeks."

"Same here."

She pressed her lips to his. "When do you go back?"

"Tomorrow."

Her shoulders sank.

"You could come with me."

She tilted her head. "You have to know I quit."

He chuckled. "I heard you got fired, straight from Porsha's mouth."

"*Pffft*. You were lucky enough to meet her?"

"Lucky. That's an interesting way to put it, but yes. When I went to your room to apologize, Porsha answered the door."

She laughed, long and deep.

He hit her with one of those arrogant smirks. "She said she gave you an ultimatum, and you chose me."

"Don't go getting a big head. It was more like I wasn't going to let her tell me what to do in my personal life."

"Whatever you gotta tell yourself." He kissed her. Then kissed her again. And again. "You should come back with me."

"I'd love to, but I need to do some job hunting."

"You could have a new job waiting. When Kingsley heard Porsha fired you, he didn't waste any time trying to dig you up. He came to me, and I told him I'd talk to you."

She shook her head, confused.

"He liked all the ideas you had. Loved your passion for your client, even when you didn't care for your client. He mentioned the possibility of a position here in LA, at Paramount."

Her jaw came unhinged. Air whooshed out of her lungs. "I — What— Are you serious?"

He nodded. "That would really be something to tell everyone back home, huh? That you're so good at what you did, you were hired as associate marketing manager of media strategy at Paramount Pictures."

Now excitement mixed with angst. "Wow, that's a long title. I don't even know what that is."

"I couldn't decipher some of the information he told me, but bottom line sounds like you'd be doing a shit ton of marketing for Paramount's Original Series."

"That sounds swanky."

"Right?"

"Should I call him? Make an appointment with his admin?"

"I say," he said, drawing out the words, "if you're interested, you should come back to Vancouver and talk to him face-to-face. I heard the hotel is booked, but I've got room for you in my bed."

She grinned until she laughed. "I like that idea, but..." She grimaced. "We need some guidelines."

He wrapped an arm around her waist and turned her toward him until she straddled his lap.

She stroked her hands down the front of his chest, the cotton tee soft beneath her fingers.

"Shoot," he said.

"I know you've been under a lot of stress, but it's not okay to take that frustration—"

"Out on you."

She nodded. "And you have to watch what you say and how you say it. You were—"

"An asshole."

She took a deep breath and jumped. "I may love you, but don't think I won't—"

"Kick my ass to Siberia."

She laughed and let her forehead rest against his. Let herself relax. Let her heart open.

He cupped her face and pulled her in for a kiss. It felt so good to be close to him again.

"I love you too." The declaration was soft and rough, and his vulnerability was heart wrenching.

She kissed him, then smiled, because everything was starting to fall into place.

Finally.

EPILOGUE

E*ight months later*

Caitlyn scanned all the boxes on her lists—still all checked off since the last time she'd looked two minutes ago.

"We're ready," Merissa told her.

Caitlyn nodded and blew out a breath. "How's Tabitha?"

"Shaking with nerves," Andi said, joining them in the backyard of Tabitha's home in the Hollywood Hills, where Caitlyn and her team—now including Merissa and Andi—had set up Caitlyn's signature press conference, warm, welcoming, and televised. "But ready."

Caitlyn smiled and headed toward the bedroom they'd turned into a makeup room. She stopped beside Tabitha's chair, giving the woman a warm smile and a squeeze on her shoulder. "You look amazing. Ready to do this?"

"No," she said, with a nervous laugh. "But yes."

"You're taking back your power."

She nodded, her auburn curls bouncing in a halo around her head. "Yes."

"You're standing up for your children."

"Yes."

"You are worthy of consideration and love and respect."

"Yes."

"Ready to tell your story?"

Tabitha's nerves melted around the edges, and she smiled. "Yes."

Caitlyn offered her hand to the mother of four boys who'd been maligned and vilified in the press by her insanely wealthy ex-husband. A man who was also trying to take her children and minimize any financial responsibility to his family.

Caitlyn had a lot of clients whose situation echoed Tabitha's. After she'd undertaken the challenge of rebuilding Kristy's reputation in the public eye, Caitlyn's business had basically built itself. She didn't even have time to entertain Kingley's offer. Women—and even some men—sought her out to right their lives. And it turned out that *did* pay the bills.

Now, Caitlyn embraced her own personal power by helping others in a meaningful way, and her team consisted of people she loved, trusted, and respected. Merissa was her manager, watching over the eight client handlers under her. Andi loved the tough stuff—investigating potential clients' backgrounds to make sure their stories checked out and that they were really in need of publicity spin, not lying, conniving brats looking for vengeance. And when Duke wasn't off doing stunts, he was her head of security.

She stopped in front of him now at the double glass doors and he kissed her before she walked through to greet journalists. "Everything good?"

Duke brushed her hair off her forehead, his gaze soft and loving, a look she loved having in her life every day. This was all part of the "more" she'd come to California to find. She just never imagined that "more" could be so incredible.

"Cam's team is holding off the vultures out front."

She shrugged. "If they had behaved themselves, they would be in."

He grinned. “You’re such a hard ass.”

She sighed, leaned into him, and pushed up on her toes to kiss him again. “Learned from the best.” Her mind veered to their afternoon plans, and she bounced on her toes. “I can’t keep my mind on what I’m doing. I’m so excited about the Canyon.”

Malibu Creek Canyon was a beautiful spot in the LA mountains with midlevel climbing opportunities over volcanic rock. They’d been scrolling through climb routes the night before and came across an image of a huge volcanic rock overhanging Malibu Creek. Caitlyn about jumped off the couch in Duke’s new place, a one-bedroom apartment only a street away from Kristy and the girls.

“You’ll let me free climb, right?” she asked now.

He hadn’t given her a definitive answer to her interest in climbing without a rope, harness, or anchors. Just her and the rock, with Duke beside her. The only reason she wanted to do it was because the rock overhung the creek, where it formed into a swimming hole, so if she fell, she’d fall in the water, and they’d planned on swimming anyway.

He smirked, but didn’t answer.

She leaned into him and tilted her head back. “Pleeeeeeease?”

Duke laughed. “As if I could deny you anything.”

They both knew he could deny her a lot—but only when her safety was at risk.

He sighed dramatically. “I’ve created a monster.”

“Can’t wait,” she said, smiling so hard, her cheeks hurt. “Can’t wait, can’t wait, can’t wait.”

“Lexi and Jax are coming too.”

She gasped. “Really?”

“And Wes and Rubi.”

She tilted her head. “Anyone else in this family crashing our party?”

He made a face. "Chase and Zahara."

"The more the merrier." She leaned into him, loving the solid wall of comfort he provided.

She'd hoped for a good life in California, but she'd gotten so much more than she bargained for—an entire family of supportive, understanding people in a gorgeous place, making more money than she ever dreamed, with more love than she'd believed possible.

He kissed her and squeezed her hand, lifting it with his gaze on her fingers. The engagement ring she'd accepted sparkled in the soft morning light, and he looked at it with wonder and a shake of his head. "Just making sure it's still there."

"It's still here." She cupped his jaw and kissed him. "And it will stay here for the rest of our lives."

"Unless you're climbing."

She laughed. "Unless I'm climbing."

ALSO BY SKYE JORDAN

FORGED IN FIRE

Flashpoint

Smoke and Mirrors

Playing with Fire

WILDFIRE LAKE SERIES

In Too Deep

Going Under

Swept Away

THE WRIGHTS SERIES

So Wright

Damn Wright

Must be Wright

MANHUNTERS SERIES

Grave Secrets

No Remorse

RENEGADES SERIES:

Reckless

Rebel

Ricochet

Rumor

Relentless

Rendezvous

Riptide

Rapture

Risk

QUICK & DIRTY COLLECTION:

Dirtiest Little Secret

WILDWOOD SERIES:

Forbidden Fling

Wild Kisses

ROUGH RIDERS HOCKEY SERIES:

Quick Trick

Hot Puck

Dirty Score

Wild Zone

COVERT AFFAIRS SERIES:

Intimate Enemies

First Temptation

Sinful Deception

Keep up to date on all my new releases by signing up for my newsletter here:

http://bit.ly/2bGqJhG

Get an inside view of upcoming books and exclusive giveaways by joining my reader group here:

https://www.facebook.com/groups/877103352359204/

ABOUT THE AUTHOR

Skye Jordan is the *New York Times* and *USA Today* bestselling author of more than thirty novels. She was born and raised in California and has recently been transplanted to Northern Virginia.

She left her challenging career in sonography at UCSF Medical Center to devote herself to writing full time, but still travels overseas on medical missions to teach sonography to physicians. Most recently, she traveled to Ethiopia and Haiti.

Skye and her husband are coming up on their thirty year wedding anniversary and have two beautiful daughters. A lover of learning, Skye enjoys classes of all kinds, from knitting to forensic sculpting. She is an avid rower and spends many wonderful hours on the Potomac with her amazing rowing club.

Make sure you sign up for her newsletter to get the first news of her upcoming releases, giveaways, freebies and more! http://bit.ly/2bGqJhG

You can find Skye online here:
Skye's Starlets | Website | Email